Royal Rebel

Love in Laandia
Sweet Royal Romance

HOLLY KERR

Also By Holly Kerr

Royal Rumble

Royal Retelling

Royal Rising

Royal Reluctance

Royal Rebel

Royal Replacement

The Love in Laandia spinoffs:

Coffee Break with the Billionaire

Babysitting the Grumpy Billionaire (coming soon!)

plus

Suitor Science series

Love & Alliteration series

Don't series

Royal Rebel

Dedication

To all the youngest daughters out there, including my Sarah

And to all the strong women who are seen as difficult and demand-ing but who are only trying to make their own way in the world

Prologue

ONCE UPON A TIME, there was a princess who lived in a castle.

And right now, she was very angry.

There were whispers among the castle staff that the princess was demanding. Her parents—the king and queen of Laandia, the small country situated between Canada and the Atlantic Ocean—joked that she was high maintenance. Her older brothers shook their heads at her moods and called her bratty, spoiled, and little sister.

I call her Lyra, and I think she's magnificent.

And have since the first day I came to the castle.

I had been three years old, still muddled and overwhelmed by the shock of being yanked out of my quiet life with my aunt in England, to living full time with my father. And on that first day in Laandia, my father brought me to meet the king.

His boss, he called him. His best friend. The king of Laandia was my father's best friend.

That was the day Princess Lyra was born—in an upstairs bedroom in the castle because Lyra was impatient even then and there had been no time to get to the hospital.

My father and I had just arrived at the castle when King Magnus practically flew down the stairs to greet us.

"Lyra is here," he all but shouted.

At me.

At least it felt like he was telling me, and me alone, like it was a royal gift he was bestowing.

Even though I had no idea who, or even what, a Lyra was.

I soon found out: the king took my father and me up to where the queen lay in a big bed with a tiny baby swaddled in her arms. The little thing was crying, wailing really, like its life was over.

That was how I got to meet the little princess of Laandia even before her brothers did.

That little baby, now twelve, stands before my father and might be just as angry as the day she was born.

"What do you mean, *Spencer* is coming to live here?" Princess Lyra demands, red-blonde hair flying around her petulant face. "What about *Sophie*? And Stella? What about them?"

"The girls will be staying with their mother."

My father sounds sad. Even at fifteen, with my teenage boy's lack of consideration and low attention span, I know my dad and I can tell this divorce isn't something that he wants.

Me, on the other hand... Signe is not my mother, and unless she's pretending in front of a crowd, or my dad, she's never really shown me much in terms of motherly affection.

Not that I know first-hand what motherly affection is. All I know is what Signe shows Stella and Sophie, my half-sisters. But I see the love Queen Selene shows her children.

Shows me, as well.

And that's why I'm not too upset about moving to the castle.

Yes, I'll miss my sisters because they are the best thing that came from my dad's marriage. But they'll still be my sisters and I'll see them all the time.

When Signe told Dad—and me—to leave, King Magnus invited us to live at the castle. This means I get to live with my best friends—Kalle, Odin, Bo, and Gunnar. And I can pretend that Queen Selene is my mother.

And then there's Princess Lyra.

Who is furious that I'm moving in.

"That's not fair," Lyra cries. "Why does Spencer get to come and not Sophie? I want Sophie, too."

She stamps her foot, her white Adidas sneaker all but glowing in the dim hallway.

Shows of temper from Lyra aren't new since I spend most of my time with one or more of the princes, with Lyra and my sisters tagging along. And Stella is just as temperamental as Lyra, to her mother's annoyance.

If it wasn't for Sophie's sweet nature, I'd think that was just how girls behaved.

"I'm sorry, Lyra," Dad says. And he really does sound sorry. "The girls will be staying with their mother."

Lyra glares at me like this is all my fault. "What do you want me to do?" I ask. "I don't have a mom to stay with."

"It's not that." Lyra's sullen expression softens. She may be a moody brat—Kalle's words, not mine—but there is a soft side as well. I think I get to see it more than her brothers. "You can stay—I just want Sophie."

"And she'd like nothing more than to be here with you," Dad tells her. "But unfortunately, that's not going to happen."

"It's not fair." Another stomp, but some of the heat disappears.

Even more when Dad ruffles her hair with a rueful smile. "No, sweetheart, it's not. But Spencer will be here. Can you help take care of Spence so he won't miss the girls so much?"

"He won't miss them," Lyra grumbles. "My brothers would never miss me."

"Oh, I beg to differ, Princess. Those boys wouldn't know what to do with themselves without you." Dad claps a hand on my shoulder, and one on Lyra's. I'm older, but Lyra is almost as tall as I am. Still waiting for that growth spurt. "I can count on the two of you to take care of each other, can't I? Be friends?"

If he only knew.

Odin

(Yes, this is Lyra's book but her big brother wanted his say!)

I smile as I open the door. "Come in."

It's an easy, welcoming smile, unlike the forced contortions of my mouth I use when pictures are taken of me, or during meetings, and at events that I really don't want to be attending. Or even when people stopped me on the street of Battle Harbour to happily inform me what the royal family was doing wrong and exactly what they should do about it.

People still stop me here in Saint Pierre, but I let Camille handle their complaints and suggestions.

She likes it that way.

I like that I'm able to open my own door without dealing with fences or security or a doorman.

Things are a lot more laid back here in Saint Pierre.

I keep a firm hand on Bea Arthur's collar, as she strains forward, tongue out. The long and lanky mutt has been known to knock over visitors in her eagerness to make friends. Tucked behind my legs, Betty White growls menacingly—or as menacingly as one can be when she's the size of a well-fed rat. I scoop her up in my other arm and she curls her lip at me.

"Stop," I caution both dogs. Camille usually locks them up when people first come over, but she's been a little flustered about all of this.

Grayson Grant steps inside. The prefect house, which Camille inherited when she took over the position from her father, is situated in the very centre of the island of Saint Pierre. While it may not be as welcoming as we'd like, Camille has been making changes, adding our own touches and personality, and removing some of her father's old-fashioned décor and traditions, and it's getting there.

I'm not sure if the dogs are helping. Betty White has a constant growl that vibrates her tiny body, giving Grayson the stink-eye as he offers the back of his hand as a peace offering.

He has more luck with Bea Arthur as her tongue makes contact and covers his outstretched hand with a fair bit of slobber.

"It's good to see you, Odin," Grayson says, discretely wiping his hand on his pants.

Grayson Grant has become the ultimate television personality. Former baseball player, Suitor celebrity, and now host and executive producer of the reality dating show. He's the Jeff Probst of the Suitor franchise, with the innate ability to befriend contestants so they'll confide in him, but managing to keep enough distance to ask the hard questions.

All with more variety in his wardrobe than the Survivor guy.

I can't believe it's been two years since my blink-and-you'll-miss-it time on The Suitorette. Did I really think I could find a wife on a reality romance television show?

Maybe if I had been actually looking to fall in love, rather than focused on heading straight for death-do-us-part, I might have had better luck.

But I did have luck, because going on the show got me Camille. That's really only the good thing about it.

That, and I made a friend.

Grayson has that "everyone likes him" quality that my brother Gunnar shares—friendly and approachable, with an abundance of charisma.

Camille says he's got "rizz."

I have no idea where she came up with that word, but it's obvious she's got a bit of a crush on Grayson.

I can't blame her because I may have a tiny bit of a crush on him, too.

Even though he saw me through one of the most humiliating events of my life, I like to think we're friends.

At least I think we've *become* friends.

I bring Grayson and his bags inside, and Camille meets us at the door to the kitchen. She uses her office—formerly her father's office, but since he's living full-time in France, it's all hers now—for meetings, but since this is Grayson's third visit and he's going to be staying here, she prefers the comfortable kitchen.

I love that she takes meetings in the kitchen. It's something my father would do if the castle kitchen didn't resemble something out of medieval times. It's been on the list to be renovated for as long as I can remember.

I also love that Camille can return Grayson's hug without her body locking up. She's lost so much of her awkward aggression since taking over as prefect.

Since we fell in love.

"Ready to get settled in?" Camille asks Grayson, her red hair clashing with her bright yellow sweater in a way that's both hard on the eyes and wonderful to see.

"Definitely." Grayson grins at my wife. "You have no idea how grateful we are that you came to us with the suggestion, Camille. Me, especially," he admits with a self-deprecating laugh. "This is my first time around as executive producer, and I completely blanked at a location. Not a great way to start."

"I think it'll benefit everyone," I say.

Saint Pierre, the tiny island nation off the coast of Newfoundland, Canada, will be the location for the next season of The Suitorette. Summer on the island is amazing, with the birds and the sun and the beach that spans more than half of the island.

And now, the world will see it.

When Camille took over from her father as prefect of Saint Pierre, she jumped in with both feet to bring out the best of the island. It was her idea to offer Oceanview, the hotel on the west side of the island, as a location for the Suitor franchise. Built by some French lord in the early nineteen hundreds, it had been turned into a hotel before World War II closed Saint Pierre to tourists.

The Oceanview limped into the twenty-first century, with a few prefects attempting renovations and rejuvenations, but it wasn't until the last few years of Camille's father's rule that things actually started to get done.

It's been restored to its former glory, but there was the issue of how do we get people to come to the island? Because more tourists would do a lot to jumpstart the economy.

This season, the contestants of The Suitorette will be staying at the Oceanview, and cameras will be showing the charm and beauty of Saint Pierre to the world.

Hopefully, this will help bring back the tourists.

Filming for the show starts in three days.

"I have to admit, I've never been much of a fan of the show," Camille confesses as Grayson takes a seat at the table. "But since Odin..." She gives me a sly glance under her lashes.

"We don't need to talk about Odin," I decide as I pull out her chair. "This has nothing to do with me."

"Oh, but we'll need a cameo," Grayson protests eagerly. "Both of you. How in a roundabout way, the show brought you together. Viewers will eat it up."

I hum my consent, not that it's up for negotiation. Camille has already decided we'll be appearing on the show. Multiple times, if she has her way.

She may not be much of a fan of the show, but she's recently discovered a love for the spotlight.

"When do the contestants show up?" Camille asks Grayson after I offer him a drink.

I also had no idea that she'd be so excited about twenty-five strangers who will be showing up on the island.

Twenty-five male strangers.

I'm not worried...

It's like Camille can read my mind because she winks at me over the cheese platter. "I love how you're doing the archetypes," she tells Grayson.

"I wish I could take credit, but it's Fiona's idea," Grayson explains as he helps himself to a cracker. "She's my wife's best friend and the biggest romance reader of anyone I know. She thought that it would be a fresh idea to have the typical characters from romance novels—the bad boy, the rock star, the athlete—"

"The boy next door, the cinnamon roll hero, the alpha male," Camille finishes, to my surprise. I always see with her e-reader, but I thought she was looking at reports and emails.

"Exactly." Grayson nods. "Fiona made me a list and I did my best to find as many as I could," he says. "But we've had no luck with the brother's best friend. I should have come to you to help with that."

I meet Camille's gaze, who is as confused as I am. "Why is that?" I ask slowly.

Grayson frowns. "We did keep this one low-key because of her status, but I thought you knew."

A weight settles in the pit of my stomach, like an anchor thrown overboard. "No. We don't know. And right now, I'm really not sure I want to."

"Who will be the Suitorette?" Camille demands. "We never asked because we thought it was a secret."

Grayson looks a little fearful. "I can't believe she didn't talk to you about it."

She? "Please don't tell me—"

"Princess Lyra is going to be the next Suitorette," Grayson finishes. "Your sister. She'll be here tomorrow to star in the show."

1

Spencer

"Eight ball in the corner pocket," I call, and obediently, the black ball rolls neatly into the pocket.

It's the only sport where I'm almost certain to win against the princes of Laandia.

And I'm fine with that. My strengths lie in other areas, but growing up so close to the family, and celebrating their wins and successes, it's kind of nice to be able to beat them at something.

"Another game?" Bo asks as he collects the balls.

I shake my head and gesture at the table across the room where Bo's wife Hettie sits with Abigail. It had been double-date night at The King's Hat before Gunnar—the youngest of the Laandian princes—and Stella, my half-sister—tracked us down.

I find now that the brothers are older, and all have girl-friends/fiancées/wives, date nights become group events. "I think we've given the girls enough time to talk about us."

"How do you know they're talking about us?"

I smile at my friend. Bo may be married and a father, but he still doesn't have a clue about women. "What else do you think they talk about when we're not around?"

"I don't know. Clothes? Tema?" Bo's smile at the mention of his daughter warms my heart.

His entire face lights up when he's with her, like a happy Jack o' lantern.

I shouldn't be surprised about his lack of knowledge: Bo and Hettie might have married eight years ago, but the union lasted only days before Hettie left the country because of Bo's grief and guilt over the death of his mother, Queen Selene.

Hettie only returned five months ago, with their eight-year-old daughter Tema in tow. It was dicey for a bit, but the family, not to mention the whole country, is ecstatic that Bo and Hettie managed to get past the secrets and serious lack of communication because they are truly made for each other.

And Tema—I seriously think the little girl could overthrow the monarchy and take over Laandia if she put her mind to it, and I'm honestly not sure where my loyalty would fall.

"They talk about Tema when we're there," I throw over my shoulder as I head back to the table where the pitcher of beer waits for us, now half empty thanks to Gunnar.

Bo might be right; I have no idea if Hettie needs to share details about Bo with her best friend, Abigail, but I can pretty much guarantee Abigail has talked her ear off about me.

"We're back." I slide onto the stool between Abigail and Stella. It's always a family affair when we come to The King's Hat, with eldest brother, Prince Kalle owning the pub, and Hettie's sister, Mabel, taking over the management from Kalle's fiancée, Edie.

"Were you talking about us?" Bo demands as he sits, crowding in between Hettie and Abigail, his shoulders dwarfing them. The latest country hit begins and the table beside us decides to sing along.

"Of course we were," Abigail tells him with a grin, and Bo looks confused.

"Don't worry." Hettie pats his hand. "I was just explaining our little plan to them."

The little plan being giving Tema a little brother or sister.

Bo wants to be a daddy—again. A fact that I think is pretty amazing.

A fact that makes Abigail want to step up *our* relationship.

And... I'm not sure how I feel about that.

I love having Abigail back in town. The four of us were inseparable when we were younger, but that all ended after Abigail left town with Hettie. Now that they're back, things have... developed with Abigail. Things that have me thinking of her as more than just a friend.

It's so easy with Abigail. She's amazing; nice, funny, smart. She's a great friend.

She's beautiful, too. I'm very attracted to her.

I stop reciting the reasons I want to be with Abigail and tune into the conversation.

"You haven't even been married for six months," Stella is saying, turning to Gunnar with an unmistakable expression of fear.

"Remarried," I correct. Eight years ago, Abigail and I witnessed a secret ceremony between Bo and Hettie, and being one of the only people who knew Prince Bo was married weighed heavy on me. But I kept his secret, even though I didn't agree with how he left/ended things with Hettie.

No one understood that. I'm just glad it's all out in the open, and they are back together.

And happy.

It makes me wonder if there's a happily ever after out there for me.

Abigail brushes my arm as she reaches for her glass and I smile down at her.

"We've missed a lot of time," Hettie explains, her hand resting on Bo's. "Speaking of which—" She glances over at him. "We should get back and check on our little princess."

"Is Dad watching her again?" Gunnar asks with a chuckle. The thought of the king of Laandia babysitting his granddaughter is amusing for all, even more so when you think about how Tema has him wrapped around her finger. The girl could ask for anything—a pony, a crown, another country—and King Magnus would make it happen.

"It's a group effort," Bo says with a worried look since he's well aware of how not only his father, but the entire castle staff, indulges his daughter.

Bo might be the worst of them all.

I know he's trying to make up for the time he missed with Tema, so no one can blame him.

"I think they fight about who is in charge," Bo adds. "Dad, Duncan, Mrs. Theissen..."

"Mrs. Theissen takes charge, for sure." Abigail laughs.

"I think so too, but the king—"

"Dad," Bo corrects Hettie with a half-smile. "He told you to call him Dad."

"He's my Lord and Sovereign King," Hettie protests. "I'm not quite at the *Dad* phase yet."

"King Daddy," I suggest with a grin. Tema still occasionally refers to Bo as Prince Daddy, but she's been dropping the prince more often these days, to Bo's delight.

The man, whose favourite pastime used to be spending sixteen hours a day tromping through the forest with an axe slung over his shoulder, turns to mush when his little girl calls him Daddy.

It's... sweet. And slightly terrifying.

"Magnus," Hettie decides. "I can manage that. We'll work on the Dad."

"Let's get back, see what the little terror did tonight."

While it is possible Tema could get away with literal murder at the castle, the little girl is still a treat, and thankfully, hasn't shown the signs of becoming the stereotypical spoiled brat.

There's a lot of talk about if Tema will take after Lyra in that matter, just because Tema physically resembles her aunt at that age.

Lyra was a lot of things, but I never considered her to be a brat. She was impulsive, often demanding and definitely liked getting her own way, but she was never a brat to me.

She was a lot of things to me, but not that.

I tell myself that it's the talk of Tema that has me sliding into thoughts of Lyra. Because of the similarities of the princesses, not the fact there's been radio silence from Lyra for the last three weeks, which is worrying. It could mean a lot of things, though:

She could be off on an African safari without cell service. She could be holed up in a hotel in Paris, working as a muse for some fashion designer, or following Sabrina Carpenter's latest tour, hobnobbing with her celebrity friends all night, and sleeping all day.

Or she could have run off with some man nobody would approve of and who only wants to use her for his fifteen minutes of fame, and she's afraid to tell me.

Tell *us*, not just me. Tell the family.

When it comes to Lyra, it could be any of those things, and more.

Contact with her brothers has always been infrequent, but it's constant with me, texting me daily or sending me silly reels or pictures. But that's stopped since...

Since Abigail.

I tell myself I don't miss getting sixteen pictures of shoes and demands to tell her which one is my favourite. I'm worried because not hearing from Lyra might mean she's about to show up on the cover of a magazine with a story about how she came between Tom Holland and Zendaya. Or have drunken pictures of her splashed over the internet. Or reports that she hosted a party that took over a high-end Toronto restaurant and caused the place to get slapped with a health warning because someone lured a raccoon into the party.

That actually happened last year. And I was sent to clean up the mess—not from the raccoon, but the media mess about how Princess Lyra of Laandia is a demanding diva whose rebellious and irresponsible behaviour made the Canadian government rethink giving Laandia their autonomy, as well as fishing rights.

I cleaned it all up.

My official job title is "lawyer", but I'm more like a fixer for the family. I deal with little things—Kalle's alcohol permit for his bar, Odin's proposal for his Viking restoration site—and big things, like Bo's secret wedding. Ever since my father brought me to live in the castle, I've been made to feel like part of the family. Still, I manage to be objective enough to see the big picture, make the tough decisions. My loyalty to them has no bounds—not just because they are the royal family, but because they're my family.

But not really.

I fix things for the family, and I do a very good job of it. And Lyra is always giving me a new challenge.

I really should track her down to make sure things aren't about to spiral out of control. "Can I get a ride back to the castle with you?" I ask Bo suddenly. I have a suite of rooms in the castle, but I divide my time between there and my apartment in town.

"You're not—" Abigail checks herself but I can see the flash of disappointment. "Oh."

Did I make plans with her? I don't think I saw that in my schedule. "I've got an early meeting with the finance minister in the morning," I tell her. "It's easier to stay there tonight."

"Okay. Sure."

I notice Hettie watching us. I'm sure this will be part of their next discussion. I lower my voice. "Are you okay with that?"

"I just thought... It's fine."

I've dated. I've had relationships. But none of them has ever felt serious. None of them has ever felt like my future is there, waiting for me to grab it.

I've never fully committed to a woman like Bo has done with Hettie. Like Gunnar has with my sister. Something has always held me back, and I've never really explored what that is.

Abigail deserves someone to be committed. She deserves someone as invested as she is. And I'm...

To be honest, I don't know if I'm that someone.

It's been a while since she's stayed the night at my place. She must be thinking of that, but I...

I can't go there right now. Not with the upcoming meeting that I still need to be briefed on, and the plans for the new hotel opening that Fenella Carrington has gone overboard with that I also need to check, and tracking down Lyra.

I can only shrug. "Early meetings," I say to Abigail with a rueful smile. "And you have the late shift at the coffee shop so you can sleep in. I don't like to disturb you."

"I'm okay being disturbed," she says under her breath.

What's wrong with me? "Tomorrow," I promise. "We'll do dinner, and then you can make me sit through an episode of The Suitor and I won't complain at all."

"Okay, but The Suitor isn't starting for a few weeks," she says, her smile not as bright as it usually is. "And it's The Suitorette this time."

"I don't know if that's better or worse."

Abigail laughs and I relax. Things are so easy with her. "It's less drama with a group of men. You'll like that."

"Sure." I roll my eyes good-naturedly. "Sure, I will."

Bo settles the bill and he and Hettie start the round of good-byes. For a moment, I don't think Abigail is going to leave—and she doesn't have to. She can stay with Gunnar and Stella. She has other friends here tonight. She can—

My phone rings.

Not only my phone, but Bo's and Gunnar's ring in unison. And behind the bar, I see Kalle reach around to where his phone sticks out of the back pocket of his jeans.

Gunnar is the first to check. "It's Odin," he says, answering the group FaceTime call. Bo and I don't bother with our phones, but crowd in beside him. "What's up, O?"

"You have no idea what she did this time," Odin rages.

She. It feels like a hand has reached inside my body to squeeze my stomach, like someone checking a melon at the market.

I don't even have to ask Odin who *she* is because I know exactly whom he's talking about.

It's the tone of his voice.

Lyra.

Did she get arrested? Is she topless on a magazine cover? Been deported from some country because she "borrowed" a catamaran from some politician's son when he was passed out on some island?

Did she get married?

Deep breaths help me deal with the stress of the unknown, but I can only manage a shaky one. "What did Lyra do this time?" I demand.

"She's going to be the next Suitorette."

She's what?

This—this is not what I expected. Lyra likes to think she's an influencer, so I can see her her going on a reality show, something like *Daughters of Wealthy and Powerful Men and the Trouble They Get Into*—if that was a real show—but The Suitorette?

Why is Lyra looking to fall in love? And on a reality show? She could have any man she wanted.

The stomach squeeze gets tighter. "Where did you get the info? Has it been confirmed?" Two very realistic questions, spoken in a calm voice. I've asked the same questions countless times for the entire royal family of Laandia, not just Lyra.

"I heard it from the horse's mouth," Odin blusters. "Grayson Grant."

Abigail gasps and clutches Hettie at the mention of his name. Both of them look too excited for this conversation.

"He's the host of the show, isn't he?" Gunnar asks.

"And the executive producer," Odin explains, uncharacteristically flustered. "Camille had the idea to offer the island as a location for the show, and they took us up on it. Shooting begins in three days and Grayson is staying with us at the house. He just told us. He thought we knew!"

"He thought you knew—?" Bo begins just as Kalle joins us.

"That Lyra is going to be on the show." Odin's voice is loud enough for heads to turn but no one turns down the volume. "She's going to be the Suitorette. She's going to star in a reality show, dating twenty-five men. At the same time."

"Oh, hell no," Kalle growls.

"We've got to stop her," Bo agrees.

Gunnar is laughing, and they all turn to me. "Spence?" Odin pleads. "You've got to— She can't do this?"

"Why can't she?" Abigail asks.

2

Lyra

"**H**AVE YOU TOLD THEM yet?" Kate asks, her normally cheerful expression showing a little too much concern for this hour.

"I have a feeling someone else will do that for me." The iPad is propped against the pillows on my bed, so it's like Kate is here to help me pack.

Or pack for me, which she's done in the past.

I love living in Chicago, but what I can't get used to is that my second-favourite city doesn't have Kate McKibbon. It's not like we're joined at the hip; I've been away from Battle Harbour for years now, but I did spend a few of those years bopping around, following Kate to school, and then on to Ottawa when she found work there.

But these days, Kate's back in Battle Harbour and I'm still living in the Windy City, with no real reason to be here.

I throw a handful of underwear into the suitcase on the bed, taking a moment to stare out of the wall of windows at the sliver of Lake Michigan I can see from my bedroom.

Along with Kate, I miss the ocean.

"Have you thought this through?" Kate asks with all seriousness.

There's a pause, and we both laugh.

A few weeks ago, Grayson Grant, the very attractive host of the reality dating show The Suitor, approached me at the wedding of a mutual friend and asked if I would consider becoming the next Suitorette.

I said yes, because why not?

Six weeks spent in the company of twenty-five men doesn't need much thinking through.

I've been the focus of cameras my whole life, and while I doubt I'll manage to find true love with one of the men—the ultimate goal of the show—it will be fun. There will be group dates, and one-on-one dates, and even overnight dates for the lucky few who manage to stick around.

It's an added bonus that the season will take place on Saint Pierre. I'll be able to explore the island, hang out at the beach and spend time with my brother Odin and sister-in-law, Camille who runs the place.

It'll be fun. At least I *think* it will be. Not that Camille isn't amazing—she is—and the island of Saint Pierre is tiny and quaint, with a small-town Battle Harbour-like vibe mixed with a little French *je ne sais quoi*.

But it is possible that living with my big brother when I'm supposed to be dating twenty-five men might be a bit of a challenge.

Odin thinks he knows what's best for me. All of my brothers do. That's what I get from being the youngest and the only girl.

Thanks, Mom and Dad.

I'm going to be the next Suitorette and I haven't given it much thought since I signed the contract. There was a clause that I wasn't allowed to tell anyone, so I used that as an excuse to push it out of my mind, and not tell my family.

The real reason I didn't tell them, is that I may be many things—willful and wayward and sometimes naughty, stubborn and wild, and often uncontrollable, according to the world's press—but I've never been a liar. And there's no way I was about to tell my family the truth.

I could tell them being on the show sounds like it'll be a good time.

I would be honest if I said I agreed to the Suitorette, because this will be an adventure, an experience, and I'm all for new things.

I like dating, I like men, and who doesn't want to fall in love?

But I might be lying if I tried to explain how my decision has *nothing* to do with the fact that Spencer is now officially dating Abigail Locke.

Dating twenty-five men under the constant surveillance of cameras will be fun. And even if it's not, the start of the season is only a few days away and I'm not about to start regretting my decisions.

I don't regret and I never second-guess.

When I was nine, I played hide and seek with my brothers and their friends. Ignoring my own rule of staying on the main floor of the castle, I snuck up to my mother's dressing room and made a nest out of her beaver fur coat. Five hours—and a nap—later, I emerged furious that Spencer didn't understand the stupid clue about where I was hiding. My parents had been away, and the castle staff and my brothers had been frantically searching for me the entire time.

When I was eleven, I stowed away on Birdie Bennet's fishing boat because I was angry that my brothers were going on their annual fishing trip with Duncan and I wasn't allowed to go.

The royal boat had to come and get me a day later.

At twelve, I organized a game of strip poker on a school bus heading to a field trip in Mary's Harbour. No skin was shown before the teachers caught us, but Danny McDermot had been *thisclose* to stripping off his T-shirt.

At fifteen, I snuck out onto the battlements with a bottle of ten-year-old Châteauneuf-du-Pape that some French diplomat had gifted my father. I attempted to send a smoke signal to Kate and might have set the roof of the castle on fire if Bo hadn't come storming up the drive and caught me.

I think it had been Spencer who told him I was there after I sent a series of half-drunken texts to him.

He got the clue where I was that time.

I've never regretted those decisions, nor did I second guess myself.

I also never took the time to think things through.

"Is there an explanation why your family shouldn't find out from *you* that you're going to be the next Suitorette?" Kate asks, as always, the voice of reason. "Because they're going to want to know."

"They don't tell me things." Am I bitter about this?

Maybe just a little bit.

On screen, Kate shakes her head. "Are you still upset about Bo and Hettie being married? Should I remind you that *no one* knew about that?"

"But it's Bo." And Spencer knew but didn't tell me. I may be a little bitter about that.

Spencer, who is my... I'm not sure what he is to me.

Not that it matters, because Spencer Laz is nothing to me now. He's with Abigail, and I say good for him.

Good for them.

My brothers—the crown princes of Laandia, Kalle, Odin, Bo, and Gunnar—are good men. Great men, even. But they are extraordinary men because our father is King Magnus and my brothers were born into a position not many men have the good fortunate to inherit in this world.

Spencer is the son of Duncan Laz, chief advisor and best friend to the king. But even without a crown, Spencer is extraordinary.

He is as brilliant and driven as a Forbes 100 businessman. As focused and loyal as a member of the Secret Service. And as savvy and sexy as any man in People's Magazine Sexiest Man of the Year edition.

He's also know-it-all, worrier, fixer of family affairs, and the best friend of *all* my brothers.

Kalle just asked him to be his best man, and this is after he did the same for Odin and Bo.

Spencer and I? We're... friends?

I'm not exactly sure what to call him.

Spencer has been my escort, date, babysitter, warden. He was my confidant, *my* best friend when I need him, and my girlhood crush.

And my teenage—and twentysomething—fantasy.

Spencer makes me laugh more than anyone else, other than Kate. He gets me more than anyone, *even* Kate. He's always been there, standing there, watching me from the shadows.

And now he's not, because Abigail Locke came home with Bo's wife Hettie, and Spencer decided he was in love with her.

Abigail, not Hettie.

It's a long story, and one I don't have the bandwidth for right now.

"Lyra," Kate chides, pulling me back from family drama, starring Spencer.

"That is the voice of the personal secretary of the royal family, not my best friend," I point out.

"Can't I be both?"

"Not tonight you can't."

I hear her sigh of exasperation, but I can't see the rolling of her eyes because I've turned to my closet, surveying what shoes to take.

"I'm heading to Odin's first thing in the morning, so I will explain everything to him," I promise Kate, dumping an armful of shoes on the bed. "He, of all people, should understand because he went on the show first, but of course, he'll want to forget all about that. But I'll tell him he gave me the idea, which will make him happy. He's always wanted me to follow in his footsteps like a good little sister."

"No, he hasn't."

"No, he hasn't," I agree. Odin may be a little stick-up-the-butt-ish for my liking, but he has always been an exemplary big brother.

They all are.

They just don't understand me.

Like living in Chicago. No one has any idea what brought me to the Windy City—except maybe Spencer.

He might be able to figure it out. If I wanted him to.

"Want to explain it to me?"

I turn back to the screen at Kate's question. "I told you."

"You said it will be fun."

"It will be."

"Lyra, you're planning on putting yourself out there on television. You're going to have to be vulnerable—"

"I can be vulnerable."

"Your shell is harder than an M&M left outside in January," Kate points out. "You are one tough cookie."

"Are you trying to make me hungry?"

"And you don't let anyone in," she finishes.

"I let *you* in."

"Because you had no choice. No one wanted to play with you because you're a princess, and no one wanted to play with me, because half of my family are the pariahs of Battle Harbour."

She does have a point. It was in kindergarten that we bonded as outsiders and if I ever became queen, the first thing I would do is exile that half of Kate's family.

"Plus, I know the secret to melt the crunchy M&M coating," Kate adds. "Not everyone will take the time to find the proper way. This is going to be new for you."

"You make it sound like I don't know how to make friends," I pout. "Gracie Abrams is my new bestie. And Millie Bobby Brown follows me on Insta. So there."

Kate is not impressed. "You're going to have to be soft. Less Lyra, maybe."

"If I'm not myself, how will they fall in love with me?"

Kate laughs, long and loud. "You know those guys will fall for you as soon as they step out of the car. That's not the point here. The point is that *you* want to fall in love with one of *them*. Right?"

"Right." I sound convincing, even to myself.

"So you're going to have to let them in. That's why you're going to do the show. Right?"

A pause.

Do I want to fall in love? Yes. Of course. Everyone needs love in their life, even the Party Princess.

I want my own happily ever after, just like my brothers are getting. Only it's proven to be a little more difficult for me.

I somehow manage to intimidate the good men, or push them away when they get too close. And the ones I should avoid with a ten-foot-pole flock around me like zombies looking for a brain. And honestly, some of them wear me down with their constant litany of compliments and presents of shiny things.

Also, it's like my heart stopped accepting guests after Mom died.

The Suitor—and Suitorette—shows may be formulaic reality television, full of needless drama and some contestants only there to find their fifteen minutes of fame, but it has worked its magic for some couples. Grayson and Bexley are the perfect example.

There may be more, but I'd have to look them up. I've watched a handful of episodes, enough to know what's in store for me, but I'm not a huge fan.

I think that's best.

"It'll be fun. I'll fall in love," I say blithely. "I'll be so soft I'll be squishy. No need to worry about anything. *No one* has to worry about anything."

I should reiterate that to my brothers. Because as soon as they hear I'm going to be the next Suitorette—and I know Grayson will tell Odin, who will tell the others—they will start to worry about why I'm doing it, how it will it work, and when I'll make a scene on television.

The why will be the big question.

All four of them have upped communication with me since Spencer got together with Abigail.

Even though they all claim that I drive them crazy, I know they all have a soft spot for their little sister.

If I told them earlier, they would ask the questions and give me the advice like they know what's best for me. They would think I'm doing this because of Spencer Laz and I'm not.

I'm really not.

And although I refuse to lie to other people, no one said anything about lying to myself.

The truth of the matter is that Spencer is with Abigail. And I need to find someone fast so I can stop feeling like I've had an essential part of my body ripped off.

Maybe not essential, like a hand or a foot. More like my elbow is missing and it's stopping me from doing things like I used to do them.

That's why I'm going on the show.

To learn to live without my elbow.

3

Spencer

"LYRA CAN'T BE THE Suitorette," Odin sputters.

Abigail leans forward to peer at the screen Gunnar is holding. "Sorry to disagree, Your Highness, but why can't she?"

All heads whip around to Abigail, who looks as surprised as Odin. "I mean, people go on that show to become famous—or as famous as you can from a reality show. Or they want to find love."

I remember what it sounded like the first time I was with Bo and he felled a tree. The crack when it began to fall, the noise when it landed, snapping branches, leaves flying.

It feels like that crack just happened to my heart, and now my branches are snapping as I land with a thud.

Lyra is looking for love.

That doesn't sound right. It definitely doesn't feel right.

And why is Abigail talking about *Lyra* and *love*? "That's why you went on it, right?" she asks Odin like he's standing here with us in the bar instead of in the kitchen in Saint Pierre. "Lyra doesn't need fame, so maybe she's serious about finding love."

I see Gunnar look at me. He opens his mouth and then shuts it, and I'm glad he does.

I know what he's thinking. I know what all of them are thinking, because I'm thinking the same thing.

It's always been assumed that if Lyra was looking for love, she'd be looking at me.

There's always been a connection between us. An understanding. We sit together during family dinners. I'm always the one she turns to with a funny aside or a complaint. I've been her escort/date/plus-one at countless events, galas and ceremonies.

She sends me pictures of her *shoes*.

Nothing has ever been said, but when you've been in love with a person for most of your life, you assume—and expect—a happily ever after one day.

And with that, my thoughts come to a screeching halt.

No one said I'm in love with Lyra. *I've* never said it. I've never even thought it.

Lyra doesn't think I'm in love with her. She's not in love with me. If she was, I would know, because men know things like that.

I would know.

We just... we're...

Friends. Princess Lyra and I are *friends*.

Who send an inordinate number of pictures to each other. And texts. Instagram reels.

Letters.

But we're just friends.

Besides, I'm with Abigail and how can I feel the way I do about Abigail and still have the assumption that a happily ever is still in the cards with Lyra?

That's not logical. Or possible. Or just—not.

I am not in love with Princess Lyra.

And if she wants to find love on a reality television show, so be it. Good luck to the men on the show, because she is a lot to handle.

Her brothers look to me to control her, which I always tell them is impossible because Lyra is headstrong and knows her own mind. If she wants to do something, she will do it.

It's the doing-it-without-me that feels a little off.

"She's going to be on the show?" I ask, just to clarify.

"That's what I'm trying to tell you." Odin is… upset. Surprising. He's the most serious of the family, other than Bo, and keeps his emotions behind the mask of the well-mannered, dutiful prince.

Not that he's a prince any longer—at least not officially. But he's still one of my best friends, crown or no crown.

"Lyra is moving into our house, because Camille did this thing and offered that the Suitorette could stay with us during the time she's on the island." Odin huffs a deep breath. "I had no idea it was going to be Lyra."

"But isn't it better that she's staying with you? So you can make sure she doesn't—" Gunnar doesn't finish the thought.

Doesn't what? Embarrass the royal family? Honestly, no one cares about that, other than the American press who have a history of promoting quasi-famous, attractive women into household names.

It's true that Lyra's claim to fame is that she's a princess. Her father is the king of Laandia. She's done some modelling, she's a social media influencer, and she gets her picture taken a lot. She's not famous.

Yet.

She is, but she's not.

But that's not why I'm worried.

"She's going to fall in love with one of these guys and we don't know anything about them," Kalle says in a tight voice.

That's sort of what's going through my mind as well. Sort of. "I'll get dossiers on them to check for security risks," I tell him.

Looking at this as a security risk gives me something to focus on.

"She might end up with one of these guys, Spence. Do you know what that means?"

I take another deep breath. And then another. I know what Odin is saying, and I don't like it. I don't like anything about this. The thought of Lyra meeting all of these men, spending time with them, kissing them—it's making me slightly nauseous.

More than slightly.

But I can't do anything about it. And I certainly shouldn't be feeling like that, not with Abigail sitting right beside me, giving me a skeptical side-eye.

I smile reassuringly at her. At least that's how I hope it comes across.

It's not like I can tell her what to do. No one can—or should—but her brothers obviously think putting their two cents in over this would be a good idea. I'm not Lyra's brother. I'm not... anything... to her. Some days we're not even friends.

Lyra has never told me how she feels about me—if she does feel anything.

And I've never told her either.

Abigail is still watching me, and she's not the only one. I smile ruefully. "It means that maybe she'll be happy," I say. "Besides, we can't stop her."

"You could!"

"No." I shake my head. "I can't."

"Odin was pretty peeved about the Lyra stuff," Bo says later when we're in the SUV being driven back to the castle. Now that Hettie and Tema are here, he's finally making use of his security detail. "Or do you think it was the Suitor stuff?"

I think Odin's reaction is that of a big brother, and not because he has a grudge against the show after getting voted off. Or sent home. I'm not sure how it works.

I don't have time for reality television nor the energy to watch the drama competition between that many people would produce.

Am I supposed to watch the show now that Lyra will be on it?

That would be a different sort of torture.

I suspect this conversation will be as well.

I'm not sure if I said goodnight to Abigail—a proper goodnight like a boyfriend would, with a hug and a kiss, and an *I'll call you later*. Because I am Abigail's boyfriend.

I am nothing to Lyra, so why is *Lyra is looking for love* echoing in my head like a sonic boom?

"What do you think about it?" Bo continues.

Bo is really going there—right now, when Hettie is sitting between us in the back of the SUV. I should have driven my own car home. "About why Odin is so upset?"

"No, Spence," Hettie says impatiently. "About if *you're* upset. You and Lyra are—"

"Nothing," I snap. I soften my voice and my expression. "We are nothing." It's not like I can say anything else. Hettie is my friend and she's also Abigail's best friend. I know what side she'd be on.

"I was going to say complicated," she corrects.

"Yeah. That," Bo agrees. "I love you and Abigail, but you and Lyra? When you see the two of you together..."

The way that Lyra always stands just a little too close to me. The way I finish her sentences and whisper comments in her ear to make her laugh. The way that we're always the last to leave a party or the dinner table.

How I find some reason to touch Lyra when I'm close to her.

Hettie sighs with frustration. "I know you and Abigail have gotten close since we've been back and I'm happy about that. So happy." She pats my knee with a big smile. "You have no idea. But Abigail aside—I care about you, Spence. And if you have *any* feelings for Lyra, whether you want to admit them or not, you need to put a stop to this."

How does Hettie know that was my first instinct? That instead of being driven to the castle, I wanted nothing more but to catch the first flight to Saint Pierre and drag Lyra home.

I've never been the Neanderthal type, and the urge to throw Lyra over my shoulder and away from all other men makes me a little shaky.

The fact I had this urge while I was saying goodnight to Abigail makes me sick to my stomach.

"Easier said than done," I mutter. "Not that I would. Or could. It's her decision."

"Yes, but you are the one who will suffer," Hettie says in a gentle voice. "Trust me on this—those years I was away from Bo, my heart broke whenever I saw a picture of him with another woman."

"Hettie," Bo protests.

"I'm not saying this to make you feel bad." She turns to him. "And thank god there weren't that many of them. But it hurt. And Lyra is going to be all over the place, and it mightbe painful. I don't like the thought of you hurt."

"It'll be fine." I sound convincing. I sound sure of myself.

But Hettie believes me even less than I believe myself.

"Oh, Spence. You lie. And you need to decide how much you can take," she tells me with another pat on the knee. "Because trust me—it won't be fine."

"Do you think she's doing this because of you and Abigail?" Bo asks.

"No," I scoff, even though the same thought has me spiraling since Odin's call.

It would be such a Lyra thing to do.

But if that's her reason, then it would mean— "No," I repeat, less forcefully this time.

If that's the reason, then I can't blame her. I told Lyra I wanted to explore a relationship with Abigail and that's what I'm doing. But still...

It's difficult to give up old dreams, especially when you're not sure that's all they are. Old dreams.

"What do you do when she falls in love with one of these guys?" Bo asks.

I can't answer because I don't know. I don't know what I would do. And I don't know what to say to Bo about this.

I should know what I would do, because I always know. Because if I don't know, that means I should have been figuring all of this out all along. I should have let myself find out what Lyra really is to me, rather than have it suddenly become this massive issue that I know will keep my up all night.

Bo just looks at me.

I finally have to turn away from his gaze.

4

Lyra

"WHY ARE YOU DOING this?" Odin demands.

I've been in the house exactly thirty-seven minutes. Time enough for Madame Carol to show me to my room, for Camille to come running and excitedly throw her arms around me.

I'm not used to an excited Camille, or one who initiates first contact. It's nice, but will definitely take some getting used to.

All this will take some getting used to.

As will Camille's dogs: tiny rat-dog Betty White who sniffs at my ankles like she's about to take a chunk out of me, and goofy, gangly horse-dog Bea Arthur. She would have knocked me over in her excitement had Camille not grabbed me.

They make the house seem fuller, more complete.

I've never had a dog before and I crouch in an attempt to make friends with Betty White. I think I like them. Even with the dismissive curl of her lip, I'm confident I'll win her over before I leave.

Kate's warning from last night still rings in my ears, following me from Chicago to St. John's, Newfoundland where I took the ferry across the St. Lawrence to Saint Pierre because I've never done it before. I had a great conversation with an eighty-year-old former fisherman and his wife eager to tell me all the gossip from Saint Pierre.

They even invited me to dinner with my "beau" after the show ends. Hope it's good that I told them what's going on.

Odin didn't pick me up at the dock, but he did send a car. I don't know if I was more annoyed or relieved.

Camille takes me down to the kitchen, where Madame Carol has a chilled bottle of Sauvignon Blanc waiting. I need the help because Odin is there readying for the attack.

The thirty-eighth minute of me being in the house has my big brother starting a tirade of how irresponsible I am to go on the show.

My brothers always think they have a right to tell me what to do.

Like they never made mistakes.

Odin, the second son, is now happily married to Camille, the new prefect of Saint Pierre. She agreed to marry him because she needed a husband to govern her tiny island nation. Technically, it's a French island nation, and Camille just looks after it, but she takes it as seriously as if she's a queen.

Camille will never be queen because Odin abdicated his position to the throne to move here with Camille and support her.

I never really saw that coming.

I may not have much to do with the running of Laandia, or give much thought to the list of events and committees and groups Duncan presents me with every year as suggestions for how I can be more involved, but I *love* being a princess.

Who wouldn't?

I have wealth and freedom and a certain amount of standing. Yes, I have a public persona that I try not to let embarrass herself, but it's not too far off of my true self to be a challenge. Doors are opened for me. Friends around the world are cultivated without too much effort. I'm welcome anywhere.

The only thing I don't have falling into my lap, is the love of a good man.

Stress on the word *good*.

Men continually tell me they *want, need, have to have me*. I've had twenty-three proposals of marriage since I turned sixteen, and the L-word has been thrown at me more times than I can count.

And because I haven't accepted these declarations in kind, I'm seen as picky, a tease, high-maintenance and a slew of other names, none of which are very respectable to call a princess.

Unfortunately, I learned at an early age that, while I am lucky to have a lot of things, respect hasn't always been one of them.

But still, I wait politely until Odin takes a breath.

"Hypocrite," I say, coughing into my hand.

"What did you say?" The furrow between Odin's eyes reminds me of our father's.

"I said, I didn't realize my big brother, the stoic sword-master and Viking ancestor advocate was a hypocrite." I glance at Camille's expression of surprise. She may be married to him but she's been hiding out too long on Saint Pierre and hasn't seen someone—me—shut my brother up. "I know it was traumatic for you, but did you somehow blank out that week or so that you were on the show? That you decided, on your own, and possibly needed to apply, to be on The Suitorette?"

"That's different," Odin blusters.

"Yes, because I am the star and you... were not," I say.

Grayson did admit that the show had considered Odin for the Suitor for the next season, but then he announced his engagement to Camille and had no need for the magic of reality romance.

Not that I think anything about this will be magical.

Or maybe it will be.

I've always considered myself as lucky, so I might find the love of my life on a television reality show.

Or...I might not.

Odin's question is the fourth time he's demanded to know why I agreed to go on the show, all worded slightly differently but with the same meaning. Before our in person chat, it was through text and email, and one garbled FaceTime call when I was boarding my plane.

I love all my brothers, but why did you birth them this way?

The silent question is directed at my mother because even though she's gone, there are some things you can only talk to about with your mom.

"Odin." I twirl my glass between my fingers. "Did anyone ask *you* why you went on the show? Or, why any of you let People Magazine take pictures of you for the sexy issue?"

"Sexiest Man issue," Odin corrects, his tone stiff like he's embarrassed.

Embarrassed to admit he *liked* being featured in the magazine, more like it.

"Full of sexy men." I turn to Camille and roll my eyes. She smiles.

My sister-in-law is totally on my side.

But Odin is red in the face and looking like he might be close to picking up one of his swords and swinging it at me, so I'd better give him something. "It sounded like fun," I concede. "So I thought I'd give it a try. I always look good on camera."

"Fun?" he splutters. "How is it fun to have your heart broken?"

"Who says anyone is going to break my heart?" I demand. "Maybe that's what happened to you, big brother—"

"Did you get your heart broken?" Camille adds, turning to him with ice in her gaze.

"No! No. I...it was..." he stammers.

"Embarrassing?" I offer

"Humiliating?" Camille raises an eyebrow.

"Mortifying?" I'm enjoying myself. "But it still turned out pretty good for you, didn't it?" I gesture to Camille, now sitting with her arms crossed. "You got the girl in the end."

"Yes, but..." Some of Odin's bluster deflates. "We don't want to see you get hurt."

"That won't happen. You should worry about the men who signed up for this." I look at Camille with an evil smile and tap my fingers together. "I'm going to go through them like a fat kid eating Smarties."

Maybe not the best thing to say in front of my brother. "Lyra! You can't say that on television. And you can't—no." He drops his head into his hands. "We don't want to see anyone eating Smarties."

"Who's *we*?" I counter.

"Me. Our brothers." Odin heaves a sigh. "Spencer."

"This is none of Spencer's concern," I say quickly, with enough chilliness in my own tone to cool this entire bottle of wine. "Or anyone else's."

"Technically, it might be your father's," Camille, who lived under her father's iron rule for far too long, says tactfully. "If he has a concern."

"Does he?" I ask Odin politely. "Because I'm sure you told him as soon as you found out."

Not that I'm completely irresponsible—I did speak to my father and the right hand of the king, Duncan, before I signed the contract. Neither of them thought there would be any problems, and Dad even told me to go easy on the guys. I told them there was a privacy issue, and the show wanted to keep it confidential until the reveal, so they couldn't say anything to my brothers.

So I may have fibbed a little to Kate—I did mention it to my family, but not *all* of them.

Because—*this*. Odin's reaction is expected. I'm sure Kalle and Bo have their reservations as well. Gunnar likes the spotlight as much as I do, so I know he won't have an issue—but they've let Odin have at it. Have at *me*, to try and change my mind.

Silly boys.

Silly, silly brothers.

"Does our father have a problem with this?" I reiterate.

"He... doesn't," Odin admits with more reluctance than Bo has being a prince. "Have a concern with it."

"Which is exactly what he said to me when I told him. So what's the problem?"

Odin stares, some unsaid accusation in his gaze. This is the closest I've seen Odin to losing his temper in a long time. "He lets you do anything."

"At least I told him," I say smugly. "He'll be ready when my old love stories come out. No offense," I add to Camille since she had been part of Odin's old love story.

Camille met Odin when she was eighteen, they shared a perfect night together, and fell in love. At least Camille did; Odin had been twenty and lacked the brain-power of a normal man in the midst of a good woman. After sharing hopes and dreams through letters, which I think is the most romantic thing ever, Odin ghosted Camille and left her with a broken heart.

Which is not romantic at all.

Fast forward ten years later, and Odin surprised us all by showing up on The Suitorette. On his date, in his attempt to be vulnerable and relatable, he told the world about his night with Camille, and how she was the one who got away.

This was news to Camille, and she was understandably furious. In an attempt to stem societal backlash that smacked him for letting such an amazing woman get away, Odin proposed an arrangement between him and Camile. I'm sure Camille would have preferred to see the slow and methodic torture of my brother, but unfortunately, she needed a husband more than she needed revenge—some archaic law states prefects must be married to govern Saint Pierre—and she agreed to marry him.

Fortunate for us.

Thankfully, what began as an arranged marriage ended in a love match when they fell for each other all over again.

Happily ever after for Odin.

Which started a bit of a trend for my brothers. Kalle, Gunnar, and even Bo have gotten their own happily ever after since then.

I love my brothers, but, c'mon.

I'm supposed to be the princess in the fairy tale, and there is no Prince Charming in sight.

The only one left in the family who hasn't found their person.

I've never handled being last very well.

"Look, Odin—" I put the emphasis on the second syllable of his name. "I'm going to assume you're fussing about this because you care, not because of some grudge you might have against the show. If that is the case, need I remind you—" I gesture to Camille impatiently. "You got the girl. And I'd appreciate if you take your huffing and puffing and step aside and let me find my boy. If he's out there. If not, I get six weeks of fun with a bunch of really cute men, and you get six weeks of my company. Everyone's a winner." I give him my big-eyed, imploring stare that I perfected when I was about three and which has gotten me out of too many messes to count. "Can you do that for me? Please? Because all I want is what all my brothers have already got. True love." Blink blink, widening my blue eyes.

And it works, because Odin gives a huff. "Fine. I just don't want to see you hurt. Or... I don't know... made fun of?"

I laugh like Nikki Glaser is roasting my last ex. "I'd like to see them try."

"Lyra..."

"No, seriously," I tell him. "I'm Princess Lyra of Laandia and I have very tall brothers, who all have awesome significant others who will *mess up* whoever dares to mess with me." I pat my brother's hand and glance at Camille. "Am I right?"

"I'm after them right after Edie, because she's…" Camille gives a helpless shrug.

"Scary as poop," I finish. "I got you. No one is going to make fun of me, O, and I'm not going to worry about getting hurt because Grayson promises these men are polite and respectful and are here for all the right reasons." I slap my chest. "Me."

Odin shrugs and I know I have him. "Thank you for your big-brotherly concern, and tell Kalle and Bo I appreciate their support—" Camille snickers at my sarcastic tone. "But chill out. Enough is enough."

He doesn't reply, and I take that as a win. "Now—" I turn to Camille as I stand, grabbing my glass of wine along with the rest of the bottle. "Want to come up and check out the new clothes I've got for the show before you feed me whatever amazing thing Madame Carol is making? If you're nice to me, I might let you borrow them."

Camille drops a kiss on Odin's head before she grabs a second bottle and follows me to my room, Betty White trotting at her heels.

I totally have the dog on my side.

5

Spencer

THE NEXT DAY, ABIGAIL asks me to meet her for coffee.

Before I can do that, I negotiate with the finance minister, sit in on a meeting with my father, the king, and the UK Secretary of State, and stay for Fenella's proposal to gentrify the neighbourhood of houses on the edge of town that have been sitting vacant for the last few years.

By the time I head into Battle Harbour in time to see Abigail, I'm ready for a break.

Twelve-or-fourteen-hour days have been the norm for me since I graduated law school, but since Abigail got back, I've been trying to cut back. It makes her happy when I'm not falling asleep during a movie.

But she doesn't look all that happy when I see her standing outside Coffee for the Sole, and her expression opens a yawning pit in my stomach. Something feels off.

Or maybe it's me.

After I got back to the castle last night, I made sure I had everything I needed for the morning's meeting. And then I spent over an hour convincing myself not to call Lyra to find out what the hell she was doing.

I couldn't, because it's none of my business. We're friends—I think—so the only reason I should call her is to wish her well.

As a pseudo-member of the royal family, I could make it my business, but it wouldn't be pretty if I got her on the phone. We'd end up fighting, like what usually happens when I question her judgement about something.

And I am questioning her judgement.

But deep down, I know there's more to my concerns about Lyra than how her behaviour will affect the royal family.

And that's why something feels off with Abigail.

I shouldn't have been thinking about Lyra. I shouldn't have let those thoughts keep me awake because I needed to be sharp for the meeting.

I need this third cup of coffee more than I usually do, and it's all Lyra's fault.

"How did it go this morning?" Abigail asks as I hug her hello.

"Fine. The finance minister was amenable to my suggestions and—"

"I meant, how did it go talking to the king about Lyra? I figure that would be a priority."

I blink with surprise. There's a crispness in Abigail's tone, like she sharpened the edges of her words. "Why would you think that?"

"You seemed upset when Odin told us last night."

"I wasn't."

"He called to tell you—"

"He called to tell *all* of us," I correct, feeling a mild panic starting to rise.

"He must have thought you'd be *something* about it," she says with a knowing glance at me. "I need a coffee and then let's take a walk. Do you have time?"

"I—sure. Of course. But I don't understand—"

"I think you do." She opens the door and heads inside the coffee shop.

Greetings ring out as we head to the counter, grouping our names together like we're a couple.

Which I expect we are.

I've never been part of a couple here in Battle Harbour. I've always been *single Spencer* while I've lived here. My relationships—if you can call them that—have been with people outside of the royal circle. My involvements happened while I was away, with women from away. I've never even brought a woman home to meet my friends and family.

There have been many who asked to meet the royal family once they heard of my connections, but they never lasted very long.

I've always felt *wrong* to have a woman on my arm walking through the streets of Battle Harbour. Stopping for coffee at Coffee for the Sole, having fish and chips after work, playing pool at The King's Hat.

It's different with Abigail because we did all those things before, when we were younger. When we were just friends. Once Hettie and Bo got together in high school, Abigail and I made up an inseparable foursome. I was a year ahead of Bo in school and I left for university right after graduation, but Bo, Hettie and Abigail stayed here, so I came home a lot to be with them.

Walking into Coffee for the Sole with Abigail now has an odd sense of déjà vu.

Only it's different.

After we get our order and chat to Silas for a few minutes—about Lyra, since that's all the town wants to talk about
now that the news about her being the Suitorette has been announced—we head across the square to the pier. It's nearly empty
at this time of the afternoon. Most of the fishing boats are out and
it's too early for crowds waiting for their catch to begin gathering.
The waves lap at the pier, a soothing backdrop for the ever-present
calls of the seagulls. Out on the water, a few boats are visible and if
I squint, that might be the blowhole of a whale.

Or it might just be a wave.

I don't often take the time to appreciate what Battle Harbour
has to offer, but on a late June day like today, it's obvious there is
a lot to offer.

"The capelin roll will be starting soon," I say as we step off the
pier onto the rocky beach.

"Any day now," Abigail agrees, pushing her short hair away
from her face. "Fenella is planning a party around it."

"Fun." The capelin are small, silvery fish that live in the Atlantic. Once a year, they move, en masse, to the beaches to spawn,
creating a wave, or roll, of fish. People catch them with hooks, lines,
nets, and buckets, and even sometimes by hand.

Their arrival in the water around Battle Harbour means the
arrival of summer, and today, the breeze is warm, the sun is bright,
and it feels like summer is beginning.

"I didn't bring you here to talk about fish," Abigail points out.
"As interesting as it might be."

"I do talk a lot about fish," I say ruefully, years of fishing dis-
putes with the Canadians, the French, and even Scotland, making

me far more knowledgeable about the animal than I've ever wanted to be. "I didn't talk to the king this morning," I add as Abigail pauses to slip off her shoes to walk close to the water. Screaming seagulls join us in the hope that we have more than coffee in our hands. "I don't know why you think Lyra's decision would be a concern for me."

"Are you in love with her?"

"I—" My mind blanks. I have no idea how to answer that. Lyra is... Lyra has always—I have always...

"Scratch that." Abigail stoops to pick up a piece of sea glass, looking out at the waves instead of me. "You *are* in love with her. The family knows it. The whole country knows it. Anyone who has seen you two together, or even a picture of the two of you, can tell." Her shoulders slump with resignation.

"Abigail—"

She turns to me and her expression...

I hope I never have to see such hurt and disappointment cross anyone's face. Luckily, she's wearing her sunglasses, so I don't have to see the sadness in her dark eyes.

I know it's there.

"I thought, maybe, because of our history, I might have a chance," she says in a low voice like she's talking to herself. "I think you started to believe it too, and then this."

"This...?" If I pretend not to know what she's talking about, will it all go away?

"The Suitor show. The Suitorette, actually. The fact that Princess Lyra is the Suitorette."

It's not going away. I'm really going to have to deal with this. I stare out at the water, afraid to look at Abigail. "Lyra can do what she wants," I offer. "It's no business of mine."

"Oh, but it is, Spencer. And now it's my business." She turns back to the water just in time to see a pelican swoop down to grab an afternoon snack.

She points it out, and I think it's all over.

But no. Abigail is just getting started. "I'm all for Princess Lyra doing what she wants," she says in a flat voice. "But her going on a reality dating show means there will be many men falling in love with her. Good for her, if that's what she wants. But unfortunately for you, you're going to have to watch that all play out. You're going to have to watch her fall in love with one of them. Maybe more. And that's going to hurt."

This is exactly what Hettie said.

I know there's always been that possibility—that Lyra will fall in love with someone else—but the blunt way Abigail talks about it, like it's a done deal, hits harder than I expect.

"I don't want to see you get hurt." She sounds so sad, like it's already happened.

"I won't be hurt. Why would I?" There are reasons, none of which I'm about to list for Abigail, or even myself.

Deny, deny, deny. It works for a lot of things.

"You really think that? What do you honestly think about Lyra going on the show?" Abigail asks.

"I don't know," I admit because it's the truth. Since Odin called, I haven't let myself process the fact that Lyra...

I swallow painfully. Still don't want to process, especially in front of Abigail.

Abigail is my girlfriend. She's the person I want to be with.

Our names sound right together when we enter a store. We hang out with Hettie and Bo, and it's fun. It's comfortable with Abigail.

"You were quiet," she persists. "You didn't say anything. That's not a good thing."

"I can be quiet."

"That's not what I mean. The way I look at it, you can deal with it in a few ways." She finally glances over her shoulder at me, like she's asking for permission to continue. I usually like hearing Abigail's theories, so I motion for her to go ahead. She holds up a finger. "You can make a big deal about it, which means that you have a problem with it."

She pauses, so I think she wants my thoughts. "I—"

But she doesn't let me finish. "And that would mean that it's obvious you have feelings for her." She holds up a second finger. "Or you can be so non-committal that I have to believe it means nothing to you, other than your best friend's sister doing something you don't agree with." She looks pointedly at me, but I'm afraid to say anything.

Abigail smiles sadly. "Or you can be quiet, which means I have no idea what you're thinking. And maybe you don't either."

"There's nothing between me and Lyra," I say after a pause. Is it too long of a pause? Does that mean something?

"Is that by choice?" Abigail asks gently. "Or because you've never had the opportunity? Because, Spence, this would be a great opportunity."

"What? How? *Why?*" The questions bubble and I'm so shocked that none of them are making sense. "What are you trying to tell me?"

"I'm not telling you anything. I want *you* to tell *me* you don't care about Lyra dating twenty-five men and possibly falling in love with them. I want you to tell me that if Lyra fell in love on that show, that you would only wish her the best. That you wouldn't regret not taking a chance with her for the rest of your life."

I pause and it feels like this one really does go on forever. I open and shut my mouth a few times before I can find the words.

"I can't tell you that," I finally admit.

From the expression on Abigail's face, I don't think they are the right words.

"Would you have ever admitted it to me? Or just let me go on thinking I was the one you really wanted to be with?" She turns to me and I have to face her. Face this.

And by the way Abigail lifts her chin, and the lack of surprise on her face, she knows. She's always known.

Everyone has always known what I've never admitted to myself.

The photo evidence of the men passing through Lyra's life, is bad enough. Lyra being the Suitorette is like an open invitation that she has given up on all of these other men.

Given up on me.

If Lyra was to fall in love with any of them, that would be its own form of torture.

I would get over it. I would deal. But Abigail is right—I would never forgive myself for not taking a chance to see what we could be together.

"I don't know..." *I don't know what you're talking about*, is what I should say. The words are forming in my head, moving to my mouth. *Of course I'm not in love with Princess Lyra. I'm in love with you.*

That's what I should say.

But it's not what comes out.

"I don't know if I'm in love with her," I confess, keeping my gaze out on a point at the horizon. How many kilometers away is Saint Pierre? I may not have spoken to the king, but I did look up Lyra's itinerary and that's where she is.

She should have arrived in Saint Pierre by now.

"Or you."

Abigail sucks in her breath but when I finally turn to her, there's no sign of surprise on her face.

"I'm sorry." I take Abigail's hand and she lets me. I want to pull it to my chest, to take back those words, but I can't.

There is love between me and Abigail, and there are years of friendship and she deserves the truth.

"I wanted to be in love with you so much," I tell her. "And I tried. I really did, because we're so good together. It's so easy with you."

"That's not why you stay with someone," she says drily but still lets me keep her hand.

"I do love you—"

"But Lyra gets in the way," she finishes. "It's my own fault. I've always known you have this weird co-dependent relationship with her."

"Co-dependent?"

She gives me a small smile. "I like to believe that's what it is. It makes me feel better."

"Abigail…"

"I know you're in love with her, Spence. You have been since you were a kid. I just hoped our history could have beat it out of you."

I laugh awkwardly. "That doesn't sound pleasant."

"Neither does hearing you admitting you're in love with her."

"I didn't admit it," I point out. "I don't know if I'm in love with her."

"But you are something." She finally pulls her hand away from mine. "And you're not in love with me."

"Abigail…"

"Please." She puts up her hand. "You love me—I know that. But as friends. I'm someone you care about. But you're not in love with me. There's a difference, you know."

Oh, I know. It's not the first time I've been accused of being a horrible boyfriend.

"I don't know what to say," I say helplessly.

"Well, you better figure it out. Because if I'm letting you go so you can find out once and for all exactly what is between you and Lyra, you better start planning. We're talking open and honest and grand gestures. And you need to tell me about it. Because I want you to be happy, Spence. It's all I've ever wanted."

I pull her into my arms, wanting to offer some comfort.

Or maybe it's me who needs the hug. "I don't deserve you," I say into her hair.

Abigail tightens her arms around my waist. "No. You don't. But I'm giving up a lot, so don't mess this up."

6

Lyra

I HAVE TWO DAYS to prepare for being the Suitorette.

I actually had three weeks, but I'm in Saint Pierre for only two days before we start filming. And it won't be televised for another month, to allow the producers and editors and everyone else involved can work their magic to take it from hours of boring video to an emotional, drama-filled, must-watch happily ever after starring yours truly.

In those two days, I've never had so many cameras pointing at me, and I'm a princess.

This is after the "make-over" that my team is tasked with performing. I like to think I'm fairly consistent in my grooming so there's not much outward difference when they finish with me, but the hours I spend being pricked and prodded *should* have resulted in some sort of transformation rather than looking like I just got a glow-up.

I have my hair cut and styled. A facial and a full-body scrub. My teeth are whitened and brightened.

Mani, pedi, and everything waxed. Then they touch up my tan with a spray.

While all this is going on, I have producers, Rue and Ria to keep me company. Grayson shows up occasionally, depending on how much privacy I need. The women don't give me that consideration.

Luckily, I quite like them both and having them around isn't a big deal. Except Rue must have a Mrs. Theissen gene because she feels the need to instruct me about everything Suitor-related.

It's helpful because as we get close to filming, I start to feel a little nervous. It's an unusual sensation for me. I do my best to push it down because I'm definitely not about to admit to anyone that I'm scared.

When I'm getting my hair cut, Grayson offers to show me pictures of the men, but I turn him down because I think it might make me feel worse.

What if I don't like any of them? What if I'm attracted to *all* of them? What if they don't like me and all decide to leave?

I don't share those thoughts either.

"If I start looking at them, I'll start sending them home now," I tell Grayson in a light and bright voice that is nothing like the queasy uneasiness inside my head. "And that won't be good for the show."

"If you're sure." Grayson frowns. "You don't think it'll be a good idea to prepare? Make some early decisions?"

"What am I supposed to prepare for? Hey, I don't like the way you look, go home? I may have the shallow, materialistic vibe, but it takes more than a funny-looking nose for me to turn a guy down."

"I don't get that vibe at all," Grayson protests.

I smile slyly at him. "Then I must be doing something wrong."

I know what the world thinks of me. People get the impression I'm all about the party, the wilder the better. That I like pretty, shiny things. That I'm high-maintenance and always need to get my own way.

And to be honest, I've never really given anyone an opportunity to see anything different.

According to Kate, that's what I'm supposed to do on the show, and that's what is making my stomach tighten into a little ball. I'm supposed to be open and honest about my feelings. Vulnerable. Show the real me.

And the thought of that is making me quiver like a little girl as the curtain rises on her first ever dance recital.

I—Lyra Bodil Selena Sif Erickson—am nervous. Who would have thought?

There are a few arguments when it comes to the gown I'll wear when I meet the men. The show wants me in a frothy, pink, princess dress, with enough tulle to outfit an entire ballet school.

I don't do pink and frothy. Makes me think of the unicorn foam back home at Coffee for the Sole.

Ria comes up with a compromise: it's a ballgown, but it's a dark indigo, with jet-black and silver beads and sequins scattered over the heavy fabric. It's fitted at the top but flares out at the waist, held up by tiny, glittery straps.

I'm the night sky. The dark princess rather than the fairy tale version. I am Elphaba, not Glinda.

I like it.

They set up an entire suite at the hotel for me, and I have a blessed few moments by myself before the men will arrive in their cavalcade of limousines. I spent most of this reprieve staring at myself in a full-length mirror, trying to convince myself that someone will find me lovable.

It's not as easy as it should be.

Outwardly, I look amazing. Alexa, my stylist, is a wizard with a makeup brush and she's highlighted everything that needs to be and hides the details that don't need to be seen. My hair, falling to my shoulders in soft waves, is almost back to my natural reddish blonde.

Strawberry blonde, my mother used to call it.

My mother...

I can never predict when it hits me, the wave of grief that feels as fresh as it was when I woke up in the hospital and Spencer told me she was gone.

I miss my mother. I miss her every single day. Some days are good, and I can be happy and social. Normal. Some are not, and I prefer to be by myself. But some days, I really, really wish she were still here, so much that there is an ache in my chest.

Today is one of those days.

I stare at myself in the mirror, my lips with the slick of Taylor Swift-red lipstick, quirking and pursing like I'm sucking on a sour candy.

No candy. I'm just trying not to cry.

"I'm doing this thing, Mom," I whisper into the quiet room. "I wish you were here. Or maybe I don't because you might tell me not to go through with it."

No, I wouldn't.

"No, you wouldn't."

Sometimes it's like I can hear her voice. I know I can't—I'm not imagining or hallucinating or believing her spirit follows me through life. But I have conversations with her—out loud for me, her responses kept in my head.

It makes me feel close to her again.

"Odin told me I shouldn't be the Suitor, but it's not like he can talk," I say to my reflection. "At least I'm guaranteed not to be sent home the first week."

In my head, Mom laughs.

"Dad was cool with the idea, because Dad is cool about everything, but the boys... They don't think I should do it. They've never really had high expectations of me being in the public eye. And this is more public than I've ever been."

Whose fault is that?

"Mine, I know," I admit. "But it would be nice sometimes... It doesn't matter." My voice drops to a whisper. "I haven't heard from Spencer. I don't know what I expected but—"

Don't give up on Spencer.

"I'm about to meet twenty-five men, one of whom may be the love of my life. Now isn't the best time to think about Spencer." I straighten my shoulders and take a deep breath. "This is going to work."

Of course it will.

A knock sounds on the door, and Ria opens it before I can respond. "You ready?" she calls, the excitement evident in her voice.

I take a last long look at myself. "Let's do this," I say.

I refused the many requests to wear a tiara.

I am wearing my mother's necklace—the oval sapphire she wore for formal occasions. It's not as big as the one in the Titanic movie, but it's a good size. And it's real.

It's like a piece of her is with me.

"You ready?" Grayson stands with me at the front of the hotel. With my heels, he's only a few inches taller than I am, resplendent in a dark purple suit.

"I'm not ready for you to one-up me, so maybe you should be out of camera for this part," I joke, giving his shoulder a push. "You look too good."

"You look amazing," he counters. "No one is going to one-up you."

"Does that mean the guys aren't pretty?"

"They are very pretty," he assures me. "First car is coming. Here we go."

The house the men are staying at is a former hotel high up overlooking the ocean. It's a beautiful spot, but the length of the drive gives my nerves too much time to ratchet up.

"Are you nervous?" Grayson asks just as the first car moves into position. I know this question is for the camera, so I turn and give him my best smile.

"Of course. My Prince Charming might be in that car, so of course I'm scared out of my mind." And then I give a laugh that sounds perfectly natural.

"When I first met Bexley, she completely blanked on my name, so don't give first impressions all that much thought. Those guys are even more scared than you are," Grayson counsels.

"What did she think your name was?" I wonder as the driver gets out to open the back door.

"I don't know," Grayson admits.

"You should ask her." And then I take a deep breath because the first man appears.

He's—he's really pretty, with dark curly hair and even darker eyes.

And the way he smiles when he catches sight of me standing there? It's *really* nice.

This is the first one, so should I admit my stomach actually flutters when he smiles at me?

"Princess Lyra," he announces when he's before me. His voice has a tinge of India mixed with British, and his teeth are very white against his skin.

He's... very pretty.

"Just Lyra," I correct. At least he didn't blank on my name.

"I am Asani. And I'm enchanted to meet you." He takes my hand and kisses it, his lips warm and dry.

I've had my hand kissed by countless men, and things never fluttered like this.

A good sign.

"Hi," I say, my smile turning foolish as I stare into those dark eyes. "And thanks. It's nice to meet you, too."

We spend a moment making small talk, but later, I won't remember what was said. There's a lot of smiling from both of us, and I'm content to stand here for another moment until Grayson clears his throat off to the side.

"Thanks for being here," I manage, trying for a polite and reluctant dismissal.

"It will be my pleasure. I look forward to getting to know you better. Can I—?" He opens his arms.

Hug. He's asking to hug me. "Of course." I step into his arms, and wow, does he smell delicious. I could stay here inhaling his jacket for the rest of the night.

But I let him go and prepare for the next one.

Eliott is next, his bashful smile charming me instantly. I'm sure his name will be followed by "cinnamon roll hero" when they show him on screen. After him is Luc P., then firefighter Dylan, who arrives in his suit so there's no doubt that he saves lives, and dentist Charlie.

He actually introduces himself as a dentist, which I don't love. I counter by asking how he likes my whitened teeth.

First car finished, I prepare for the next batch.

There are too many for me to keep track of all of their names, but there are several that are memorable: Boone, bald and brawny and covered in tattoos. He rides up on a motorcycle and we have to shoot his entrance again because I head straight for the bike when he swings a leg over, all ready to jump on for a ride.

I've always had a thing for bad boys.

Then there's Basher, who commandeered a tour bus, which, given the size of the island, is impressive. He's the drummer of Water Rhinos, whom I'm proud to say I've actually heard of.

"My father will love you," I tell Basher. "Or maybe not, depending on how much he remembers from his time in his band."

They have a man who plays tennis, a basketball player who towers over me, and Tanner McGainey. "I know your brother," is how he introduces himself to me. He's big and broad and shaggy-haired, with a crooked nose.

"Lucky you." I roll my eyes. "Which one?"

"Prince Kalle. Hockey. We played Juniors together," Tanner says, with an adorable *aw shucks* attitude. "He's going to hate that I'm on the show here with you."

I smile and touch his arm. "That's Kalle's problem, and I don't concern myself with my brothers' problems."

Jon is big and broody, but I like the way his gaze flicks around before landing on me, like he's checking the perimeter in full-protect mode. He's supposedly an alpha—I had to ask for clarification from Ria when she told me, since all I could think of is the alpha of a werewolf pack.

I'm surprised by a few of them: Leo, whom I instantly recognize as not only a former child star on the show *Time to Go*, but as a recent finalist on *Dancing with the Stars*.

Grayson gives another clear of the throat when I keep talking to Leo—mainly me asking what it was like to be a part of Dancing.

I'm still high from meeting him when the fourth car arrives, bringing fellow Laandian Lucas Nyle.

"Oh, my god!" I cry, hands slapping against my mouth.

"Boy next door," Lucas says, arms wide. "Or as next door as you can get when you live in a castle."

I went to school with Lucas, and I'm not surprised when the first thing he does is admit that he's always had a crush on me. I always knew he had a crush on me.

A girl can tell these things.

It's not until the fifth limo that I get the first real shock of the evening.

Ashton Carrington gets out of the car.

"No," I cry, starting to laugh. "Oh, hell no!"

Ashton spreads his arms. "Babe!"

"No way!"

"Why not?" His mock hurt expression doesn't deter from his model-looks.

A producer thrusts a microphone in my face and Ashton stands by the car, waiting for my reaction to be recorded. "Lyra? How do you know Ashton?"

"I know his twin sister, Fenella. She lives in Battle Harbour and has transformed the town. My brother used to race cars with him. I've met Ashton a few times."

I've made out with Ashton a few times, but I'm not about to admit that on camera.

Because we know each other, and Ashton is the last to arrive, they give us longer. Or maybe it's because Ashton blatantly ignores Grayson's warning cough.

But finally, I shoo him into the house, sensing Grayson needs a minute with me.

And I need a minute to process what just happened.

I just met twenty-five men. Not only am I supposed to remember their names, I also have to choose the first three to send home by the end of the night.

"So?" Grayson asks.

I manage to give him a grin. "This is going to be fun."

7

Spencer

I DON'T GO TO Abigail's that night because there is no longer any Abigail to go to. No more Abigail to hang out with, spend time with. To make up the fun foursome with Bo and Hettie.

What am I supposed to tell Bo? And Hettie. She'll hate me for breaking Abigail's heart.

It doesn't have to be this way. It doesn't have to be like this. If I can get my head straight, I can fix this. Get this question answered, the one that's been stuck in my head since I was a kid, and make it right with Abigail.

Only, as amazing and incredible as she is, it will never be right with Abigail.

Because of that one silly question: will there ever be anything between Lyra and me? Like a future? A happily ever after, for all the romantic softies out there.

I am not a romantic softie. I never have been.

There have been women in my life: Coral, when I went to boarding school in London; a brief fling with Rachel when I was in Toronto at university.

Abigail.

Lyra.

They are the main ones, the ones that left a mark.

I wasn't looking for a future with Coral or Rachel. I never planned on one with Abigail— we were friends who might have become more, but then she left.

And then she came back.

If she hadn't left with Hettie, would that have become serious? Would I have had these thoughts eight years ago, trying to decide if I want to let go of my dream of a life with Lyra?

Because that's what it is.

Deep down, I dream of a life with Princess Lyra of Laandia. That's not unheard of. Lyra is gorgeous and smart, vivacious and daring and bold and funny. She speaks her mind, she does what she wants and asks for forgiveness later.

And there's more to her than most people see.

I was three when my father brought me to Battle Harbour. My mother was British, Dad from a nearby town in Laandia, but they met in Barcelona at the final concert of Kräftig, the heavy metal band Dad and Magnus started when they were young. It had been a one-off concert to celebrate an anniversary of their first platinum record.

The two of them broke up the band. Magnus left when he took the throne, and then Dad put in the final nail after Magnus convinced him to return to Laandia to help him rule.

There was never any question of Dad not standing at Magnus's side for whatever he needed.

My mother's name was Siobhan, and she met my father at a party after the concert. And then Dad went back to Laandia while my mother returned to London, and they didn't give that night another thought until Siobhan discovered she was pregnant.

She had the baby—obviously, because it was me—but she died in an accident when I was four months old. Her sister raised me, never telling my father what happened until I was almost two. It was another year before my aunt allowed him to be a part of my life, and six months later, after Duncan married Signe, mother of my half-sisters, he went to London to bring me back to Laandia.

I was a three-year-old boy, taken from the only home I'd ever known to travel to a new country with a man I knew nothing about, only that he was my father.

I didn't even know his first name until we got here, or that he was best friends with a king.

It went much better than it sounds.

I loved my life in Laandia, but I was always curious about England. After much discussion, Dad agreed that I could go to boarding school outside London. I stayed for six years, returning to Battle Harbour for holidays and vacations, and ended up with a cordial and affectionate relationship with my aunt that I still have to this day.

I returned to Laandia for high school and moved into the castle with my father when he divorced Signe. I stayed in the country for university but went to Toronto to law school, and had a brief stint in Ottawa working for the Canadian government. But I've always felt like Battle Harbour was home, and that had more to do with family than any length of time I've spent in the town.

My family, as well as the royal family.

After work that night, instead of sitting with my laptop and responding to emails, I head straight to my bedroom. As well as a suite of rooms in the castle, I keep an apartment in Battle Harbour, a few streets back from the square, in an old Victorian house that was made into a tri-plex.

There are no apartment buildings in Battle Harbour, only converted houses and the second floors above the stores.

There's never been a need. The age group that would move out of their family's home for independence often moves straight out of Battle Harbour. The younger population has been decreasing for years as the lack of opportunities becomes apparent.

I've been working with the king to stop the flow, and we're beginning to see some improvement, but not enough. There's more work to be done, especially to bring in new families.

Having Fenella Carrington move to Laandia was a big help.

But I don't want to think about what else needs to be done tonight because I want to focus on something other than the fate of the town right now.

At the bottom of my tiny closet is a shoe box, and I pull it out.

Doc Martens. It's funny that I've never owned a pair in my life, but it's the box of the brand of shoes that holds my memories.

I've never been one to keep sentimental things, but there are a few items that matter. Inside the box is a tattered stuffed rabbit, missing an eye. A colourful Swatch that has long stopped telling the time. A handful of guitar picks. A CD Stella burned for me, full of music she insisted I listen to. A bright, chaotic painting on a tiny canvas, a cork, and a handful of letters.

The letters are from Lyra.

I pull out the bundle. It's been years since I've read them. They were written in a different time, when I was a different person, but I've still kept them.

They show a different side of Lyra, one that she hides from the rest of the world. If it's even still part of her.

She wrote to me every week for the six years I went to boarding school. She started up again when I went to university, even though email would have been easier. At least a few times a month, I would receive the cream-coloured envelopes embossed with the castle address, but with my name scrawled in purple ink. There are some from the two years I lived in Ottawa.

I've kept them all.

And now I sit on my bed and reread them all.

Most make me laugh—a younger Lyra with her random thoughts and comments about her brothers and life living in a castle. But it's the longer letters that I pay the most attention to—the ones she wrote a few months after the death of Queen Selene.

Eight pages of solid pain and guilt, and Lyra never hesitated, sharing every single thing she was feeling about her mother, the accident, and what she was afraid of. She told *me*. Not Kate, not her brothers, but me. Her brothers' best friend. The person who has known her the longest.

A friend who isn't really a friend because it's more than friendship that binds us.

Only I don't know how much more.

There's always been a connection between Lyra and me. There is a lot of frivolous garbage on the pages of the letters—here is one where she detailed a concert Bo took her to, giving me comments on every song in the playlist. There's another where she shared the plot of several movies. But there's a lot of Lyra in here.

And there's a lot of me. Things I never told anyone.

Thoughts about my mother. What I remember about living with my aunt. Missing my sisters when I was away.

Missing her.

Lyra always signed off with a scrawled pink heart and an L. There was never any mention of what we felt for each other, just that the connection was real and we both acknowledged and appreciated it.

It was friendship, but it was more. I've never tried to figure out the words to describe it, other than a friendship.

Sitting on my bed, letters in a clumsy pile beside me, I can see the ocean from my window, a sliver of dark blue under a moonlit sky.

The stars are bright and I have a sudden urge to tell Lyra, to find out if they're just as bright in Saint Pierre.

Maybe Abigail is right.

It's time to find out what exactly is between Lyra and me.

8

Lyra

I THINK THAT WENT well.

Grayson and Rue had explained the concept of this season: that the men selected for the show will all be romance novel types or something like that. I've never been a reader, but Sophie is, so I asked her for a breakdown of what to expect.

Sophie had been very thorough in her explanation of the archetypes, so when I walk into the hotel lobby after Ashton arrives, I look at the men and categorize them with a label in my head, like what will be shown on the screen when they're each introduced.

I'm going to have to pick one of these men, so I'll need more than a label.

When I walk in, every single man there jumps to his feet. There is so much admiration and appreciation thrown at me that it's palpable and slightly overwhelming.

And I'm used to being admired.

I accept a glass of champagne from Luc P. — no, Luc C. My nerves have settled but this is just the beginning.

What am I doing?

You've got this.

And I take a breath before the second part of the evening begins.

"Hi, y'all," I manage and immediately kick myself. Where did the southern accent come from? I try again. "Hel-lo. Welcome to my world."

I was supposed to say, *Welcome to this season of The Suitorette*, but the way the guys cheer, it's obvious my way is better.

"Let's get this party started," I add and turn to the first man I lay eyes on. Gord? Or Marc? I'll figure it out. "Come talk to me."

His chest puffs as I lead him away from the others.

Throughout the next four hours, I manage to have private conversations with eighteen of the men. By the time the producers call it a night, it's after two a.m. and I'm exhausted. For once, I may be completely peopled out.

But at least I've kept busy; the guys are forced to sit around and wait for their turn to talk to me. A group sets off on an exploratory mission through the hotel; a few of them spend the time drinking, which makes private time interesting.

I'm kissed: by one of the drunk guys—to my dismay. Basher, the drummer—not really dismaying at all, and Rand, who gives me the sloppiest and yet sweetest kiss I've ever received.

I don't bother trying to talk to Lucas and Ashton because I know them. Ashton understands because I hear him laughing as he holds court, but I get sad eyes from Lucas every time I step a foot back in the room.

It's like the worst kind of event at the castle, where all I want to do is take off my shoes and have a dance before I go to bed, but there are so many dignitaries I have to talk up first.

I do take my shoes off half-way through, which leads to Jon, the big, broody guy, giving me a foot rub.

I'll be keeping him for a while, just for that.

Finally, Grayson, Rue, and Ria get me out of there. I'm spent, but the adrenaline keeps flowing during the ten-minute drive back to Camille and Odin's.

Lucky them—they're asleep when we get back, but lovely Madame Carol is still awake to offer us coffee or tea.

Because I don't get to go to bed. Now the work begins.

Ria has a list of names—on Bristol board written in coloured markers, no less—and we go through them and make notes on each to help me remember.

I've already forgotten too many of the men.

"Is there anyone that you're ready to rule out?" Rue asks after we finish that part. She's making her own notes via iPad.

"About half of them," I tell her as I yawn without covering my mouth.

"Seriously?" Her eyes pop open. "I thought this was a great group."

"Sure, but I'd rather get rid of half of them. It would make narrowing them down so much easier."

"Do you see potential with anyone?" Ria asks, marker poised like she's about to put a star beside the names I give her.

"Basher seems fun." She does star him. "Jon rubbed my feet."

"Likes foot rubs," Rue confirms as she taps on her keyboard.

"Rand," I decide. "He made me laugh. So did Asani. But get rid of the drunk guy who slobbered all over me."

"I thought that was Rand?" Ria frowns.

"Yes, but he was sweet about it. Drunk guy had too much whiskey. I don't drink whiskey."

"I think that was Luc C.," Grayson offers.

"No, it was P.," Rue corrects.

"Couldn't you find more with different names?" I complain. "Two Luc's and a Lucas— how did you get him here, anyway?"

"We contacted the school in Battle Harbour and asked for volunteers. We got about six of them, and after interviews, decided on Lucas."

"I'm not sure I'd pick Lucas," I admit.

"He said he always had a crush on you," Ria protests.

"He also had a girlfriend three out of the four years of high school, so who's he lying to?"

Rue makes a note. "We tried to get a brother's best friend, but we were turned down."

Brother's best friend? That would be— "He—really? He said no?"

Utter desolation crashes over me like a hurricane-size wave and I blink away the sudden sting in my eyes.

Spencer said *no*.

Of course he did, because he's with Abigail. He doesn't want *me*, he's never wanted me. He wants her.

I clear my throat twice before I can manage anything else. "Oh."

Not much else to say.

There must be something else to say, because all three heads whip around.

"Jonathan McKibbon," Grayson supplies. "That's your friend Kate's brother? He's friends with Prince Kalle. I guess we could have used him as *best friend's* brother, but he wasn't interested."

I let out a shaky laugh. Jonathan. Not— "Thank god for that," I say with more emphasis than is necessary. It's better that than letting the relief show that it wasn't Spencer who refused.

Did they even ask him?

I'm not sure if I'm more relieved or disappointed, but definitely curious about what he might have said.

I should already know—he's with Abigail, so he would have said no. He said no when I asked him to come to the wedding with me, so of course he would refuse.

This isn't Spencer's thing anyway. He's too much of a fixer. He'd take over the producing of the show before he got to go on one date with me.

Not that there would be any dates, because Spencer would never agree to this.

A little voice that sounds awfully like my mother reminds me that I wouldn't have agreed to this if Spencer had come to the wedding with me.

Or if I had ever told Spencer how I felt about him.

That would mean admitting it to myself first, and I've always steered clear of that.

"We need to send three of the men home."

I focus on what Rue is saying, how tomorrow morning there will be one red rose left outside a room, yellow roses of friendship for the men I'm sending home, and pink roses for everyone else.

The flower shop in town must be making a killing from this show.

"What do you want from me?" I do my best to keep my mind off the *did they or didn't they ask Spencer* dilemma and the frustration I feel that it's even an issue.

"We need you to pick the three that are going home, plus the one who gets the first date," Grayson says. He looks more exhausted than I do, his natty suit jacket thrown over a chair, shirt sleeves rolled up. This needs to be finished for the night.

I lean back in the chair, tilting my head to look at the ceiling. "I'm so tired I don't think I can remember enough names for that."

"I know it's late, and there are a lot of them, but if you can't remember their name or some trait, it's a good indication you don't want them here," Rue points out.

"That's a good way of looking at it, but I still feel I like need to phone a friend." Another yawn. "Can I ask Camille?"

"We're your sounding board," Ria says in a firm voice. "And time's up for three of them, so make your choice."

I finally decide to send Desmond home because I found him too smooth; Eriq, who it turns out, was the slobberer; and Waylon because all I could think about when I saw him was the country singer, Waylon Jennings.

My father used to make us listen to old country music.

Plus, Waylon looks like a cowboy, and that's never been my type. He's cute, but a cowboy can't handle me.

I'm honestly not sure how many of these men can.

After I give the exit orders for them, it's time to pick who gets the First Date Rose. Who gets the first one-on-one date with me?

Grayson explained how it used to be—in other seasons, the one to get the First Date Rose was notoriously the first to be sent home. That it was basically picking who was the next to leave, but giving them a bit of hope before they got kicked off the show.

I have to think back, but I don't think Odin got the First Date Rose. I think his was the second one-on-one date.

Either way, I think I'll keep this little tidbit to myself, lest he be even more anti-Suitor.

Grayson also assures me it is entirely my decision, that he doesn't want the producers to have that much say about who stays and who goes.

They also don't give their opinion on whom I should pick. This is good because it's my love story, but my eyes are bleary with lack of sleep and the faces of the men keep swimming through my mind, and I really wish one of them would just tell me who to pick.

I finally decide on Asani because I remember him. "And he was the first to meet me, so I think I should pick him," I finish giving my reasonings.

"Are you interested in him?" Rue demands.

"Sure."

That must not that been convincing enough because Ria gives it a try. "Are you interested in anyone?"

"The only thing I am interested in right now is my bed, so if that's all..." I stand, swaying tiredly. It's been a long day, and the producers still have to deliver the flowers early in the morning.

Unlike the Bachelor, this show doesn't make them stand around in suits looking miserable as I slowly make my decision. The men will check the hall outside their rooms in the hotel tomorrow morning to see who gets what, and cameras will be there to catch the reactions.

I'm off the hook until my date with Asani.

I use that time to get some much-needed sleep.

9

Spencer

THE NEXT DAY, I send a text on the group chat BROBEER.

I'm still not sure what I'm doing, but whatever it is, it has to do with their sister and the princes deserve to know what I'm thinking.

Even if it wasn't about Lyra, I'd still want to talk to them.

Kalle has the obligatory pint waiting as I slide onto one of the stools before the bar. Bo and Gunnar are already there, playfully arguing about some childhood slight. Odin sent his regrets from Saint Pierre. I'll call him later.

"Are you here to tell us what Lyra is up to?" Kalle asks, planting both hands on the bar as he leans over it.

He took over The King's Hat after he got out of sports, and before he got into being a prince. He hired his best friend, Edie England, to run the place.

Fast forward, and Kalle and Edie are now engaged, the royal wedding fast approaching. Edie handed over the management to Mabel Crow, sister of Bo's wife, because learning to be a queen takes up a lot of time.

These days, Kalle and Edie both spend more time with their royal duties but both still like to show their faces at the pub as much as they can.

And thanks to the free beer, we still meet here when there's a reason to.

Kalle's question stops the discussion. "I haven't heard anything," I tell them. "And I don't expect to."

"Odin says she's in Saint Pierre," Bo offers.

"That's where you're going to get the info from. It's supposed to be radio silence, kind of like all of them are sequestered. At least that's what I remember from when Odin did the show."

"But he wasn't gone for that long," Gunnar points out.

"I don't think he appreciates people bringing that up," I say, picking up my glass.

Gunnar and Bo follow suit, and Kalle waves at us to wait while he pours himself a beer. And then we drink in unison.

I wonder what it would be like to slowly sip a beer with the princes.

Kalle is the first to admit defeat this time, unusual because even all these years, there's no way I can keep up with the steel-lined stomachs of the Erickson brothers.

And Lyra. She can almost drink her brothers under the table.

"Too much head," Kalle grumbles as I set my glass down, a respectful half empty.

Gunnar gives it a good try, but only Bo is able to finish the entire pint with one breath.

"Do you know how many pints we go through when you guys do that?" Edie asks, standing beside Kalle and pulling glasses and bottles down. "They see you do that, and everyone here wants to try."

"It means we sell more." Kalle refills Bo's glass. "Good for business. Speaking of Lyra business—"

"Which we weren't," Gunnar interrupts.

"Which we are," Kalle counters. "Apparently, the show asked some guys from here to join the cast. Some kid Lyra went to school with, and Jonathan."

I watch Edie mix drinks and process what Kalle just said.

They asked some guys from Battle Harbour.

Not me. No one asked me. Did Lyra give suggestions? Did she have a list of men she wanted to get to know, and I wasn't on it?

"That would have been hilarious," Gunnar says, not bothering to hide his laughter. "Lyra can't stand Jonathan."

"Lyra can't stand a lot of people," Bo points out.

Lyra never would have suggested Jonathan McKibbon. Never. Ever.

"Odin said they were looking for architecture types?" Gunnar shakes his head. "I don't get it."

"Archetypes?" Edie suggests, trying to hide her smile. "Like characters from a book."

"I thought these were real guys."

"They are, but they've got certain types—athletes, and heroes, and brother's best friends," Edie explains. "You need to read more romance novels."

"And have Duncan looking at me from the cover every time I pick it up?" Gunnar shivers. "No, thank you. Besides, I don't need to read any romance. It's not like I need help in that department."

Edie rolls her eyes and I try to smother my laugh. Kalle doesn't even try.

Bo, on the other hand, is still on the Lyra topic. "They didn't ask you?" he demands of me. "If they want these types of guys? You're our best friend so—"

"No. I'm with Abigail, though." I swallow painfully. "Was."

Bo holds my gaze for a long moment.

"Was with Abigail," I admit. "She, uh, ended things yesterday."

"Why?" Gunnar demands. "Did you do something?"

I glance at Edie, who is looking at me with as much confused concern as the boys. It's never me that needs to get stuff off my chest. I'm always the one listening to Gunnar or Kalle... even Bo sometimes, although his lack of romantic entanglements over the years makes sense now that I know he was still completely in love with Hettie the whole time.

"Lyra." My shoulders slump. "Abigail thinks there's something there."

"Because there is," Gunnar says with emphasis.

"I don't know," I argue. "Can you actually see Lyra and me? We fight all the time."

"I don't want—" Kalle, in full big-brother mode, begins to bluster, but Edie holds up her hand.

"When you and Lyra are together, you lean toward each other," she says simply. "It's quite fascinating to watch. It's like you both have some magnetic pull."

"We don't."

"You kind of do," Gunnar agrees. "I've seen it too, but I just thought she lost her balance."

"Or drank too much," Bo adds.

"But she doesn't..." I trail off as Gunnar raises his eyebrows. "Does she?"

"That's the question, isn't it?" Bo asks. "And it seems that's what Abigail is telling you to find out."

"How am I supposed to do that?" I scoff. "Lyra is on Saint Pierre, surrounded by cameras and men. All these men who want to fall in love with her. How am I supposed to figure out anything?""You need to get on the show," Gunnar suggests.

Me as part of The Suitorette? That's the last thing I want. Constantly being on camera and media attention and lack of privacy aren't things I strive for. But it kind of makes sense in a strange, there-may-be-aliens-out-there type of way. Like it's completely crazy.

Why would I want to do that to myself?

Edie gives me a knowing smile as she takes the drink to a table across the room.

"What show?" Bo asks with confusion.

Gunnar punches his shoulder. "What show do you think? I thought it already started."

"You're going on The Suitorette?" Kalle all but shouts. "Lyra's show?"

"What?" Bo blusters. "How? Why? *Abigail.*"

I take a gulp of beer for courage and hold up my hand. "One at a time. The Suitorette show. It makes sense. I think... I think I'll offer myself up as the brother's best friend, if that's what they're looking for."

"Are you serious?" Bo asks.

I nod slowly, still not certain, but leaning that way. "And it's over with Abigail," I tell him quietly. "Her choice."

"Were looking for," Kalle points out. "They *were* looking for a brother's best friend."

"They won't say no to him. So you're going after our sister?" Gunnar folds his arms over his chest. "Rebound much?"

"It's not like that."

"Can we not call her 'your sister' in this conversation?" Bo begs. "Just Lyra is good. I don't want it to get weird."

"Is this going to be weird?" I ask. "Because that's why I'm here, to give you a heads up. And to deal with any fallout."

"How can we deal with fallout when you haven't done anything?" Kalle points out. "Or have you?"

"You broke up with Abigail?" Bo demands. "There'll be fallout from that from Hettie."

"It was Abigail's decision," I say in a heavy voice. "She told me to go figure things out with Lyra. And now I need to know what you guys think."

Kalle looks at Bo, who turns to Gunnar. "Are you asking for our approval?" Kalle asks.

"I don't know how I feel about this." Gunnar scrubs at his forehead. "You've always been paired up with Lyra in my mind, and then you weren't."

"Because he was with Abigail," Bo growls.

"And now I'm not. Still friends, still care about her, but we're over." It's easier every time I say it.

"Hettie's going to kill you," Bo warns.

"No, she won't, because it wouldn't have been fair if Spence had stuck around when he had feelings for Lyra."

I turn to Kalle, the biggest, the broadest, and the smartest. According to him, anyway. "You can see it?"

"A blind man could see it," Gunnar drawls.

Kalle frowns. "This is our little sister we're talking about."

"She's a handful," Gunnar adds. "And like Bo said, let's use her name rather than focus on the sister aspect."

"She deserves to be with a man who will make her happy," Bo corrects. "You think that's you?"

I run a hand through my hair. "I don't know," I admit. "Maybe?"

"Are you asking for our blessing?" Kalle wants to know. "Because I did that with Edie's dad and it didn't go down like this."

"I'm so sick of everyone getting married," Gunnar bursts out, dropping his head onto the bar. "There's so much pressure and me and Stella are *not* there yet."

The outburst temporarily silences us. "Dude," Bo says finally. "This isn't about you."

Gunnar lifts his head. "I know, but I had to get it out there. So. Much. Pressure. Please don't marry her," he begs me. "At least not right away."

"I think that might be getting a little ahead of ourselves," Kalle cautions, which mirrors my thoughts exactly.

"When you know, you know," Bo says sagely, pushing his glass back to Kalle for a refill.

Also my thought.

"I don't know what will happen, but I want to see her." I take a deep breath, wishing we were talking about just a girl, rather than their sister. But Lyra has never been just a girl, and that's the whole problem. "I want to spend some time with her. I need to see if I have to fight for her, if this is my last chance."

"Leaving it a bit late, aren't you?" Bo asks drily.

"Maybe. Hopefully not. I just don't know, you know?"

"I've never known you not to know something," Gunnar points out.

Bo huffs a laugh.

"Are you all right with it?" I ask, turning to each of them.

Regardless of how he feels about Abigail and me, Bo is the first to clap a meaty hand on my shoulder. "Yes." His voice is gruff. "You're our brother."

"And if you and Lyra got together, that would make it really real," Gunnar adds. "Not that it's not real."

"All of us would be honoured to call you brother-in-law." Kalle offers me his hand.

"But don't get married," Gunnar groans. "Don't do that to me. Not yet, please."

"I'm not promising anything," I tell Gunnar. "But okay. I'm going to do this." I finish the rest of my beer too quickly and it almost comes up my nose. "I'm going to Saint Pierre to fight for your sister."

"Best of luck." Kalle raises his glass and the others follow. "You're going to need it."

10

Lyra

I TELL MYSELF I picked Asani because I'm interested in him. That I'm attracted, intrigued. I was swept away by our first meeting, our conversation at the cocktail party, and that I can see a future with him.

I could have picked any of them—Tanner, Basher, sweet and funny Rand. Eliott. Even sad-dog-eyed Lucas, but the way he looks at me might have been too much for an entire date.

But I picked Asani.

I keep listing the entirely plausible reasons so I can forget that I decided to give Asani the First Date Rose because he was first out of the car, and that seemed fair. It takes courage to go first and he should be rewarded.

It's not a great reason, but at least it's a start.

The show gets me a snazzy convertible, thinking it makes good video to show me speeding around the roads of Saint Pierre. I agree that it does.

There aren't a lot of snazzy any things on Saint Pierre. Most of the vehicles are either pickups or tiny compacts, and all have seen better days. But I like the red Audi convertible waiting for me the next afternoon, although I push it a bit on the short drive and the drone filming above me barely keeps up.

Whoever designed the hotel did an amazing job because it feels like any place in the South of France. Luxurious, with a lobby to the water and a bar at the back. The pool is off to the side via a winding path set into the manicured lawn.

Not many things grow in the soil of Saint Pierre, but they've managed to find flowers to bloom in containers set along the path.

I find the men by the pool when I arrive to pick up Asani, all in various degrees of undress. Some are in the water, some lounging around it. Someone has created a mock gym near the deep end, and a number of the men are flexing with weights.

I'm sure this scene will take up many minutes in the episode because there's so much to look at.

And I'm looking.

I didn't see the men yesterday, and even though first impressions have faded and most of their faces have blurred, I can guarantee I won't have the same problem with their bodies.

These boys have been hitting the gym.

Asani stands off to the side, patiently waiting, as I greet the others, wearing off-white linen pants and a patterned shirt that would be perfect for a Caribbean vacation.

I wear cut-offs and a tank top with a loose white shirt. Alexa still took her time to make sure I'm "camera ready".

I told her I was born camera ready.

Asani's smile is warm and he smells amazing, a mix of cloves and citrus, and I breathe deeply as I give him a hug hello, conscious of the gazes of twenty-one other men.

It's not an unpleasant sensation, knowing these men are here just for me.

I give them a bright smile as I take off with Asani, excitement at war with apprehension and making my stomach tingle and tighten.

Here we go. Lyra's journey to love starts now.

Good luck, my darling girl.

Most of the men I've been involved with—whether they are men I've picked because of interest or friends or acquaintances I've asked to take me to events or premieres or social gatherings where I need to be seen—know the rules of dating Princess Lyra.

There must be fashionable attire since many pictures will be taken. There will be alcohol served, and drinking will be monitored so no drunken situations will occur. Conversation will be limited to small talk and pleasant discussions so there will never be a question of having a picture taken with an embarrassing expression.

Why did Princess Lyra look sad with so-and-so? Did he break her heart? Is she carrying his baby? She looks drawn and tired and has lost weight? Is she taking Ozempic? Is she gaining weight?

I long ago stopped reading the comments that inevitably follow whenever a picture of me with a man shows up online.

There will be more than pictures of my date with Asani. There will be video so people can rewatch it as many times as they want to dissect every word and expression.

Or maybe not, Maybe I'm putting too much importance on myself.

But I don't think so.

I come from a famous family; not only that, but it's a family that is liked and admired and followed by millions. My brothers seem to grasp the importance of this. Or maybe they have been able to separate themselves from being part of the Laandian royal family.

I never have, which is why there are rules and no reading of comments

But this is not a normal date, so I'm not exactly sure how to proceed. Or what to expect.

There are no paparazzi in sight as I drive us to the tiny airport, just the cameraman. I think his name is Johnny.

I should really find out.

"Where are you whisking me away to?" Asani asks, linking hands with me as we cross the tarmac to the tiny prop plane.

"We're going to look at birds," I tell him cheerfully.

As we board the plane, I explain to Asani that the nation of Saint Pierre is an archipelago, made up of islands. The bird sanctuary—which Camille herself started—is on the mostly uninhabited Miquelon.

It's a short flight across the water to the island and the first thing I notice is that Asani holds my hand like he expects me to be frightened.

It makes me want to pull my hand away from his grip.

I've been in planes my entire life, some even smaller than this. I've *flown* planes my entire life, even though I've never followed through to get my pilot's license like Bo and Gunnar. But even before my brothers started flying—and teaching me something every time they took me up—I had always pestered the royal pilots to let me push the buttons, touch the rudder, let me take the controls for just a minute, please.

I was with Spencer when he took the second flight of his life, when he returned to London for boarding school. He was a frightened seven-year-old, already regretting his decision to go to school away from his family, and I was a four-year-old, cocky with my experience flying in planes.

The cockiness didn't last long when I realized Spencer was scared.

I made him watch videos with me, and he shared his headphones as we listened to music. I curled up on his shoulder for my nap. I didn't leave his side until we landed, and then my mother had to physically pull me away because I hadn't realized Spencer was staying there, that he wouldn't be coming home with us after the quick visit with the Windsors.

I cried all the way home.

Maybe it's because my head is full of those memories, but I spend more time talking to the pilot during the flight than Asani. I notice the cameraman doesn't film that.

I wonder how long it will take before I forget he's even around. Grayson assured me I would, but I'm very conscious of him.

Or maybe I'm very conscious of Asani.

He's super polite and attentive, asking questions and listening carefully to everything I say. I wonder if this is nervous behavior for him, or if this is what I can expect if I make Asani my forever guy.

That will take some time—viewing each of the men as a potential person to spend the rest of my life with.

Right now, I'm not convinced about Asani.

"Do you like birds?" he asks after we land and get a tour of the area they call the nursery, where the eggs lie under warm lights, and baby birds get their start in life. After that, we head to the medical area where the injured birds are taken care of. It's a well-run organization but still loud and slightly chaotic when a gull is brought in with the remains of a plastic bag caught tight around his wing.

"Who doesn't like them?" I counter. "You're a doctor, aren't you?"

"A surgeon," he says proudly.

And yet, Asani doesn't give the injured birds a second glance.

I do like birds. I'm sure I'm not the sort of person that anyone would think of being a birdwatcher, but there's always been something about watching them fly.

It's like they're calling to me to come with them.

I don't tell Asani that.

But these men took time out of their lives to come on the show. They have given up a lot to take a chance on love.

To take a chance on me.

I thaw slightly. "Why did you decide to come on the show?"

"To find true love." He smiles.

It's truly a devasting smile.

We spend a few hours on Miquelon. I like the fresh air and being close to the water. I miss being close to the ocean when I'm in Chicago. And this is my ocean, a little south of Battle Harbour. Rough and wavy, always in motion, the dark blue water suggesting hidden depths, and so much below.

"It looks dangerous," Asani says as we walk along the water. He's back to holding my hand again, consistently tugging me away from the waves rolling along the pebble-strewn beach.

I'm not sure if it's protective of me or he just doesn't want to get his pants wet.

"You don't like the ocean?"

"I prefer pools," he offers.

I get the sense this isn't a perfect date for Asani. He acts like being outdoors is a chore, something he's not accustomed to. I can see him on a golf course, or maybe a picnic with a curated basket of artisanal meats and cheeses.

The cameraman—Johnny—motions us back. Ria met us here, as well as another man and woman with cameras and technical stuff, plus Alexa, to touch up my makeup. I've followed all the instructions given today—to walk where they want me to walk, to look at what they decide they need me to look at. They tell me when to smile up at Asani, and how close to stand to him.

It's not really a date, but rather a series of logistical exercises to make two people look good together.

I'm not sure any exercise would make me feel comfortable with Asani, and I'm not sure if I can blame Johnny and the rest of the audience, or just us.

There is no us. I don't know what I should be feeling, but I do know it should be *something*, and not this mild irritation, like there's a pebble stuck in the sole of my shoe.

I've already decided that there will never be an us, but I still have to get through this date.

"Look at all the birds," I cry as we reach the stretch of sand beside the centre. Hundreds of seagulls and other birds I don't recognize perch along the beach. Some of them walk along the water, some sleep on warm rocks.

An air of devil-may-care fills me and I stop to take off my sandals.

"What are you doing?" Asani asks.

"Waking them up. I used to do this with my brothers." I tug his hand. "Come on."

"No."

"It won't hurt them."

"I don't care. I am not running pell-mell into a group of birds like a child." His face is set and he's not as pretty anymore.

He actually stopped being pretty earlier today.

"Pell-mell," I say lightly, trying to ignore his implication that I am childish. "Good description." And then I turn and run through the birds with a whoop of laughter.

The result is a cacophony of sound and movement as every bird reacts to my sudden presence. Some take off with an offended shriek, some shift onto another rock.

A few actually seem like they're playing, flying away only to suddenly dive-bomb me, and sending me racing away with a screech that echoes the birds.

I spend a few minutes running across the sand with the birds, laughing like a child during their first trip to the playground. And then I see the seals basking off the shore and I spend more time watching them.

I motion Asani over to see them, but he stays where I left him, arms folded across his chest, with an expression like a disappointed father.

I notice Johnny filming him standing like that.

Gunnar and I would run with the birds every chance we got. Sometimes Kalle would join us, occasionally Bo. Never Odin, or Spencer, but Spencer would always hold my shoes.

He would cheer me on. It wasn't that he couldn't be childish—it wasn't often, but there were moments when his mischievous side emerged—but he hated the idea of a bird pooping on him. One summer, it was as if every time we played outside, he would get dropped on.

I finally, reluctantly, head back to Asani.

"That was great," Johnny calls out to me. "I got most of it."

"Good, because I'm not doing it again," I tell him, grinning at Asani.

"Is that something you enjoy doing?" he asks, not bothering to hide his annoyance.

"Yes." I raise my chin. "I enjoy being childlike and having fun."

"It's just not... not very princess-like."

The red flag swings high and there ends the journey for Asani. "I've never really followed the stereotypical princess behaviour," I drawl. "Nor am I about to start." I head back to the car waiting to take us to the plane.

"You have bird poop on your shoulder," Asani calls after me.

When we get back to Saint Pierre, I tell Ria the date is over.

Even though I didn't mean to, it seems that the First Date Rose curse is still alive and well on my season.

11

Spencer

Before I do anything Lyra-related, I visit the castle to see my father.

My father doesn't really have an official title, nor a job description. They call him the right-hand man of the king, but no one really knows exactly what he does.

He does a lot.

Duncan Laz has been at the side of the king of Laandia since before Magnus was king, guiding, advising, and supporting him in everything he does.

The fishing dispute with Canada? Duncan was behind the scenes researching the issue, talking to the right people, and creating the talking points so Magnus could nail the negotiations.

When the queen suddenly passed away? Dad, with Mrs. Theissen's help, organized the funeral, dealt with the outpouring of grief from the country and basically ran Laandia for weeks while the family grieved.

When Bo had a secret wedding eight years ago—

No, that was me. My father had no clue about that.

I head to the castle after beers with the boys. Bo offered to fly me down to Saint Pierre first thing in the morning, and there is much to be done if I'm going to take a few weeks off.

I'm really not sure how much time I'll need because I have no idea how long Lyra will want to keep me around.

If at all.

I manage to avoid most of the staff and residents of the castle as I slip upstairs to Dad's office. He has a suite of rooms on the top floor but his office is down the hall from the king's. It's the one hallway that doesn't look like a castle, renovated under the former king. I've always thought it looks a little like a corridor in the White House.

No one really likes it. I much prefer the rest of the castle, which is why I set up an office on the main floor, conveniently close to the kitchen.

The door to his office is open but I knock anyway.

"What's up?" Dad runs a hand through his grey hair. People say a lot of things about Duncan Laz but the one thing everyone agrees on is that he is a seriously beautiful man with great hair. "Long day. You here for work or just to say hi?"

I shake my head. "I cut out early. I needed a meeting with the boys."

He narrows his silvery eyes and motions me to take a seat. His eyes are the same colour as mine—flashing grey one moment and green the next. We all got the good hair from Dad, but mine will never hang loose to my shoulders as his does. Even after all these years, my father still looks like he belongs on a romance novel cover, albeit a little tired with a few extra lines around his eyes.

"Was that meeting about Lyra?"

Dad's abrupt question throws me. I know what I came to say to him, and planned how to say it, and I wasn't going to start with Lyra.

I thought I would slowly get around to her.

Dad leans back in his chair and crosses his arms. "I wondered if her going on that reality show might light a fire under you. Guess it's better late than never."

My jaw drops and I'm silent for a full minute. "What do you mean?" I finally manage.

"Spencer Xavier Laz, do you honestly think that there is anyone in this place who doesn't know that you're completely crazy about our princess?"

"I—what?" I give my head a shake. I'm not usually so tongue-tied.

Dad chuckles. "You want me to call in Magnus? We've been expecting this day since you first crawled up on the queen's bed to see Lyra when she was born."

"I never—"

He reaches into a drawer and pulls out a business card and carefully sets it before me on the desk. "Grayson Grant's number. I'm assuming you're on your way to Saint Pierre?"

There's no sense denying what he says is right. I have been crazy about Lyra my entire life, and I've spent that much time trying to pretend it isn't so.

Accepting it is like opening a door to a room that has sat musty and dark for years, and I laugh because it's a relief. "How did you know?"

Dad grins. "Oh, my boy. Everyone knows."

"Except for me, I guess."

"You have been a bit distracted. What about Abigail?"

"She's the one telling me to figure things out once and for all."

"I knew there was a reason I liked her. It's a shame though. I'll be sad to see her go. But what else can you do?"

"You think so?" I lean forward, resting my hands on his desk. "That it's a good idea? Me and... me and Lyra?"

It's the first time I've actually said it. Our names have been linked many times, but never by me.

Me and Lyra. Lyra and I. Spencer Laz and Princess Lyra of Laandia.

It might need some getting used to.

"It wouldn't be my first choice," Dad admits.

"Why?" I demand, my voice rising.

Dad waves away my concern. "It's nothing about Lyra, just that it can be hard to live as a royal. We may be close, but you and I still have a life outside the castle."

"Really?" I raise a skeptical eyebrow because Dad spends more time on Laandian business than even the king.

"Well, we could," he concedes with a rakish smile. "We still have our privacy. But if you take this step with Lyra, you'll lose all that. I don't think you realize that."

"I know what I'm getting into."

"Maybe. Those boys on the show have no clue, though. I knew there'd be a reaction from Lyra when you got serious with Abigail, but no one could have expected this. Not that there was any way to stop her, mind you." This is said with true affection rather than resignation. Duncan is Lyra's biggest champion. He would never pick a favourite member of the family, but if he were ever forced to, I really think it would be Lyra.

He presses his fingertips together. "Are you sure about this?"

"I'm not sure about anything," I confess.

"But you know you need to go after her?"

I stare at the white card on his desk. GRAYSON GRANT with a rose above it. "I'm not," I say with confusion. "Yes, I'm headed to Saint Pierre for a few weeks, but I'm not going to stop Lyra from being on the show."

Dad laughs. "It'd be fun to see you try. No, you're about to throw your hat in the ring. I understand. It's your only option. And I say—what are you waiting for?"

I'm not waiting, more like taking a breath because there's a possibility that my life is about to change.

I've never wanted to be a prince. I see how all four of the Erickson brothers struggle with their duties and responsibilities as members of the royal family. I've done what I can to help them, and that's been enough.

Sometimes I wonder if I should have taken a different path, one that led me away from the family. It had been my choice—my father told me enough times how demanding it was being so close to the family. Rewarding, but it's clear that it takes a lot out of him.

One could say it destroyed his marriage, but then, if you look at his ex-wife, it's clear the fault doesn't lie solely with him.

I shake my head with a grin. "You sound like Magnus."

"Or maybe he sounds like me. But Spence, you need to know, once you walk out of this office, things are going to change."

"I know."

"Those boys say a lot of things about their sister, but they're fiercely protective of her. I know this, because so am I. I don't want to see her get hurt. No one does."

"I'm not about to hurt her."

"I don't want to see you get hurt either."

"I think that's more likely to happen," I say grimly.

There are a few possibilities here: My life will change the moment I walk onto the set of that show. Either I can win Lyra's heart, or she sends me packing without letting me take a shot.

Or I take that shot and find out it's not going to work. That's a possibility as well. But I'm not looking at the third option, just the first two.

They are terrifying enough.

"I don't know what goes on in that girl's head, but there is a lot of you in there," Dad continues while I fight with my fear. "Have you spoke to your sisters? Sophie might have some insight how to best win her over."

"No offence, but if I can't do it myself, I don't deserve her."

"That is true. She's just had her first date with a guy."

That jolts me and I stand up. "I don't want to waste any more time."

"I concur. I don't think you should." He stands up. "Keep me posted."

"I'm not sure I can, but I'll try to get in touch with you and let you know if anything happens." I take a deep breath. "And if nothing happens... well, I'll be home in a week or so."

He nods. "One more thing that's going to change? There'll be no more hiding in the shadows for you. You do this, you better be all in. For all of it."

That doesn't help.

But the arm slung around my shoulder does as he walks me to the door, as does the hand splayed at back of my neck as my father hugs me. "Good luck, my boy. I'd say you don't need it, but this is Lyra we're talking about."

12

Lyra

THE SECOND DATE IS a group one. I think carefully about who to bring on this date, unlike picking Asani because I was tired and wanted to go to bed.

Asani left without saying goodbye. I can't say that I'm surprised.

He would have hated this date as well, because we're going whale watching today.

Growing up in a country on the edge of the Atlantic Ocean means that whale watching isn't a once-in-a-lifetime experience. I've gone out on a boat at least once a summer for most of my life.

There's something about being in the middle of the ocean, close to the giant, magnificent creatures, that does it for me.

Birds and whales. Who would have thought?

I take my time deciding, because I don't want a dud out on a boat with me.

I pick men whom I see a potential to have a relationship with. There needs to be attraction and interest. Intrigue would be better. Fascination would be the best, but I tell myself I just don't know the men that well yet.

I settle for men that I'm curious about, and I hate to admit that it takes me time to decide on my choice for the seven I invite to go with me.

Ashton Carrington is the last one to greet me this morning when I pick up the group, his smirk widening when I pull him aside.

"Do you really want to be here?" I demand without any preamble. "Because this doesn't seem like your thing."

The smirk vanishes. "Are you going to send me home?" The usual self-satisfied expression disappears as well, and Ashton looks almost worried.

"I'm not picking you at the end," I warn him.

I've known Ashton for years. We run in the same circles and his sister Fenella is one of Gunnar's best friends. Ashton is model-handsome, a racecar driver, and comes from a family worth billions.

Despite all that, I already know he's the last one I'm ever going to pick.

There's a flash in Ashton's eyes that I don't want to see—it makes me wonder if maybe he has an ulterior motive for being here, one that might be me...

But then it's gone and Ashton laughs, his low, billionaire-playboy chuckle. "I'm hurt."

"You're not. Why are you here? It's not like you've ever had problems finding a date."

"Are you kicking me out already?" He gives me a cocky smile, but his eyes are still wary because, to Ashton, being sent home would mean a failure, and Ashton Carrington doesn't fail at much.

"Because I've got a pretty big wager that I'll make it to the last four."

"You came here on a bet?" There's only amusement, no anger, because the relief that Ashton isn't actually interested in me washes it out.

"It's as good a reason as any. What's yours?" he counters.

I thought a lot about Ashton last night. I thought a lot about all of the men, and about sending Asani home so quickly. And it got me worried that there may not be anyone here for me.

No one who might love me.

The thought of going through all of this—of spending time with the men, trying to be myself with them, but not too much, starting to care for them—only to not end up with anyone because they can't love me is not a pleasant thought.

The reality of that might break my heart, but the optics of it would do more than that. If the world thought I was unlovable...

I glance over Ashton's shoulder at the men waiting impatiently for me and give them a little wave. "Do you get along with the other guys?" I ask instead of answering.

"Are you serious? They love me." His eyes light up. "Do you want me to spy for you?"

I laugh at his reaction. "You're way too excited about that."

I don't want a spy, but I might like a back up plan. Going in to this, I knew there's no guarantee that I'll fall in love with someone. Or maybe I will, but there's no certainty that the man will feel the same. So maybe things can go wrong and there's a chance that I'll end up with no one.

Ashton could be that back up plan. It would be easy to couple with Ashton, and then uncouple a few weeks later, to save face.

He knows the rules because he would follow them too.

I should keep him around at least for that.

He clutches his chest. "You want to be my friend? Someone to tell all your deep, darkest, sexy secrets to?"

"Don't make me regret this," I warn.

Ashton laughs and it's a good laugh. It makes me think for just a moment if—

Nope. We had that moment a few years ago and—just no.

"I'll stick around," he says like it's actually his decision. "But you have to give me a good one-on-one date."

"I don't have to give you anything." I laugh and shoulder my way past him. "Let's go find some whales."

It's a good group with lots of laughter as we drive to the marina. We take a Zodiac tour because of the small group, which means more speed and more splashes. It's the best time of the year to see whales, and it doesn't take us long to find the first pod of humpbacks.

Tanner, the laid-back hockey player, is as excited as a little girl with her first boy band crush when the first whale breaches, the powerful body crashing into the sea with a white-plumed splash that is a little too close for comfort.

Leo screams when the wave hits us, which makes me laugh.

I like the way Jon stays close—like he's a bodyguard that I actually want to protect me— and how both Boone and Ashton try to stay cool and casual, but are as excited as the rest of us.

We manage to see two different pods of humpbacks and a fin whale in the distance. Rand insists that he sees a dolphin, and Jon agrees, so our driver heads over to find a friendly dolphin who swims alongside us for a while.

I wish the water was warm enough for me to swim along beside her.

Closer to shore, we see porpoises and seals and so many birds. It's a good day—a fun few hours on the water. I like these men. I'm comfortable with them all; I can say with certainty that I'm attracted and interested, maybe even intrigued enough to want to find out more about them.

Is this how it starts? Tiny flicks of interest that I either snuff out or fan into a flame?

Is the spark strong enough with one of these men?

On the ride back, I'm in one of the SUVs with Eliott and Rand and my cheeks hurt from laughing by the time we get back to the hotel.

It was a good day, maybe a great day. Once I rid myself of the smell of salt and sea, and let Alexa do something with the windblown mess of my hair, I'm going to explore more of the tentative connections I'm developing with these men.

For the first time since arriving, I feel hopeful.

Maybe this will work.

Grayson waits at the door of the hotel as we tumble out of the SUVs. The men talk over each other, with big smiles and a comradery that comes from sharing something special. They trail after me like an excitable band of puppies as I head over to Grayson.

"Good time?" Grayson asks.

"The best."

There are two camerapeople off to the side, and out of the corner of my eye, I see Johnny lift his camera and start filming.

I don't think anything of it until Grayson starts speaking.

"Before you go in," he says, raising his voice over the laughter. "We have a new addition to our group." He says this to the men, eventually shifting his gaze to me.

I can't read his expression, but something pricks at the back of my neck.

"Somebody new is here?" Leo demands.

"No," Boone grumbles.

"No way," Jon agrees. "There's enough of us now."

"Who?" Rand wants to know.

Ashton just slides his gaze to me, eyebrows up and questioning.

"Why?" I manage. I like the group I have. I don't want to have any more choices.

"Before we started, we looked for a specific archetype that we all felt might be a good match for you," Grayson says to me. "We didn't have any luck then, but now..." He trails off with a grin.

I don't like that grin.

I don't like this at all.

"I don't want—" I try, but words fail me.

Because stepping through the door of the hotel, is my brothers' best friend.

Spencer Laz.

My breath leaves my lungs in a huff and a gasp, and all I can do is stare. A murmur of protest begins behind me at Spencer suddenly appearing like he's my Prince Charming sent to rescue me from I don't know what.

Spencer is here.

And then my stunned mind gets dark as images of my father lying in the hospital flash before me. Of Bo or Gunnar in their planes.

Of Kalle— My heartbeat begins to race and I can't keep up with it because there are so many reasons for Spencer to be here and they have nothing to do with what Grayson was trying to say.

"What happened?" I demand in a high-pitched voice that I don't recognize as my own.

Spencer steps forward. "It's okay," he soothes like he knows what I'm thinking. Because of course, he does. He's Spencer and he knows me almost better than I know myself. "Everything's okay."

I take a giant step back because in my stupor, I've moved halfway toward him. "Why are you here?"

A hand on my lower back, two bodies flanking me. My step back takes me into a welcoming embrace of men.

"Can we talk?" Spencer asks.

"Tell me why you're here."

"That's what I want to talk to you about."

There's a low growl/grumble from behind me.

My heart stutters as I realize these seven men are... *protecting* me? Guarding me? They are not going to let Spencer anywhere close to me until I give the go ahead.

He looks like he doesn't know what to do. Uncomfortable. Awkward. This isn't Spencer. Spencer can do anything, can fix anything. He always knows what to say.

"We found a brother's best friend to join the group," Grayson cuts in loudly. "Spencer will be joining us. I'm not sure we need introductions—"

Grayson is watching this. All the men are watching.

The cameras are recording and here I am, freaking out about Spencer randomly showing up like this.

Joining us.

I take a deep breath. Spencer looks the same as he always does—dark hair that starts out perfectly coiffed but always ends up flopping onto his forehead—but different. He's wearing a suit from his collection, but even without the tie, he looks out of place amongst the others.

He looks good, but then, Spencer always looks good. "Hi," I finally manage.

"Hi." His relief is palpable. Did he think I would send him home without hearing what he had to say? "I need a minute with you," he says.

I'm not sure I want to hear what he has to say.

This is a lot. I've had a really good day, and I've just begun to think of *what ifs* with some of the group. I like the way Jon takes care of me, and how Rand makes me laugh. I've enjoyed discovering how Basher drums with anything he can get his hands on, and that, for such a big jock, Tanner is sweet and childlike.

He would run through the birds with me.

But Spencer is here, and he's going to ruin everything.

"I don't have a minute," I snap without thinking. "I have to—I have to get ready. There's a party and I— What are you doing here, Spencer?"

He stares. He swallows. He takes a deep breath like he's drumming up his courage, which is so not Spencer.

This is not a Spencer thing to do.

"Lyra. I, ah—" Spencer holds out his hands. "I'm here for you."

Silence. And then a seagull screams in the distance.

"No," I say instinctively. "No way."

13

Spencer

"DUDE, THAT'S WHAT SHE said when she saw me too."
One of the men laughs and I do a double take when I
see Ashton Carrington is here.

There's a lot more than just Ashton, but right now the seven
she came in with are flanking Lyra like she's their prized possession,
one they don't want to share.

"Lyra, please? I just need a minute." I hate the note of pleading
in my voice, but I should have expected it. Lyra will not make this
easy for me.

She might make me beg.

Am I prepared for that? How far am I willing to go?

"Lyra, Spencer approached us about joining the show."
Grayson Grant is going to need the talents of a very expensive
mediation lawyer if he wants to get this on camera. Which I know
he does—The other producer—Rue or Prue—practically jumped
up and down when I got there and they started planning our
"reunion."

"I realize this is unconventional," he continues, "but because
of your history with him, we made an exception. Won't you listen
to what he has to say?"

Lyra *snarls* at Grayson. "He has a girlfriend."

"Not anymore," I say quickly. "Abigail and I—"

"Did *you* break up with her?"

"Can I talk to you alone for a minute?" I plead.

"There is no alone here."

"Well, away from your..." *Guards* is what I want to say because I think the huge guy behind Lyra is growling at me. "From your friends. For just a minute. Please, Lyra."

At least Grayson is on my side, because none of the pack is. The host inclines his head, and with a frown reminiscent of seven-year-old Lyra, she stomps over to one of the pillars.

A cameraman follows her. I guess that's what she meant about never being alone.

I signed up for this—better get used to it.

"Guess she didn't like the surprise," I say lamely, as I head over to her.

"None of us likes this surprise," one of the men snaps. I don't bother to look back to see who it was because now I'm standing in front of Lyra, and she's all I can see.

Lyra, who has her hands on her slim hips, and an expression that would evoke fear in the bravest of men.

It's not the first time I've seen it. "Talk," she orders.

She looks... she looks amazing. Reddish hair swept up into a ponytail, a scatter of freckles across her nose from being out in the sun. Her white tank top hugs her curves, the pink strap of her bikini slipping down her shoulder.

I've argued cases in courts of law. I've given interviews on camera. I've made speeches, introduced each of the princes at events at one time or another, as well as the king. I'm articulate. I'm a good speaker.

Then why can't I get the words out? Why is it so hard to tell Lyra how I feel? How I've always felt. "I thought we could ... try."

Her blue eyes narrow. "Try what?"

"Try to be together. As more than friends."

"I wasn't aware we *were* friends." She tugs up her strap angrily. "What about Abigail?"

I shake my head. Based on Lyra's reaction, I don't have time to go into details, but she deserves something. "Abigail saw that I had issues about you going on the show. We decided that I need the space to finally figure out what it is between us."

While that may not be exactly what happened, it's a good recap.

Lyra studies me for a long moment. There's no hint of a smile or a welcome light in her eyes. She looks at me like I'm a stranger.

I've also been the recipient of *that* look before and it's not pretty.

"I wasn't aware there *was* something between us," she finally drawls in an icy voice.

Something snaps inside me. It's one thing when we both have been denying a connection, but now that I'm here and willing to take a chance... "This—" I gesture to the space between us that seems to be shrinking since both of us have started leaning toward each other. "This is something. You're lying to yourself if you think there's nothing between us."

"Apparently *you've* been lying to me for years, so what's the difference?"

"I've never lied," I tell her. "And I'm here now to find out once and for all if you have the same feelings for me that I do for you."

Unless it's just me. Oh god, please tell me it's not just me.

For a moment, a heart-breaking moment that seems to drag on forever, I really do think that's the case. Then Lyra opens her mouth.

And shuts it.

It seems like I'm not the only one at a loss for words.

"Why now?" she finally manages.

I can only shrug. "Has there been a better time?"

And that's all I get to say.

The producers break us up, sweeping me aside as they whisk Lyra away from me.

From all the men.

At least they get hugs, and I grit my teeth at seeing Lyra being passed around from one pair of arms to the next, a few of the men managing to kiss her cheeks.

Whatever anger she feels toward me doesn't transfer to them.

Lyra climbs into an SUV, leaving her guardians slowly circling me like they're a pack of hyenas and I'm a wounded antelope.

At least the cameras are still rolling, so I think I'm safe enough.

"Who are you?" A tall, tattooed man wearing a black tank and pink, patterned shorts steps forward a growl. He looks like he enjoys snakes and motorcycles and possibly bar fights.

Maybe not safe enough.

"This is the fifth prince of Laandia."

"You're Leo Whyte," I say with surprise, recognizing the speaker from a television show, some sit-com Abigail made me watch.

"I am." But there's no agreeable grin on his face like he always wore in the show. "What are you doing here?

"His Dad was in the band with the king," comes another voice, and I give a start to see the drummer of the band Water Rhinos standing there, fingers drumming on his thigh. "Didn't you grow up with the royal family?"

"You grew up with Lyra?" Scary guy demands.

"Kind of."

"He's the brother's best friend," a tall blond with an open, handsome face says. I'm glad he's not recognizable. Where did they come up with these guys?

I nod. "I'm Spencer Laz."

"I know this isn't ideal for you," Grayson takes pity on me, as the mutters become louder. "But I know you all want the best for Lyra. She needs to have all the options as she travels on her journey to find love."

Who writes this stuff?

"And Spencer is an option," Grayson continues. "They have a shared past—"

"What kind of past?" Ashton Carrington smirks at me.

"A history," Grayson says firmly before I can answer. "And as long as this is what Lyra wants, we need to give her the respect to explore every possibility."

"What if she doesn't want to?" demands the growly man.

"Then Spencer will say goodbye," Grayson confirms. "It's her decision."

"So you didn't bring him here to make trouble?" asks a tall, shaggy-haired man who also looks vaguely familiar.

"Is there going to be trouble?" Grayson asks, looking at the group and then at me, waiting like a primary school teacher for us all to shake our heads. "I suggest you get changed because Lyra will be back soon to finish your date with the cocktail party. And Spencer, you'll be with the rest of the men tonight."

"So he's not showing up and getting a date right away?" asks a red-haired man.

Grayson shakes his head. "No, Spencer will wait to get a rose like everyone else. I'll come in with you and get things smoothed over," he says to me. "I'll see the rest of you later."

He inclines his head to me and I follow him into the lobby of the hotel.

I knew Odin and Camille have put a lot of hope and faith in the Oceanview being able to bring in tourists to Saint Pierre, and from my first sight of the newly renovated place, I think they were right to focus on it. The lobby is light and airy with a wall of glass doors open to let in the ocean breeze.

There are a few men scattered around the lobby, lounging in comfortable chairs with books or notebooks. Grayson says a few words and they drop their belongings to follow us out to the pool area.

There are no electronics allowed. That's going to be more difficult than winning over Lyra for me.

"I'm not questioning your decision to come," Grayson says in a low voice to me. "But I need to warn you that this might not be easy."

"Has she already found someone?" I ask, throat dry at the thought.

"She might have made connections with a few of the men."
A few? "She looked happy," I say. "Before she saw me."
"Sounds like they had a good day. They went whale watching."
"Lyra loves that."

"This is why we wanted you here," he tells me as we step outside. The pool area is full of men—swimming, sleeping, lifting weights.

These are my competition.

"You know Lyra better than anyone else," Grayson continues as a few of them call out greetings.

No one looks very welcoming to me.

"I hope she might be able to open up with you here. Come on over, guys," he calls. "I want you to meet someone."

"Spencer?" calls a voice. A man wearing a bathing suit louder than living in a castle full of kids pulls himself off a lounge chair and makes his way over to me.

"Lucas Nyle." I recognize him right away since I've made a point of knowing most of the residents of Battle Harbour at least by sight. Lucas was a few years younger than me in school. He was in Lyra's grade, if I remember correctly.

"What are you doing here?" Lucas demands with a nervous laugh.

Does no one think I could be here for Lyra?

"This is Spencer Laz," Grayson calls out. "He's a good friend of Lyra's brother. Brothers," he corrects. "He's a little late to the party, but he'll be joining you all in throwing his hat in the ring for Lyra."

At least these men aren't glaring at me, but no one is very excited to see me.

Except Lucas. "Spencer, dude, I never thought I would see you here." Lucas extends a hand like we're friends.

We're not. If we were, he might not be surprised to see me.

"I didn't think I'd see you either," I say.

"Yeah, well when they asked for the boy next door, I jumped at the chance. Lyra's always been pretty special. But you should know that already. This guy is like the fifth prince of Laandia," Lucas tells the others, slapping me on the shoulder. "We gotta hang out with him because he's got the inside track."

I've had to deal with all sorts of people, so I know it's hard coming back from a bad first impression. And unless Lucas stops talking, he's not coming back from this.

He doesn't stop. Instead, he starts spouting Battle Harbour gossip about me. And Lyra.

I'm not sure if Lucas is trying to make himself look good by knowing all this information about me, or showing the others that I'm a threat.

"I thought you had a girlfriend?" I interrupt Lucas. "Or was it a fiancée?"

Lucas's face drains of colour. "No—no, no. No, we broke up. A long time ago actually."

"Is that so?"

Along with knowing the residents, I make sure I'm kept informed of what's going on in town. I also have staff who love to gossip.

"Sad, but I... I said I'm coming here. I'm going to take this chance with Princess Lyra, and that's it," Lucas says in a hearty voice, not like a man who broke up with a woman for a one-in-twenty-five chance with Lyra Erickson.

Like me. I don't sound like that. I'm determined, but I also miss Abigail.

"That's too bad," I tell him. "You guys were together a long time."

"Well, I'm moving on with Lyra. I hope."

Grayson looks at us out of the corner of his eye, and I can see that Lucas's time here will soon come to an end as clearly as if I were predicting the future.

I also get the feeling it's not going to make me any more popular among the men.

14

Lyra

GRAYSON IS USING MY snazzy convertible, so I'm escorted back to Camille's in one of the SUVs.

What the hell just happened? And why, when I haven't been alone in days, is there no one in the car for me to ask?

None of the producers ride back with me, which is a smart move for them, since I'm in a mood.

I don't know exactly what kind, but it's definitely a mood.

Seeing Spencer was like someone slapped my face, then gave me the biggest bear hug. I'm so *angry* that he showed up *right* after I had such a good date. Right after I started thinking that maybe things will be okay, and maybe my person could be here.

But the anger can't wipe out the sheer delight in seeing him. The relief that he was there. That he came for me.

I try not to focus on that because how can I be furious with a silly grin on my face?

And I want to stay mad. That's what my head thinks is a good idea. A great idea. Because—why? What is Spencer trying to prove?

But then my heart gets in the way because of that one line. "I'm here for you."

What does that even *mean*? He's had his whole life— my whole life—and now, when I'm looking at moving on, away from thoughts of him, he's here.

I know what it means. I've had men declare their feelings for me. I've had proposals of marriage, offers to buy me anything from jewelry to small islands. I've had offers to buy *me*.

But Spencer Laz, whom I have known my entire life, showing up to join the cast of men vying for my heart? I never saw that coming.

That doesn't mean I never secretly hoped for a grand gesture from him. I just didn't think it would be this. Now.

I thought I had accepted that he had found love with Abigail, that she was his future, which left me adrift to find my own.

Did I think—deep down with the things I never speak about, like thoughts of me somehow becoming queen of Laandia—Spencer and I would end up together?

Yes. Yes, I really did think that.

And then I didn't.

And now I don't know what to think.

It's a quick drive back to the house with my thoughts racing.

I tumble out of the car when we arrive, jumping out before it even comes to a complete stop. Camille and Odin are waiting for me in the kitchen, along with Bo.

Bo is here, along with Hettie and Tema. For a moment, I'm even more confused until I realize he flew Spencer to the island.

Tema is the only one who reacts, throwing her arms around my waist to give me a tight hug. I haven't known her long, but we were quick to bond, being Swifties and fans of LEGO flowers sets. I make a point of sending her something in the mail every few weeks and she responds with texts of her pictures and what books she's reading from Bo's phone.

I breathe into her little girl smell—sunscreen, strawberry shampoo and Jolly Rancher gummies—and take a moment.

No one says a word until Hettie pulls Tema away from me and leads her from the room.

"Spencer showed up," I say unnecessarily when they disappear.

"I flew him over," Bo tells me.

"Why?"

"Why did I bring him?" Bo asks.

"Why is he here?" It comes out as a bit of a screech, like one of the seabirds from my visit to the bird sanctuary and both Bo and Odin grimace.

Camille pulls out the chair beside her. "What did he say?" she asks as casually as if we're discussing the weather.

I shake my head. "I can't sit. I need to move. Possibly hit something." I stalk across the room. Sitting quietly has never been a thing for me, especially not when I'm upset. Or confused. "I didn't talk to him. Much."

"I thought that was the whole point," Odin demands.

"Well, it was a bit of a shock to see him there, and you know, I've got stuff to do," I tell him sarcastically. "I have a cocktail party to host, and I really need to stop smelling like whale."

"Did you see whales?" Tema calls. She's still in the doorway with an embarrassed Hettie.

This is going to be awkward because Abigail is Hettie's best friend. I haven't warmed up to Bo's wife like I should because of that.

"I did," I tell Tema. "You can come help me get dressed, just give me a minute to figure out my life."

"Okay!" she cheers.

"Why don't I show you to Lyra's room?" Camille offers and leaves to escort my niece and Hettie.

I owe her one because I don't want Hettie to report back to Abigail.

Once they've gone. I turn to Bo. "What did he say?' I ask, taking the screech out of my tone.

"He contacted Grayson, said he wanted to come on the show," my brother reports.

"He *wanted* to come on the show," I repeat, shaking my head in pure disbelief. Spencer cares so much about privacy that I never expected there would be even an alternate universe in which Spencer would show up on a reality show. But he's here.

He's here.

It doesn't help the confused collage of my thoughts.

Instead of my room, I head straight to Camille's office. There's a landline there, and since my phone was confiscated when we started shooting, this is my only way to communicate with the outside world.

And there's one person I really want to communicate with.

Sophie answers on the first ring. "I wondered if I'd hear from you," she says with a smile in her voice. "What's going on?"

"Can you tell me?" I beg.

"Did you talk to him?"

My shoulders droop, relieved that Sophie seems to know about Spencer showing up so I don't have to tell her the story. Because I'm not sure if I'm the good guy here? Or the villain.

Should I have stayed to talk to him? Should we have worked things out right then and there?

Would Spencer have told me that he's had feelings for me this whole time, instead of vaguely suggesting that there is the potential that he might have feelings for me. Maybe.

It's something he needs to figure out.

And that's why I'm going to stay mad.

"No, I didn't talk to him," I say a little too vehemently. "I'm supposed to be with seven other guys tonight and I can't just stop and say, hey dudes, gotta go talk to this guy here."

This is your show. You can do anything you want.

"You can do anything." Sophie echoes my mother's imaginary voice. "Don't worry, I'm coming to you. I've already asked Gunnar to give me a ride to you tomorrow morning. I'll be there first thing. We'll figure this out," she soothes.

"How am I supposed to figure out your brother?" I demand, but the thought of Sophie here does calm me down. The only thing better would be Kate.

With the two of them, I can handle anything, even the sudden earthquake that is my love life.

You can handle everything, even on your own.

I blow out my breath in a raspberry. "Can you at least tell me what he's doing here? All he said was about *maybe feelings*. What about Abigail?"

"They broke up," Sophie reports. "How do you feel about him?"

I want to feel nothing. I've always tried to feel nothing and the stupid idiot won't let me. I even asked him to go to a wedding with me and he said no because of Abigail. What was I supposed to think about that? I remember what they were like hanging with Bo and Hettie years ago. It made me sick to see them together.

Because I wanted that with him.

"You know," I murmur.

"Ah—no, I don't," she says. "No one does because you refuse to talk about him. The chemistry between the two of you is amazing, Lyra. It always has been. But the only thing you ever say is that he's "Just Spencer.""

"He *is* just Spencer."

"Well, Just Spencer just showed up on your doorstep, hat in hand and ready to woo you. I can't even picture that image in my head," she adds, giving an audible shiver.

"See? What am I supposed to think if you can't even? He's your brother."

"*That's* what I can't even," Sophie wails. "He's my brother and you're my—are we best friends again?"

Despite my turmoil over Spencer, Sophie's question brings a rush of warmth to my chest. Sophie had been such a big part of my childhood, and then she wasn't. Spencer came to live at the castle, and I lost Sophie in the bargain.

We both did.

"You're the one who stopped being my best friend," I tell her primly. "But since that was all your mother's fault, I suppose I can forgive you."

I will never forgive her mother for causing the rift, not only between me and Sophie, but between Spencer and his sisters but Sophie is easy to forgive.

"Sooo kind of you," Sophie teases, the warmth in her voice matching mine. "But back to Spencer?"

"I've always wanted him, Soph," I admit, more to myself than to her. "What am I supposed to do now? I've got all these guys here and some of them are—I can see potential. I really can. But now that Spencer is here..."

Nothing is a sure thing, and while that's never been a problem for me before, right now it's making my mind race in crazy circles.

"Give him a chance," Sophie tells me, sounding more rational and mature than your usual twenty-five-year-old woman. More rational and mature than me.

"That's all he's asking for," she continues. "Just like the other guys. See if there's something there."

"And if there's not?"

"Then you'll finally know."

15

Spencer

I'VE FINALLY MADE A move, and I'm not allowed to see Lyra.

I'm not invited to the cocktail party that night. After I unpack and change, I'm offered food made by one of the men, and ushered into a back room of the hotel, where the laughter of the lucky few who get to spend time with Lyra, drifts in from the lobby.

"This is the worst part," Lucas tells me, settled beside me by the door.

There are pool, ping-pong, and foosball tables, but I refuse to join in, just sitting like I'm in the middle of a pout.

It seems like Lucas has appointed himself as my guide here. I'm not impressed since having him stuck to my side is keeping the others away. It could also be because I'm sitting like a lump, but no one initiates a conversation. They watch me like I'm about to freak out or something, but no one says anything.

It's a little unnerving. While I'm not here to make friends, I do need to find out about my competition.

I hate that I now have competition for Lyra.

"Are there any good parts?" I ask him, watching as a really good-looking guy cleans the pool table with two shots.

Everyone here is good looking.

"Going on a date," Lucas offers. "They seem like they're having fun."

We saw a glimpse of Lyra when she came back to the hotel for the remainder of her date. She had changed into a white jumpsuit, and I knew just from the quick look that it was backless.

Long and lean, prowling into the lobby like an exotic white wild cat.

Sexy as hell.

It's strange allowing myself to think of Lyra as sexy. I would always censor my internal comments when I thought of her.

And yes—I often thought of her.

A burst of laughter pulls me back into my misery. "Is it going to be like that all night?" I scrub at my face. I need to get myself out of this funk. I shouldn't have expected Lyra to greet me with open arms because I've never given her a reason to think I wanted to be greeted like that.

Or that I would ever show up here at the very moment she's returned from a date with seven men.

Who would ever expect that?

"What happens now?" I ask Lucas, who is looking at me too closely. It's like he's storing all the information on me and the show away to let loose when he gets back to Battle Harbour.

I considered how I would appear on television if I joined the show, but I didn't give much thought about what the people of Battle Harbour will think of me.

What will they think of me if I don't end up with Lyra?

"On their date," I add. Is it better to think about what Lyra is doing at this moment or about the embarrassment of returning home with my tail tucked between my legs?

It's really a toss-up.

"They… talk?" Lucas guesses. "This is the first one. The guys get a chance to spend time with Lyra. Have you not seen the show?"

"I saw it when Odin was doing it, but that's it."

"They kiss. Sometimes."

"They're kissing Lyra tonight?" The thought of that makes my blood boil. I know Lyra has kissed men. I've kissed women. I was just with Abigail but still, now that I'm here, the thought of any of those men I saw with Lyra earlier touching her… kissing her—

No. It's wrong.

Any man doing that is wrong because Lyra is mine.

She's not mine. She can do whatever she likes, with whomever she likes, and that realization just… sucks.

I'm not usually unreasonable but it's as if stepping out of Bo's plane in Saint Pierre has turned me into a different person.

A person who gave up a good relationship with an amazing woman for a chance with Lyra.

I've become someone who is going to have to dig deep to find out if the feelings I have for a princess are real or just a fantasy.

A person who has willingly volunteered to be on a reality show.

Who is this person? Because these are not things that I do. I end relationships because we have nothing in common, ending things before they get too serious to save the pain.

I go above and beyond in my work, but never discussing my emotions. Not even acknowledging them.

And I don't even watch reality television.

I lurch to my feet because if I sit here any longer, my head might well explode. "I'm going to look around," I tell Lucas.

"They said we're not supposed to go near the lobby," he calls after me. I give a wave that I heard him.

But that's exactly where I go.

It's like I have a homing beacon attached, bringing me straight back to Lyra. I find the corridor that leads to the lobby and stay close to the wall as I check it out.

There is a small group of men sitting on the double couches by the fireplace, all with drinks in their hands and laughing.

A few more stand by the front door. Plotting an escape? Or waiting for someone to return.

At first glance they look like they're enjoying themselves, but the laughter sounds forced, and the smiles are too bright for the way their gazes scan the room looking for something.

Looking for Lyra.

I sense her before I see her.

She walks back into the lobby with one of the men, a tall, gawky-looking redhead. Her arm is tucked in his, and the way he's looking down at her—

He's looking at her like I want to look at her. Like she's the most important thing in the room.

In the whole place.

The white jumpsuit is shot through with silver thread so it looks like it's glowing in the lights. It's tied around her neck, doing *things* to her cleavage that I've never considered before.

I've considered her cleavage, and the rest of her body before, but I always told myself I wasn't allowed to think of her like that.

Lyra's hair floats past her shoulders in a cloud of reddish-blonde waves, smiling like she's exactly where she wants to be. And the way she looks up at the guy beside her...

I'm done denying. It hurts.

I want Lyra to look at *me* like that. Just once, so I can see what it's like to be her whole focus. Lyra has smiled at me countless times, looked at me with dancing eyes, laughter curving those lips into a wide grin, but those times were never just about me. There was always someone with us, someone watching, taking pictures. Judging.

For once, I'd like to be just with Lyra Erickson. Not Princess Lyra of Laandia.

Someone hands her a fresh drink and she smiles at *them* too. Why did I bother coming to check on her? She's having the best time, not even giving a second thought that I'm not there.

I wonder if she thinks of me at all.

And then she sees me.

All it takes is her throwing back her head mid-laugh and glancing over at the doorway where I'm standing. I never realized that I've inched around, obvious to anyone who looked over.

I pull back around the corner with a muffled curse, wondering if I should try and get back to the room, or wait until Lyra disappears with another man for some one-on-one time.

I don't have time to do anything because suddenly Lyra is standing in front of me.

The drink is gone and her arms are folded across her chest. If I was in a courtroom, I'd say she was a hostile witness.

"Did you need something?" she demands in an icy voice. The white material of her jumpsuit folds and flutters, and it's all I can do to keep my focus up on her face.

She's wearing the red lipstick that brings all attention to her lips.

I'm allowed to think about her lips now.

"Just looking around," I manage. "I took a wrong turn."

"Nope. You were born with a compass in your hand, plus I'm pretty sure Odin showed you the plans for this place, so you know exactly where you're going."

"I don't remember that—"

"Plus you've been standing here since I got back with Rand." She cocks her head. "You're not the only spymaster in Laandia, Spencer. The only thing I haven't been able to figure out is the real reason you're here."

I've never been so glad that my teenage growth spurt gave me enough height to still have a few inches over the tall and slender Lyra, even in her heels.

Taking a quick glance down, I notice the tips of her gold strappy sandals under the hem of the pants. Her toenails are painted a periwinkle blue.

"I told you," I begin, dragging my gaze back. Lyra claps her fingers in front of my face and I step back in reflex.

"Not here—*here*," she hisses. "Is this some sort of big-brother move where you're trying to stop me from kissing someone? Because—been there, done that, and *not* about to stand for it again."

It's funny that she went back to the same memory that I did. The summer she turned thirteen, Lyra decided she needed to have her first kiss—her first *real* kiss. She had a list of boys whom she deemed suitable, a list that Gunnar somehow got a copy of.

We spent that summer blocking every opportunity Lyra had for being alone with anyone on that list.

Her brothers thought it was hilarious, but I was more satisfied knowing she wasn't going to be kissing anyone.

Especially, since I considered that her first kiss had already happened, and it had been with me

"It's not that," I tell her.

"Are you aware that your right eyebrow twitches when you lie?"

This is the first time I'm hearing this. "Is that why you could always beat me playing poker?"

"No, that's just because I'm a better card player than you could ever hope to be." Those glorious red lips are still frowning at me.

"Okay, fine. I'm not lost," I concede.

"If you plan on staying, you better lose the brother's best-friend-protective deal," she warns.

"Why wouldn't I stay? I told you, I want to see what there really is between us."

Lyra's face softens, losing the irritated gleam in her eyes and some of the haughty poise she was born with. "You keep saying that," she says in a quiet voice.

"Because it's true. That's why I'm here." I reach out, my fingers practically tingling with the need to touch some part of her.

I manage a slight brush of one of her fingers. How could I have denied myself the opportunity to focus my attention on her lips? Being close enough to her for her perfume—sweet cherry blossoms—to invade my senses?

"I've been an idiot," I say aloud.

"I'm not arguing with you."

I smile, holding her gaze with a gentleness I've never felt before. "It's nice not to argue with you."

"I don't want that," she says in a quiet voice.

"You want to fight with me?"

"I want you to be *you*, not some stranger who thinks he has to act in a certain way for the cameras. You know me better than anyone, Spencer."

"Do I?"

"Yes." Lyra leans towards me, like a tall flower bending in the breeze. "So you should know that you being here makes me angry."

Her perfume, those lips, what she's saying has the effect of making my head spin, leaving me very confused and somewhat unsteady on my feet. "It—what? I thought—"

"That's the problem. You didn't think—about me. About what I need, what I want. You just thought about how you might be about to lose something incredible that you never had the courage to go after."

"Lyra..."

"I'm not finished," she says, her voice crisp and curt and sounding very much like her mother's. "*I* know how I feel about you, Spencer. I've always known. It's only you who needs to get his head on straight."

All of the air in my lungs expels in a huff. She knows how she feels. Does that mean—

But she's still not finished. "You will not be getting any special treatment until you figure all this out." Her finger juts out and pokes me in the chest. "If it were up to me, I wouldn't even give you a date. I'm not wasting time here. I'm not giving up opportunities with the other men—who all know why they're here, and that's because of *me*. I'm not picking you over them just to have you decide at the last minute that I'm not who you want. Because—" She takes a step forward and pokes me again, harder than before. "You have been picking everyone else over me for my entire life."

"I haven't."

"You have. You picked my brothers. You picked my father when you told him I snuck out of the castle to go to that party."

"You were sixteen!"

"You still picked him. You picked Abigail." Her face crumples in an un-Lyra like expression and I instinctively reach for her to comfort.

But she steps away, schooling her face into her usual coolness. "I'm not some rebound either," she continues. "If you're here, you're over her. If you decide to stay, you better start putting me first, Spencer. I won't stand for it any other way. And don't waste too much time, because I'm not waiting for you."

"There's the talk *I* wanted." With that, she sweeps back into the lobby.

That's when I see that her jumpsuit *is* backless, and the cameras have caught the entire exchange on film.

16

Lyra

I HEAD STRAIGHT FOR the back doors of the lobby after my chat with Spencer, desperate for some air to cool the heat of my cheeks. That was—

That was badass. Even I have to admit that.

I did not fall into Spencer's arms. But I'm not denying that it was tempting.

Earlier, at Camille's, after I talked to Sophie, I called Kate. She made me understand that while I might be touched that Spencer would travel so far out of his comfort zone to come here, I was allowed to be angry at his timing.

"You can be angry with him, even if you're happy to see him," Kate had told me. "You give him a chance if that's what *you* want to do, not because you feel obligated."

"I don't feel obligated to do anything," I argued.

Kate sighed. "Lyra, you're a princess. Your whole life is an obligation. But you're out of Laandia now, away from the castle. You don't have to be Princess Lyra there. Try to be Lyra Erickson for a bit."

"No one wants Lyra Erickson."

"If they don't, they don't deserve you," she had said heatedly.

I told Spencer that he knew me better than anyone, but was that true? Did he just know Princess Lyra better than most? And what about Lyra Erickson? What did she think about Spencer showing up?

She's mad at him.

Which is the reason behind my little speech, most of which, I imagine, Spencer was not expecting. I could see it on his face; his expression was that of every man who had ever been attracted to me. The connection is there—the attraction, the chemistry, or whatever it can be called. It's always been there.

While we've both openly denied it, I've always known that Spencer and I would be good together. The fact that he's only realizing this after I made a point of trying to forget him is... For such an intelligent man, Spencer is a dimwitted nitwit whose understanding of the female species can be compared to the Wi fi signal here—weak, spotty, and basically non-existent.

Maybe more than that, but I'm not giving him too much credit at this moment.

Both of us have been idiots, but Spencer more than me.

Today was a good day, and tonight had been even better. Good conversations, a few real connections, and yes, some kissing—Jon (amazingly thorough) and Leo (somewhat lackluster). I've laughed and told stories and I was one hundred percent Lyra Erickson, and they still seemed to like me.

I liked me.

And then I saw Spencer and now everything is mixed up.

"Where did you sneak off to?" Ashton says suddenly from beside me. "Jon was about to send off a search party."

I clutch my chest and try to control my jumping heart rate. "I was just—Spencer." I grind my teeth. I'm glad it's Ashton who found me because I need a minute before I rejoin the group.

"You talked to him?" he asks under his breath.

I nod, keeping my face away from the cameras like the professional I am.

"What's his sister like?" I turn to him with confusion. "You're pretty good friends with her, aren't you?"

Where did *that* come from—? "No," I say automatically.

"Can you not use other words with me? I really don't like it. *No*," he says mockingly.

"How about *not on your life*. You're not nice enough for Sophie."

"I'm nice." Ashton pretends to be offended.

I raise an eyebrow.

"I'm nice enough."

"Again—no."

"See? You say that a lot, you know."

"I'm very good at saying no."

"Is that what you told the wannabe prince when he asked for the next date?"

Even though Ashton has no chance with Sophie and if he does continue to suggest he might, I will personally see that every single tire is slashed before his next race. "Spencer doesn't want to be a prince and he didn't ask for a date."

"I'm sure he thinks he's getting it."

"I'm pretty sure he doesn't now."

Ashton laughs under his breath. "So here's me trying the friend thing. Ready to learn all your deep, dirty dark secrets."

"I don't think anything is dirty dark, but sure. Go for it."

Ashton is easy. I know what to expect from him, and even when he's at his most flirtatious, I know nothing serious will ever happen between us. It makes him comfortable to be around, a quiet island in a sea of complications.

Not that my relationships with the other men are complicated, but this is only the beginning. And now that Spencer is here...

"What do you think of your boyfriend being here?"

I stifle my groan. "I really don't want to talk about him."

"That's all anyone is talking about. You got to give me something to report back to the guys."

I round on him. "I thought you wanted to be my friend, to hear my secrets. Secrets that you would keep secret."

"Is that a rule or something?" But he nudges my shoulder with a smile as he says it. "I'm not anyone's first choice to confide in, so give me a break."

Is this Ashton trying to make me feel better? Weird. I roll my eyes. "Yeah, yeah. Here's something. Spencer is not my boyfriend."

"That's not what my sister says."

I keep my mouth shut. Fenella has her finger in all of the pies in Battle Harbour and I'm sure she's heard all the stories about Spencer and me.

"Do you want him to be?" Ashton continues in a lazy voice. "Do you want him to be your boyfriend?"

I have to think about that because it deserves more than a snappy reply. "I want him to figure out what he wants."

"That's awfully nice of you. This is your show, you know, and if the dude didn't know where his head is before he stepped foot in this place, you should send him packing. There are other guys here who know they want you."

It's like he's repeating my own words back to me. And it does calm me down, strengthens my resolve.

This is *my* show. This is my life.

"Do you?" I ask. While I'm on a roll, I might as well double-check that I don't need to shut anything down with Ashton. He's rich and good-looking, and I'm sure there's more to him than meets the eye, but it will be difficult enough for me to open up to these men to show my true self. I don't want to have to coax anyone else into doing the same thing.

Not even Spencer.

"Want you?' Ashton lifts an eyebrow. "What's the point when you say you're not picking me at the end?"

I feel bad about that. I've never got the sense that Ashton was interested in me more the publicity I could bring him.

That we could bring to each other.

"I don't think you really want to end up with me," I say as cautiously as if I'm picking gravel out of road rash because if I've read Ashton wrong, this might hurt.

Ashton shrugs. "You sound worried. Are you already regretting friend-zoning me?"

"Honestly, no. I think we'd be good, but it would blow up so fast and so spectacularly and we'd get a lot of publicity about it and that would be good for the show. But this is my life, so no. But I will keep you around."

"Because I'm such a charming and devastatingly handsome person?"

"No, no and no. I guess you are a person, so only two nos this time."

Ashton slings an arm around me. "Are we supposed to kiss now?"

"And another no. You know, I think that *is* my favourite word when it comes to you."

Laughing, I let Ashton lead me back to the others. I can't help myself and give a sideways glance to where Spencer had been lurking.

He's gone.

But he's still here.

17

Spencer

L AST NIGHT DID NOT go as planned.

Not that I had much of a plan, it turned out.

I'm regretting being so impulsive. There should be no question if I want to be with Lyra. I should have had all that figured out before I set foot on Saint Pierre.

It's not fair to Lyra, and I feel bad about that.

But in my defense, time was of the essence, so I'll have to work fast to discover what I want. Lots of self-reflection, internal monologues, and second-guessing myself before I find my true self and what will make me happy.

That's what would happen in a romance novel, according to my sister Stella. I managed a quick call to her before I got here, and like always, she wasn't the most positive about the situation.

Today, I'm not feeling that positive about it either and while a lot of that has to do with my conversation with Lyra last night, some of it is the fact that I woke up to a roommate this morning.

It's been years since I've shared a room, and I don't have great memories of the arrangement.

I was asleep before my roommate returned last night, one of the lucky ones who was on the group date with Lyra. It's not until

I wake up that I get my first sight of the red-haired man as he pulls a shirt over his head.

It takes a minute before I can come up with a name. Rand. "Hey," I mutter sleepily.

He turns with a smile. "Get up, dude. They're giving out the flowers in five."

"Flowers?" I sit up and wish for coffee.

"It's how we find out who stays and who goes. And who gets a date." He motions to the door. "We need to be out there and camera ready."

Camera ready. I wince as I'm faced again with another part of my plan I didn't think through. I'm about to spend six weeks in front of a camera, my every facial expression visible to television viewers.

And there will be a lot of viewers because people are going to want to see Princess Lyra find her Prince Charming.

Not only do I have to be on screen, but I have to make sure I look good.

In five minutes.

I hit the bathroom.

Thanks to living in the castle and my friendship with the princes, I know how this works. Give them the good profile, make sure I'm standing on a slant, and do everything I can not to be at the end of a group photo.

I'm not vain, but I'm human. Especially being around the royal family—I may not be on their good looks level, but I never want to look like a pauper next to the princes.

In four minutes, I manage to brush my teeth, fix my hair and get dressed, mirroring Rand's shorts and a polo shirt. I also wake up enough to offer him my hand. "Spencer Laz. I didn't get a chance to introduce myself last night."

Rand grins. "Oh, I know who you are. The ex-boyfriend."

I shake my head. "Just friends."

"Damn, *I* was hoping to do the friends-to-lovers trope."

"I don't know what that is."

"It's where the friend slowly becomes something more. Didn't you do your research before you came?"

"It was a bit of a quick decision," I admit.

"I'll try to fill you in after we see who gets sent home." He jerks his head to the door. "Ready for this? There'll be a camera when we open it."

"Seriously?"

"Uh huh. Try not to seem miserable if you don't get anything. I saw Lucas's face yesterday when he didn't get the date rose and it was hilarious. I hope they save it for the show."

"Lucas Nyle?"

Rand pauses with his hand on the doorknob. "I'm supposed to play a nice guy, so don't get me started on him."

"Noted." Good to know I'm not the only one with the not-so-great opinion of Lucas.

He gives me an encouraging smile before he opens the door. "A guy like you shouldn't take too long to get used to the cameras, so don't worry."

No one has ever told me not to worry, because that's what I do. I worry about the royal family, and fix what is fixable.

But I'm not sure how to fix this.

Taking a deep breath, I follow Rand out into the hall, coaching my expression into one of pleasant and mild excitement. He was right—a cameraperson stands off to the side, recording everything about this moment.

This is going to be hell.

The reveal has already started down the hall, with under-the-breath mutters heard as a disappointed man scoops a yellow rose from the floor.

"That's Mac. Or Max," Rand whispers. "Yellow means friendship in flower language, so Lyra is sending him home."

I watch as more doors open. Two more men—Mac this time, and someone named Devon—get a yellow rose, as well as Lucas Nyle.

I guess I didn't have to share my thoughts of him with Lyra after all.

I watch as the men give those going home one-shouldered hugs and pretend to be upset.

Maybe they really are upset. Odin told me that during the short time he was on the show, he saw friendships develop. Being cooped up in a hotel together would have to be the reason for that, because I don't think competing for the same woman makes anyone friendly.

Still, the only ones who are truly upset are the ones going home. I'm sure the rest of us feel the same elation that it's not us.

It's not me.

There are two pink roses outside the door, one for Rand and one for me. Pink means we can stay.

A red rose outside your door means you get a date.

It's not me going home, but it's not me going on the date with Lyra, either.

Rand scoops both of them off the floor. "Looks like we'll be roomies for another few days," he says, handing one to me. "You're the second one I've had, so it's good that I'm not going to be seen as a bad-luck charm."

"He already went home?"

"Yes. Asani. He didn't even make it through the first date. I was hoping you'd at least make it twenty-four hours."

"Hopefully more than that." It's very difficult to keep the disappointment from my face, but Rand acts as if he's used to being the focus of cameras.

Maybe he's right and it won't take long to get used to the constant surveillance.

But it will be impossible to get comfortable with the idea that Lyra can send me home at any time. As someone she's turned to for advice in the past, I know there's no chance of taking on that role here, because this is about me.

Lyra can decide I'm not worth the effort of keeping me around anytime she wants to, and I don't blame her. She can do the same for any of these men.

She must love the control aspect of it.

The only thing I can do to convince her to keep me around is to show her I'm all in. There is no time for self-reflection or internal monologues—I have to make sure she knows I'm here for her, for an honest-to-goodness chance at a future with her.

Maybe if I hadn't spent my life denying it, I wouldn't be standing in a hallway with a bunch of strangers holding a pink rose.

I take a deep breath, and then another, because this feels like a moment. An epiphany, where I finally pull my head out of the sand.

Or pull it out of somewhere else.

I want Princess Lyra.

And I'm going to do everything I can to get her.

I join Rand as the men stand around and talk. "So, who gets the next date?" I ask.

18

Lyra

S ophie and Gunnar haven't arrived before I take the car to the hotel to pick up my date, and for once, I wish Gunnar had more of Odin's punctuality.

I'd really like my friend here.

My friend, who is also Spencer's half-sister, so maybe I'm better off with Grayson and the Rs as a sounding board. Sophie might well be working for Team Spencer.

She better not be.

Not that there is Team Spencer versus Team Lyra. There are no teams—yet. There's just a confused Lyra. And an unsure Lyra. And a really-want-to-know-what's-going-on-in-Spencer's-head Lyra.

All of which are not fun Lyras.

I push all of that down deep as I drive over to the hotel to pick up my date for the day.

I told Grayson even before Spencer arrived to give the next one-on-one date rose to Basher. The drummer impressed me with his easy-going ways and cute smile. Plus, I'm the daughter of a former rock star, so why wouldn't I want to spend the day with a musician?

Who to send home was the easiest pick. I gave Grayson Mac's and Max's names because even after almost a week into this, I still can't tell them apart. Devon got the yellow rose because he can't seem to look me in the eye. I can be intimidating, but if he's already scared of me, there's really no chance for us.

Not that there was much of one, anyway.

Lucas had been on my list to go home since day one because I remember six-year-old Lucas with his finger up his nose at the end-of-year concert, and if I remember that, I'm sure the rest of the town would as well.

And I want Battle Harbour to be proud of me.

I'm making my own decisions, based on what I want and don't want. And what I think is good for me. Lately though, thoughts about my image have been clogging up my mental feed. I've always tried to keep a *don't care* attitude about what people think of me, but I think it's time to tone down society's idea of me as the Party Princess. The demanding, high maintenance royal rebel needs to go.

Because everyone, eventually, has to grow up.

I'm not sure if my decision to be the Suitorette helps or hinders, but at least I'm taking control of my life.

I'm proud of you, I imagine Mom saying.

"Maybe, but what do you think of this guy?" I murmur as I pull up in front of the hotel. Basher is waiting for me, arms waving as quickly as his hands fly around his drum kit.

Basher isn't the most attractive man here—unfortunately, that is Ashton, with fireman Dylan a close second—but there's a coolness that I'm drawn to, like a younger Keanu Reeves mixed with a pre-Pirates of the Caribbean Johnny Depp. He's got swagger, but with a cute smile and lots of energy. He seems like he enjoys life, and that is tops on my list.

"Hey, hey, Princess," Basher greets me, jumping in the car before it comes to a complete stop. "Let's get out of here before the masses find us."

"Where is everyone?"

"They told me to wait for you inside and I... didn't." His smile veers into mischievous territory, and I start the car with a laugh.

"Wave to the camera then," I tell him as Grayson and Johnny burst out of the door.

Today's date is parasailing and there's not much time to talk as I drive away.

Rue and a cameraman are waiting for us there at the marina where we catch the boat, and they hop aboard with us. I've been parasailing before, but never over the Atlantic. Even in July, there's a hint of chill in the air and the Atlantic is much darker than the bright blue of the warm Caribbean and just a little foreboding. All I can think of is that I don't want to end up in the water.

Hasan hooks a Go-Pro to the harness before we're lifted into the air to catch the gasps and giggles and even the quick kiss Basher gives me when we're flying high in the air.

I don't mind the kiss too much. In fact, the whole day does the trick in getting my mind off Spencer.

Parasailing, a quick walk along the beach where I ask so many questions about Basher's life in the band that Rue tells me to stop so Basher can ask me something.

He counters with questions about my dad's life with the band.

Basher doesn't mention Spencer or any of the other men, and I appreciate it. It's too easy to get caught up in my thoughts and that wouldn't be fair to him. After I change into a clinging, one-shouldered green dress, we meet at the public school for the second part of our date.

"Couldn't get enough of me?" Basher teases as he takes my hand to walk through the doors. Holding hands with him would take some getting used to, with his rings and calluses from holding drumsticks. His hands are always in motion, like he's playing air drums. "It's been a while since I've been in a school," he adds, looking around at the posters and pictures and tiny lockers as I lead him to the gymnasium.

"This date is nothing school related," I promise as I let him open the door for me.

"I wondered if you knew what's going on."

"I might. Just know this involves music."

A table is set up in the middle of the gym, and on the stage at the back of the gym is—

"Dude!" Basher cries. Letting go of my hand, he rushes to the stage where recording artist Denzel Duke has just launched into his latest hit.

"Basher!" Denzel stops playing as Basher jumps on the little stage. I watch with surprise as the two men hug, slapping shoulders noisily.

Hasan gets the entire thing on film.

It turns out Basher and Denzel have known each other for years, so what was supposed to be a romantic concert with slow music and champagne becomes a reunion.

And a jam session.

Basher is quite happy to leave my side and climb behind the drum kit when Denzel suggests it. I'm happy as well, because watching him play really increases his sex appeal.

After a few songs, it gets even better; Basher gives me the sticks and gives me an impromptu drum lesson.

All for the camera. Rue loves it.

Eventually, we leave the stage for Denzel to perform, swaying together in the darkened gym.

"Sorry about that," Basher murmurs into my ear. "I got a little carried away."

"It was amazing," I tell him. "Who gets a lesson from Basher Doyle?"

"Denzel's a good guy. I can't believe he's here."

"I love it. Spontaneous, completely unscripted. It'll be good for the show."

"But not for me." He pouts. "It was great, yeah, but I missed out getting to know you."

"What do you want to know?"

"What it's really like to kiss you? Not when we're flying fifty feet in the air. And don't say you feel like you're flying," he adds with a smile.

"It'd be a good line."

"I don't want lines with you. I want the real deal."

I motion to the stage. "That was the real deal. Think you're up for the challenge?"

"I'm willing to give it a try." And then Basher brushes his lips against mine, soft and gentle, and unlike what anyone would think a rock star's kiss would be like.

I have kissed a few rock stars in my time and it's very different.

Basher pulls back with a smile, like he's waiting for me to refuse, but I tell myself not to.

Earlier in the day, Rue told me to feel free to kiss when I felt like it, but there needed to be a kiss near the end, for the audience to feel invested in the relationship.

This is that moment and so I lean in and kiss him.

It's brief, closed mouth, the perfect TV kiss.

I've been kissed by a lot of men. It's one of my favourite things to do, which isn't surprising, since it's really the *only* thing I do. I might have a reputation, but it's not based on much, because I can count on one hand the number of men I've been with and I'm not using very many fingers.

There's a spark with Basher, and I lean into it, waiting for it to catch fire.

It doesn't.

Frustrating, because Basher is fun and sweet and funny and hot. Plus, I was vulnerable with him and talked about my feelings, and it wasn't even that difficult.

But the spark fizzles out. Is that because Spencer is my fire-break, steadily burning all the brush and fuel so a simple spark won't be able to build into something more?

I wonder if that's always been my problem.

It's a good kiss, but I can't stop thinking about what Spencer will say when he sees me kissing Basher.

I shouldn't care, but I do.

It's not a good thing to think about one man while you're kissing another.

19

Spencer

I'M NOT SURE I can handle the sitting around.

Lyra is on a date with Basher, and I'm stuck at the hotel with the other guys. We're all waiting for it to be over.

Waiting, and dreading when Basher comes back to report.

The men are scattered all over the house—some in the pool, a few working with the weights. There is laughter and music from the kitchen, and a small group hangs out in the lobby, ready to be the first ones to see Lyra when she drops off Basher.

We missed her earlier since Basher had been waiting outside and they drove off without giving anyone time to say hello.

Some of the guys are upset about that, but I'd bet it's just Lyra.

If I were a producer of this show, I would have made her sign an ironclad agreement to follow each and every instruction. Even though that still might not have gotten her to follow the rules.

Lyra does what Lyra wants. It's how it's always been.

Since I've been here, I've been thinking about her a lot.

Lyra is seen as demanding, constantly in search of adventure, new experiences. Her life is a quest for fun. A rebel in the royal family.

But being here—cut off from the outside world, including the work I know is piling up—means I'm alone with my thoughts for the first time in years. And I've done a lot of thinking about Lyra, about how she's not as demanding as everyone thinks she is. She's definitely a smart, strong, tenacious woman because the daughter of Magnus and Selene Erickson could be nothing else. I've been fortunate to see a different side of Lyra, but now I wonder if there's more to her than even I realize.

Demanding and difficult could be a way of wrestling for control over her life.

Being the child of a king is a challenge and I've seen the princes struggle with their duties and responsibilities in their attempts to have a life somewhat separate from their royal personas. But it must be even more difficult for Lyra—not only is she a woman, but she's a strong one who knows her own mind. She's never sidestepped obstacles, but dealt with them directly, even bulldozing them. All amazing traits for women, but even today, not all society sees strong women as a positive thing.

She lost her mother, but rather than letting that define her, letting her grief change her into an entitled, spoiled woman who demands sympathy, Lyra put in the work to deal with her emotions instead of pretending they don't exist. A public melt-down days after the queen's funeral, questionable relationships, and bad judgements made it obvious that she needed help with her grief, and she got it.

I respect her for that. Admire her.

Princess Lyra is an incredible woman, and I can't wait for the chance to tell her that.

I don't think it will be tonight, though.

Instead, I spend the evening lounging on a couch before the fire with Rand, who has become my newest shadow since Lucas left.

I don't mind Rand following me around.

With us are Boone, Jon, Dylan and Leo. Even for someone who grew up with princes—all sexiest men of various years—there is a intimidating amount of attractiveness and testosterone in this group.

I should have expected that.

"So you and Lyra were pretty close?" Tanner asks, joining me on the couch. He hands me a beer, and I accept it gratefully.

"Sort of," I hedge, not wanting to give them too much information. "She was always there."

"And you didn't notice her being there?" Boone raises his eyebrows.

"I did... and I didn't." It's surreal talking about my complicated history with Lyra with men who might have feelings with her as well. The cynical side of me worries that they might use anything I tell them against me, but the other said tells me I have to trust.

"She had her life, and I had mine and once in a while, we'd come together." I press my hands together and push them off each other. "We had fun—"

"How much fun?" Leo asks with a lascivious grin, but his eyes are serious.

"Not fun like that," I assure him. "Plus, we usually ended up arguing."

"She's a scrapper." Boone smiles, and it's more disconcerting than his scowl. "I like that."

Rand goes around and asks them what brought them to the show. One thing I like about hanging out with him is that he talks a lot—and I find out a lot about the others.

"I was sort of pushed into it by the guys in the fire station," Fireman Dylan admits. "We did one of those calendars, and women would DM me, and even show up at the station. It was fun for a while, but I've never been big on dating."

"Well, that certainly opens up room for the rest of us," Rand drawls. Dylan is one of the better-looking guys here.

"I want to settle down," he argues. "No more dating."

I wonder if Lyra will ever settle down.

"My sister made me do it," Boone offers in his gravelly voice. "I don't say no to her."

"Same with mine." Heads turn in my direction since it's the first time I've given anything. "Half-sisters, but still sisters. I'd do anything they tell me to. Not that they told me to do this. This was all me. They were very surprised."

"I've got brothers, and they told me I didn't have a chance," Rand says cheerfully. "What about you?" He turns to Leo. "Need a little more reality after your dancing debut?"

Leo shrugs apologetically. "My agent suggested it. Gotta find a way to bridge the kid actor to the leading man. But knowing Lyra was going to be the Suitorette was definitely a bonus," he adds.

"My daughter told me to do it." This is from Jon, who wants to be the leader of the group. I laugh when I think of him trying to control Lyra.

And then I feel sick to my stomach.

It's a regular occurrence when I think of any one of these guys taking Lyra from me.

Never exactly *taking*, since she's never been mine, but winning her heart, in Suitor terms. I feel sick at the thought of any of them walking away with her, because there's an excellent possibility that any of them could.

King Magnus would approve of them asking for the hand of his only daughter.

The realization that I *like* the competition is worse than the waiting.

"You have a kid?" Rand asks with enough surprise for the rest of us.

"She's six and wants to be a princess."

"She'll love Tema then. Lyra's great with her. She's Bo's daughter," I say, inwardly cursing about giving any information.

I may be friendly with these men, but we're all after the same prize.

"What else can you tell us about Lyra?" Leo demands.

I shake my head. "Nope. You find out what you want on your own."

"Dude," Rand pleads with mock seriousness. "There's a bro-code."

"Really?" Leo asks.

"No," Rand admits. "It's every man for himself."

"And may the best man win," Jon adds. "She deserves only the best of us."

That's sweet. I don't think I can be that honourable. I want Lyra to be with *me*, even if I'm not the best one here.

The realization doesn't make me feel good. "Is this what it's like?" I demand, unable to keep the note of sudden irritation from my voice. "We just sit around and do nothing when she's out with other guys?"

I'm irritated because I hate the thought of Lyra with anyone else. With Jon's daughter. Helping Leo with his career. Bringing a smile to moody Boone's face.

I hate this whole thing.

Why can't I be the one out with Lyra tonight? We could talk and sort things out and then—

And then I don't know what would happen. How would it work if Lyra picked me out of all these men?

What would happen if Lyra picked me?

What would happen if she didn't?

"That's what you signed up for." Boone has a resting scowl face, the bad boy of the group, and definitely gives off that vibe even when the cameras aren't rolling. "Feel free to take off if you can't handle it."

"Did you sign up for it?" Fireman Dylan asks me.

"I'm here, aren't I?"

"Could be a royal family thing," Leo muses. "You could be here to check up on Lyra."

"You think I'm some sort of spy for the royal family?" I manage a laugh, but it's not the first time I've heard that. "That's not how the king works."

"How does he work?" Jon wants to know.

"King Magnus?"

He nods. "Does he agree with all this?" He waves his hand around the room and I get that he's not talking about the newly renovated hotel.

"Lucas tried to tell us about him, but I think he was full of it," Dylan leans against the wall.

"And he's gone now," Boone points out. "Lucas. You have something to do with that? Not that I'm complaining."

"Lucas was full of it," I tell them. "He claimed a longtime crush on Lyra, said he broke up with his girlfriend, but I don't think he really did. He's never been a fan of the family. I'd say he was here solely for the attention, or that he was out to embarrass Lyra somehow."

"So you are here checking up on her?" Jon doesn't sound happy about that possibility.

"No, I'm here because I'm an idiot." I've never been one to admit my shortcomings in public, but saying it out loud doesn't make it any less true. "I should have told Lyra a long time ago how I feel about her."

"Cameras should have been rolling for that little confession," Leo says ruefully. "You'd be even more of a contender."

"His name is already pretty far up that board." Dylan grimaces.

There is a whiteboard at the end of the hallway by the kitchen. Every morning, there's a few names written on it, those men considered as front-runners.

Basher was obviously top today after getting the date rose, but my name has been on it since I got here.

I shrug. I suspect it's the producers who decide who's on the list, not Lyra. "We've got a history. I'm not apologizing for that."

"Everyone likes a second chance romance," Leo muses. "But did you even have a first chance with her?"

"I met Lyra the day she was born," Why am I telling them this? And I've never once told anyone how I feel about Lyra. "She's always been a big part of my life. And no—this would be my first chance, because I never took one with her in all the years I've known her. I'm in the same boat as you are."

"No, you're an idiot because you never made a move on her," Jon points out. "Why now?"

"I'm afraid of losing her." Just the thought of it has my head falling into my hands. "Any one of you could leave with her and I'd end up being the brothers' best friend who just let it happen because I was too afraid to shoot my shot."

Boone rumbles. "You got it bad."

I lift my head. "Don't you? Because every one of you should have it bad for Lyra. If I lose her, I want to make sure it's to someone who loves her like she deserves to be loved. And if you're not here for the right reasons..." I let the words trail off.

"Is that a threat?" Boone demands.

I've stood up to the king of Laandia as well as his sons, so I look the brooding bad boy straight in the eye. "It is. I won't let anyone hurt her."

The room is quiet for a moment. Then Jon gives a guffaw and rises to his feet. "Good. Feel like a game of pool?" And then he walks away, expecting me to follow.

Which I do, because anything is better than sitting there talking about my feelings.

Dylan, Leo and Boone come with me and the act of hitting small balls into pockets seems to put me in a better mood.

Possibly because I'm a good pool player.

"I wonder what they're doing?" Leo finally asks in a morose voice.

"They're having a good time," I tell them, lining up my final shot. "Lyra doesn't know how to do anything else."

"They're having a good time," I tell them, lining up my final shot. "Lyra doesn't know how to do anything else."

20

Lyra

THE NEXT DAY, THERE are no dates.

The only thing on my schedule is a photo shoot at the hotel, which Camille loves. The show hasn't been televised yet, but the traffic on the websites has already picked up, both for the hotel and the tourist site for Saint Pierre.

I want to help Camille promote her island, so I'm game to go along with everything the producers want to show off the beauty of Saint Pierre. And I'll promote my season of The Suitorette, because other than Spencer's surprise arrival, it's been a lot of fun.

It was a great date with Basher yesterday, maybe one of the top ten best I've ever had. He ticks a lot of my boxes: interesting and exciting, we have lots in common, and he would understand my world and bring a new slant to it. He was all in for the parasailing and he's the one who suggested we change up the date with the jam session. I got to play the drums with Denzel Duke. The entire day was amazing.

Kissing him should have been just as amazing.

And it's not that Basher can't kiss—the man has moves—but he can't kiss *me*.

Or rather, I didn't want him to kiss me. And that's a problem when you're the Suitorette.

I blame Spencer.

Having him here is like being picked up in a bar while your ex watches. It's awkward. Uncomfortable. And you really want the pickup to happen because that ex broke your heart, and he should be forced to watch while other men find you fascinating.

Not that Spencer is my ex. He's not. Nothing has ever happened between us. There have been a few pecks over the years—one which was embarrassing because it happened in front of my brothers and his sisters during a game of Spin the Bottle when we were very young.

There had been a few almost-kisses over the years, but an almost isn't a kiss. It just leaves you frustrated and with a heightened sense of anticipation about when will be the next time it almost happens.

It's those almost-kisses that have haunted me over the years.

What Spencer and I have done is share. We've confided in each other about everything and anything. In a lot of ways, he's just as much my best friend as Kate, and now Sophie.

But having a best friend like Spencer has led to years of confusion. I know he cares about me. I know he loves me in his own way, but why can't he *love* me?

I've wondered and wanted and hoped because Spencer Laz has always been my Prince Charming. Only, I've never told him because *brother's best friend*. And because I honestly never thought he felt the same. Or could ever feel the same. He's as thick as thieves with my brothers and there's no room for me in that huddle.

And there's always been a part of me who thinks Spencer just mirrors the relationships I have with my brothers. Does he think of me as another one of his sisters? Am I simply an aspect of his friendship with them?

Could he ever see me as anything else?

I have never lacked self-confidence, but thoughts of Spencer have always left me

flustered and uncertain.

I don't like it.

So when he went full steam ahead with Abigail a few months ago, I told myself enough was enough. I was not waiting one more day for him to realize we could be the power couple of our generation.

If not that, then at least we'd be good together. I thought I could make him happy—but I stopped thinking that because I had to leave happiness up to Abigail. I tucked all my Spencer thoughts into a neat little box and shoved them deep. And then Grayson came to me.

And now we're here and I don't know what to think. I wish I could say, *You're too late. I'm over you.*

But unfortunately, that wouldn't be true.

And there's a little voice that hasn't shut up since he arrived.

What if you're meant to be with him?

I think that's my mother's voice. Or maybe it's mine.

Whoever is talking to me, it makes me want to see Spencer today.

"Can I hang out with the guys today after the photo shoot?" I ask Grayson over breakfast. The guest list staying at the house has expanded with Bo, Hettie, and Tema still here, as well as Gunnar and Sophie, who arrived yesterday. Camille seems flustered by the extra people, but Odin is his usual organized self. And of course, it's Madame Carol who does the lion's share of the work.

Grayson fits in nicely. Ria spends most of her time with Rue at the hotel, but Grayson likes to hang around here. I've suggested he bring his wife here to stay with us as well.

"Tomorrow is the next group date," Grayson reminds me, smiling his thanks as Madame Carol refills his coffee cup. He's much better looking without the cake of makeup they slather on him when he's in front of the camera, a fact that Madame Carol seems to appreciate.

There were no roses given out this morning, which is good because I didn't know whom I would have sent home. I'm keeping Basher, even after the kissing thing, and no one is on my radar to get rid of.

I think that's more because I haven't spent enough time to get to know them.

"But I want to hang with them *today*," I say with exaggerated excitement. "I need more time with them off-camera, with no tripping over each other to pull me aside. Just to get to know them better."

"We've never done that before." Grayson sounds worried at the thought.

I smirk. "You've never had me as the Suitorette."

"I want to come," Tema pipes up. "I want to see the suitors because I don't know what a suitor is."

Tema sits at the far end of the table. I thought she was all about gulping down her waffles rather than paying attention to us.

Sometimes I forget how good her listening skills really are. "It's like a boyfriend," I explain.

"I thought it was like a suitcase." Tema's eyes widen. "They're all your boyfriends? Everybody at the hotel?"

"Please, god no," Bo mutters.

"I'm not sure *she's* a good idea," Grayson mouths the word. Obviously, he doesn't have children because Tema picks up on the word right away.

"I'm the *best* idea," she declares.

"Aunt Lyra has to work," Hettie cuts in.

"But she can help me," I argue. "I think it's the *best* idea." I grin at Tema.

"The two of you should not be alone together," Bo mutters under his breath.

"Tema's a great judge of character," I tell Grayson. "Out of the mouths of babes and all that. She can help me narrow my choices. And it'll give me insight on the guys because if they can't figure out how to look after my niece, then I shouldn't keep them around."

"They're not here to babysit," Bo rumbles. "And I don't want them to be. And you're not here to do that either."

"I'll come to keep an eye on Tema," Sophie offers. "Are you okay staying here for another day?" she asks Gunnar.

She stayed up for hours with me last night, wanting to know everything about the men, including my thoughts on Spencer. Sophie is definitely on Team Lyra, but there's no question of her fierce loyalty for her brother.

I understand brotherly loyalty.

"I can handle that." Gunnar grins. "But I'm telling Stella it's your fault I'm not coming home to help her set up the new dog kennel."

"It's settled." I give Grayson a toothy grin. "Me and my girls are coming to hang with the boys today. Tell them to prepare for my arrival."

I can tell Grayson has no clue what to do with me.

"Hey, boys!" I cry, after the photoshoot. "How's it going?"

My voice rings out over the pool area and I swear, every head turns in my direction. Smiles and cheers and—the men look so *happy* to see me that it fills my chest with a warmth that comes from being liked.

I'm liked by many but not everyone, and I've accepted that fact. But the mad scramble to get to me, like baby goats trying to be the first in line for food, makes me feel good.

"I told Grayson I want to hang out here today with you," I tell them amidst the cheers, and I hold up a hand as Phillippe is the first to make it to my side. "All of you. This isn't a group date and we're all friends here, so we'll all share and there'll be no dragging me away for a little *tête à tête*. Because there will be no kissing today."

There are several boos at that news, including Phillippe, who actually tries to nuzzle in to kiss my cheek.

I push him away.

"And along with me, I've brought a couple of friends." With that, Tema gives a yell from where she's hiding by the door, and with a running leap, cannon balls into the pool.

Phillippe is in the splash zone.

"That's Princess Tema," I say, amid the laughter. "And this is Sophie—" I reach behind me and pull her to my side. "And you're going to entertain us today."

The men quickly rise to the challenge.

Tema is constantly surrounded by men doing their best to keep up with her in the pool. Hettie—whom I didn't invite because on a rare note of compassion, I thought it might be weird for her to see Spencer there for me—gave me a tube of sunscreen and a hat and asked to make sure she wore both.

Rand—being a redhead—takes it upon himself to keep reapplying the Coppertone every ninety minutes. He somehow manages to get her out of the pool, slather the stuff on every part of Tema not covered by her rash guard, and then they'll head in for a snack while it absorbs.

This gives the other guys a much-needed break, because ninety minutes of Tema is a lot.

Tanner takes the lead in pool time, which means he doesn't get a lot of time with me. I respect that. Apparently, he has amazing breath control and can stay under long enough to swim across the length of the pool after Tema.

I also respect the way he looks in a bathing suit.

Jon takes command of the kitchen and the grill, making the most delicious lobster rolls and fish tacos. He has a handful of sous chefs—whether they volunteered or were conscripted—and I make sure to spend time in the kitchen to show my appreciation.

It's an easy, comfortable day.

I've always been at ease with men because I grew up with four brothers. But while my brothers teased and tormented, indulged and tried their best to influence, these men just want my attention.

And it seems like they will do anything to make me happy, whether it's bringing me fruit plates and margaritas, looking after Tema in the pool, or keeping Sophie surrounded by her own group of admirers.

Spencer is there, hanging on the outskirts, but I can feel his gaze. Like I told him, I won't give him special treatment, but I keep track of where he is and what he's doing.

It's not until after lunch that he finds me in the hot tub.

"I thought you were crazy bringing Tema with you," Spencer begins, sinking into the warmth beside me. Bubbles and waves surround me as he takes the spot Charlie just vacated.

Eliott sits on my other side, his arm close enough to touch my shoulder. His face is red from the heat, and he looks like he's ready for a break, but too stubborn to give up his spot beside me.

"Tema is my niece. I'm not apologizing for not being Abigail, the perfect wannabe-mother," I snap. Both of us are surprised by the vehemence in my tone.

"I'm not comparing you to her." Spencer looks over at Eliott. "I'm sorry, but would you mind giving us a minute?"

"Your cheeks look a little red," I add with a smile. "I'm getting out soon, too."

Eliott nods and climbs out without a word to either of us. I wait until he's out of earshot. "You really think you don't compare me to Abigail?" Sarcasm is not a good look for me, but it serves its purpose.

"I never meant to hurt you with her." It's a different voice for him—deep and emotional. Spencer is very good at what he does because he's able to keep his emotions separate and invisible. It's one of the reasons why I never knew how he felt about me—if he felt anything—because most of the time, his face is devoid of emotion.

I'm very emotional, just a ball of them that makes me hard to deal with at times.

I know this about myself.

Spencer inches closer and suddenly I feel the touch of his hand under the water. I pull away, but he grasps my fingers before I can get away, and then his hand is holding mine.

The simple touch of my hand in his brings heat to my eyes.

I've held hands with men before, so why should this make me cry?

But this is Spencer. It's Spencer, and he's here with me, and I'm so confused and afraid of saying too much that it's hard to breathe.

"You didn't hurt me," I lie and try to move my hand out of his.

"I don't believe you." There's a battle going on between our fingers under the water that no one can see.

It's just like our relationship—if you can call it that. No one sees the letters I write to him, the texts he sends me. The memes and reels and silly pictures that fly between us.

The way he makes me laugh over the stupidest things.

"I don't care." I set my jaw and refuse to look at him because he'd be able to tell I'm lying in a heartbeat.

"Lyra," he urges. "I'm trying here."

"Rebound much?" I give up the battle of the fingers and let him take my hand again. It does feel good to let him hold it. I watch Tema in the pool with Tanner and Leo, notice how Ashton seems to follow Sophie around, and laugh at how Basher was put in charge of the music, but everyone keeps complaining because all he plays is Denzel Duke.

I watch everyone and everything except Spencer beside me.

"It's not what you think between me and Abigail," he says, his thumb making circles on my wrist; a touch that would be much more of a distraction if I didn't want to hear what he is saying so badly.

"I didn't give much thought to the two of you at all," I declare.

"I don't believe you," he repeats.

"Again—I don't care. And I think I've proven that by deciding to be the Suitorette."

"I think that proves that you do care," he says ruefully. "Look, we don't have to talk about why you wanted to come on the show, but I need you to know that I'm here for you."

"So you said."

"And you don't believe me?"

I finally turn and study his face, the silvery grey eyes that I know as well as I know my own. "The only thing I'm sure about is that I've known you literally my entire life. And in that time, you've never once treated me as anything other than your best friends' little sister. I find it hard to believe—and yes, a little suspicious—that you suddenly show up now, when I'm in the process of moving on."

"Why do you need to move on if you've never had feelings for me?" Spencer interrupts.

"I never said I didn't," I point out. "*You* did."

"I said I wasn't sure—"

"Which pretty much means you didn't. Why now? It's like the worst timing for me. Can't you see that?"

Spencer has always understood me and if he doesn't see this—see that he's here for himself, rather than me—then I don't know how to make him understand.

I could send him home. That would make him understand.

But I can't do that.

"What about you deciding to move on just after Abigail and I get together? What about that timing?"

I jerk my hand out of his grip. Maybe he deserves to be sent home.

21

Spencer

I'M NOT PUTTING UP with Lyra talking in circles. It's like she's not listening, and I'm being honest and straightforward about everything.

Now.

Finally.

It's always been that way with us—two steps forward and one giant leap back. Lyra would send me a letter a week until she got upset with me over a perceived slight, like when I invited Bo and Odin to my place in Toronto for the weekend but not her.

She pushes for more than the friendship that I have with the princes, and I've never been certain if it's because she's jealous of her brothers or it's something she really wants. The princes, because of their interests, have had a kind of freedom that she's always craved. She puts herself in the public eye, and with that come restrictions and scrutiny that any beautiful woman would have to deal with, regardless of whether she's a princess.

I've spent too many years with these kinds of upsets with Lyra, but I'm not about to put up with them anymore. The stakes are too high. There's too much history between us for this to be easy, but she's too important for me not to put in the effort.

I fumble for her hand under the water. It's easier to say these things when I'm touching her. And once I admit I want to touch her, it's like I need to touch her all the time.

I think not touching her might drive me crazy.

"Did you think about how your decision to be on this show would hurt me?" I ask. "To open the doors for all these men to have a shot with you?"

Her blue eyes widen. "Are you trying to guilt me?"

"No, just being truthful." I blow out my breath as I capture her hand. "The only good thing about you doing this is that it's going to make me be honest with you."

"Are you telling me you weren't honest before?"

"I wasn't honest in that I never told you that you are the woman I compare all other women to."

There. I said it. I'm not sure which one of us is more surprised.

"And no one has ever measured up," I finish in a rush. "No one. You are the gold standard, Lyra. You have ruined me for other women. If I get involved with someone, it's only because they remind me of you. The only reason I was with Abigail is that we were such good friends, and then we crossed the line and I was too comfortable to stop it."

"You were comfortable?" Lyra whispers, her lip curling with disapproval.

"I know, it's horrible. It wasn't fair to her or myself. Abigail is an incredible woman, but she's not *you*. And that's why I'm here, because I've never been able to find someone just like you. Because there's no one. No one with your sense of adventure, or your passion for life, and definitely no one with a connection as strong as the one between us. That's why I've been dreaming about having moments like this with you for my entire life."

Lyra's lips part and fall open as if in slow motion. Her gaze searches my face like it's struggling to find the truth in my eyes.

That was the truth.

This is what raw honesty is like with Lyra.

"Moments like what?" she whispers.

I clasp our fingers together. "Moments like this where we're not fighting."

"We do fight a lot," she admits.

"That's because you're exasperating." But I smile as I say it, rubbing my thumb along her delicate wrist.

"*You're* exasperating."

"That's a childish comeback. You don't have anything else?"

"You're a lot of things."

"All of them bad?"

She shakes her head.

"Do you believe me that I'm here for you?" Slowly, she nods. "And I don't expect special treatment, and this isn't a rebound or some sort of spy mission—"

"What?"

"One of the guys asked that. You." I pull our hands out of the water and rest them against my chest. "You're the only reason I'm here. And yes, the timing is bad, but what else is new? I think the timing has always been bad for us."

"Maybe," she concedes, and she doesn't pull her hand away.

Of course, that is the moment that we're interrupted.

A shadow falls over us and I look up to see a dripping Basher beside the hot tub.

I never would have imagined a drummer being so muscular. "Do you know Princess Tema has never been on a slip and slide?" he demands.

I'm so caught up in Lyra that it takes a moment to understand what he's saying. "A what?"

"Slip and slide. That's what they're called, isn't it? Those yellow plastic things that you get wet and then slide down."

I blink. "I don't think that generation even knows what it is."

"But I do." Lyra squeezes my hand before pulling away to climb out of the hot tub and immediately the water feels cooler when she's not beside me. "Don't you remember that super-hot summer when I was ten and Bo and Kalle made us one on the castle lawn?"

"You were nine," I correct.

"Nine. Tema needs that experience, so let's build her one," Lyra decides.

That's all it takes to set a plan in motion—Lyra is the queen of our little bubble of reality and her every word is law.

She announces what she wants, and as Tema jumps up and down with excitement, the men move into action. I'm left with red legs from being in the hot water for too long, and a smile on my face because it seems I'm finally getting somewhere with Lyra.

Boone, with his construction background, takes the lead. Deciding the slope of the lawn beside the hotel is the perfect angle, he disappears into the hotel for a few minutes, returning with a roll of plastic and a hose.

"Get some soap to make it slippery," Lyra instructs.

"Not too much," Tanner warns, Tema perched high on his shoulders. "Don't want the little miss to go flying off."

"But the little miss wants to go flying!" Tema cries and Tanner jogs along the grass with Tema's arms outstretched to take his place in line for the slip and slide.

Jon insists on going first to check for safety, with Fireman Dylan waiting at the bottom in case of accidents. It's all very organized.

After a few of the men run and slide down the plastic, ending up at the bottom dripping with soap bubbles and howling with laughter, Tema insists on taking her turn.

They all cheer her on, but no one as loudly as Tanner.

"I can't believe you kissed him," I mutter, not letting Lyra get too far away from me. Lyra turns to me in surprise. "Why do you say that?"

"I didn't hear it from him, in case you're wondering. He's a good guy," I say reluctantly. "But I guess the guys report to each other on who gets a kiss."

"Do they give details?"

I shake my head. "If they said anything disrespectful about you, I would see them out of here."

She rolls her eyes. "You can't always protect me, Spencer."

"I can, and I will."

"Were you jealous?" The flirtatious voice is new. I've heard it before, but never when Lyra speaks to me. I've always thought it was because Lyra refused to flirt with me, but maybe that's what we've been doing, all this time.

Regardless of what Lyra's definition of flirting is, I'm not letting the voice get to me. It's hard enough to stand here with her in her bathing suit.

Bikini. Blue.

I shift, taking a step closer, but not nearly as close as I'd like to be. "I'm not answering that because I told myself I don't want to fight with you today," I say, keeping my gaze on her face and not on the other men looking at her.

"Why would telling me you're jealous make us fight?"

"Because I would follow up with how I don't want you to kiss anyone but me ever again."

She drops her gaze to my lips and my heart leaps like Tema jumping in the pool. And then she smiles. "You know, if you were to say that, it will only make me kiss more of them, don't you?"

I heave a sigh. "Yes, I know, because you hate being told what not to do."

Lyra laughs and in the middle of the chaos and uncertainty of a reality romance show, I realize I'm happy.

I'm happy with Lyra. I always have been.

"Lyra!" Tanner shouts. "Come take your turn."

"Coming!" She takes two steps away from me, and my heart gives a lurch. Time to share her—at least while we're on camera. And then she turns around, facing me as she walks backward.

"I never kissed him, you know." Giving me a wink, she jogs away to join the group.

"You really had to say no kissing today, didn't you?" I call after her.

22

Lyra

I'M GLAD THERE'S NO cocktail party tonight because after a day in the sun, I'm exhausted.

Tema falls asleep on the short ride back to Camille's and Sophie looks like she's about to drop off beside her.

But it was fun. Totally worth it, especially since not one bit of Tema is sunburnt, thanks to Rand.

"I didn't think I'd have a day like that," I say over the wind rushing through the open windows.

"It was a good day," Grayson agrees. He's driving because I had more than a couple of drinks. "Didn't you expect to have fun?"

"I always have fun, but today was spontaneous. Unprompted. That's what I like."

"Like the Denzel Duke date."

"Like the Denzel Duke date." I tap my fingers on the window. "Turns out, I'm pretty good on the drums."

"I expect you're pretty good at anything you put your mind to," Grayson says with a fond smile.

I also never expected to feel so much affection for Grayson Grant. Having him and Ria stay at Camille's is good in that I've gotten to know them both better than if they were just producers on the show dictating what I can and can't do.

I really don't like being told what I can and can't do.

I glance into the backseat. "When are you heading home?" I ask Sophie.

She makes a face. "Tomorrow. Gunnar says he needs to get back."

"You could stay and fly back with Bo and Hettie," I suggest.

"We've got a pretty special date coming up. It might be helpful if you were a part of it," Grayson suggests.

Sophie's eyes light up. "The wedding dress date?"

It's also good that she's such a big fan of the show. Although if I watched the show more, then maybe I wouldn't change things up so much.

Who am I kidding? I'd still do it my way.

"I have to admit, the producer side of me wasn't a fan when you suggested today, but we did get some great footage to use."

"Always important," I tell him drily. "I like seeing the men when they're not competing for my attention. Some of them seem to have become friends."

"That's always good to see. There's so much infighting when we have the group of women on The Suitor, but viewers like to see the men bonding."

"The bromances," Sophie adds from the back. "Like Rand and Jon."

"Jon could eat Rand for breakfast, but they're so cute together," I laugh. "And Tanner with everyone. He's such a big puppy."

"We should have used him for a golden retriever rather than the athlete," Grayson says, making the turn into the prefect's house. "Have you given much thought about your next one-on-one date?"

I have given so much thought about the next one-on-one date that it's laughable that Grayson can't see that.

Or maybe I'm a better actress than I've ever given myself credit for. "I'll let you know tomorrow after the group date," I tell Grayson. "Then everyone will have had a crack at me."

I've been looking forward to tomorrow all day—at least all day since the hot tub. All the men who haven't had a date with me get to come, which means Spencer will be on tomorrow's group date.

Spencer. I want to go on a date with Spencer.

I'm surprised how much I want it.

Seeing him today—even the argument in the hot tub—proved that there is so much the two of us need to unpack. And me thinking about starting a relationship with another man before that is resolved is silly.

I can't wait.

23

Spencer

R and and I are the second ones to make it into the hall in the morning.

I really want time with Lyra.

Seeing her yesterday, but not having her to myself; talking to her but getting into another spat in the hot tub? The whole day was frustrating.

But fun.

That's where my mind went when I collapsed into bed last night. After Lyra left, we continued on with the party. Rand found another keg of the king's honey lager in the bar, Jon fed us some really good burgers, and we divided ourselves up. There was pool, ping-pong and foosball inside, water polo and tennis outside. Everyone played, with the exception of Leo, who passed out on a lobby couch, sunburnt and clutching his empty pint glass, and Jon, who announced himself as judge and umpire when needed.

Fireman Dylan won it all, and someone scrawled his name on the whiteboard before we crashed last night, crossing out mine.

I don't like to see my name with a thick black line through it. I also don't like that I'm part of a handful of men who haven't had a date with Lyra.

That changes today.

I actually forget about the cameras as I snatch up the red rose on the floor outside my door with a whoop.

"Good job, dude!" Rand cries, thumping my shoulder.

"Nice." Ashton smirks. "You can join the pack of boyfriends."

I still. "You're not all her boyfriends."

"Oh...but we are," Ashton assures me. "That's what we'll be called when the show airs. Can't wait, can you?"

I don't like that at all.

"Except for them." Ashton gestures down the hall, where Marc, Gord and Luc P., have received their yellow roses of friendship. Shoulders slumping, they begin the round of goodbyes.

"She's really narrowing it down," Rand says.

"That's a good thing, isn't it? Less competition?" I quickly do the math in my head. With the latest three being sent home, that leaves only fifteen of us.

"But I like those guys." And Rand moves off to say goodbye.

"He's too nice for the show," Ashton drawls. "Where's his killer Win The Woman instinct?"

"Please tell me you don't have that." Ashton would be a formidable opponent if he cared enough to compete. The only thing I've seen him try to win were car races. The rest of the time, he has a *laissez-faire* attitude, to go with his *don't care* nonchalance.

His sister, Fenella, has a fire within her, and I wonder what happened to Ashton's.

Ashton lifts a shoulder. "Lyra already told me I'm not making it to the end, but she likes me, so she's keeping me as long as she can."

That's the first good news I've heard about Ashton. "Why are you staying, then?"

Another elegant shrug. "Got nothing better to do. Plus—" He winks and I have a curl of dread. "Maybe your little sister will stop in for another visit."

I point my finger at him. "Stay. Away."

Ashton's laughter follows me back into the room as I go to change for my date.

I can't believe how excited I am to see Lyra.

A short time later, seven of us meet in the lobby, the only ones still here who haven't been on a date with Lyra. And one—Derrick—who hasn't even had much of a conversation with her. The plan is to spend the day at the beach and then visit the brewery in town.

I'm not sure if there's a cocktail party after it, but I vow to take every minute I can with Lyra.

Easier said than done.

A van transports us to the beach west of town, and it's busy with chairs and blankets dotting the sand. Lyra meets us there, wearing a pair of high-waisted denim cut-offs and a red bikini under a white cotton shirt.

I let the others greet her first, listen to their compliments and cheesy lines, and then I step up. "Is that the bathing suit you had in Mykonos two Christmases ago?"

Lyra's eyes narrow and I know she's remembering the vacation. The king had chartered a yacht for the royal family, and included my father and me. I have a lot of memories of that trip—midnight swims in the Mediterranean, great food, and visits to the island's nightclubs, where I negotiated with a local for the hand of Lyra.

And back on the boat, laughing as Lyra slapped at my chest for daring to try to sell her off. "You know I was only joking," I finally told her. "You're worth so much more than he could have ever paid."

"How much am I worth?" Her fingers had curled into my linen shirt, and with a flash of heat, I wished I had her hands on my bare chest.

"Everything," I whispered, my hands finding her slim hips. And I had leaned in, so close that I could taste the sweetness of her breath. So close that our noses had brushed. So close that it would have been natural for our lips to touch, to move together—

And Gunnar had interrupted, and Lyra pushed me away, stalking back to her cabin.

That wasn't the first almost-kiss, but it was the most intense. The whole time we had been drifting closer together, only to have something, or someone, interrupt and push us apart.

I really think if Lyra hadn't been distracted the next day by friends on their own yacht, something might have finally happened.

But it didn't happen, and here we are.

There is a lot of history between Lyra and me, and I want her to remember it all, just like I'm doing.

"I got a new one." Lyra plucks at her strap and I can't stop staring at the streak of red against her tanned shoulder.

"Too bad. It was always my favourite." I hold her gaze until she swallows, and I look away.

Lyra decides we're going to play volleyball. We break into teams, and I'm on Fireman Dylan's team, who, after what I saw last night, seems like he excels at everything.

I'm also glad that Lyra is on the opposite side of the net, so I can watch her without totally messing up my game, like Luc C. does.

I don't like Derrick's steady stream of inane compliments, or the way Phillippe puts his arms around her to demonstrate a serve.

"She was captain of the volleyball team in high school," I call out. "She can serve by herself."

"Practice makes perfect," Lyra simpers, leaning back into Phillippe's chest.

It's not a good game for me. I can't relax around her because I don't know how to react when she constantly smiles at the other men. The way she laughs at their jokes.

The way she looks over at me, an unreadable expression in her blue eyes.

I've always been able to read Lyra, but now, here, she's a mystery to me.

One that I want to solve.

24

Lyra

SURROUNDED BY THE MEN, as well as the townspeople on the beach—some of which try very hard to get in front of the camera—I'm very conscious of Spencer.

After the game, I led the group into the water like some bikini-clad Pied Piper. Most of the men had never swum in the Atlantic Ocean, not to mention in the Gulf of St. Lawrence, and the shock of the cold water proves to be a challenge.

Spencer dives right in like I knew he would. A date at the beach gives me the opportunity to see him shirtless.

Again.

There's no shame in this because I could feel the heat of his gaze as soon as I showed up in the red bikini.

And yes, I picked the colour and the style because it resembles the bathing suit I wore when we went on the Greece trip.

Am I trying to tease and tempt? Possibly for revenge?

All yes.

I remember every moment of time I spent with Spencer and how close we came to—

To what? What were we close to? All I know is that I took the coward's way out when we were at the tipping point. Instead of leaning over to see *what if*, I backed away.

I ran, or as much as you can run when you're on a yacht.

But Spencer never chased. He never pushed.

The only pushing we do is to push each other away, and I'm having a hard time stopping that practice.

After the swim, and once we pull clothes over still-damp bodies, we walk into town. It's an odd pack moving along the boardwalk—seven men with me in the centre and clearly the focus, as well as three cameras recording every word and expression.

We stop in a few places: Dylan wants to check out the firehall, Liam stops at a market stand to buy late-season strawberries for me, Phillippe plucks a rose from someone's bush in the front yard and presents it to me with a flourish.

Picking a stranger's flowers is something I would do—and have done—but I don't think it's a good move for the show.

Finally, we end up at the local brewery and I laugh at the scuffle of seven men all trying to sit next to me, like a game of musical chairs and me as the last chair.

We start with a tasting fleet. The mood is casual and fun, even though I don't like how Phillippe hovers, like he's blocking access to me. Liam holds his own on my other side, and he is so *sweet*.

Too sweet for me, but better than the handsy Luc C. I might have accidentally-on-purpose elbowed him in the water earlier.

Once we've tasted the choices, I decide on a pint of hibiscus lager. After we're served, across the table from me, Spencer raises his glass of stout. "Shall we?" The challenge is there in his eyes.

"What's this?" Charlie wants to know.

I touch my glass with Spencer's. "We shall. On three. One, two..." I tip the frothy beer to my lips and drink deep.

"Hey, slow down," Phillippe warns.

The beer chug race is what my brothers and Spencer do when they're together, and occasionally, they let me join in. To have Spencer instigate...

It's on, because he can never finish a pint in one go. Neither can I, but I'll give it my all.

I lock gazes with Spencer over the rims of our glasses and try not to laugh as his eyes bulge slightly. He makes it over halfway before admitting defeat and slamming down his glass.

I last a second longer.

"Ha!" I wipe my mouth.

"I don't know whether to be afraid or turned on," Dylan chuckles.

"I've always said I could drink you under the table," I say.

"I'll take a round with you under the table," Phillippe says, pressing his leg against mine. I move it away.

Spencer inclines his head. "I bow to your greatness."

"As you should." My teasing smile is just for him, but then I bring the others in. "I grew up with four brothers and a father who has a micro-brewery," I say. "They all like their beer."

"Isn't it *five* brothers?" Derrick asks with a glance at Spencer. "That's what they call you. The fifth prince. You grew up together, so you should—"

"I stopped thinking of Lyra as little sister a long, long time ago," Spencer interrupts, his gaze still on me.

"How long?" I have to ask.

"You were fourteen. It was the Sea Queen dance, and you wore pink."

I laugh, because he *remembers*. "My Barbie pink dress," I say proudly. "Mrs. Theissen said it would clash with my hair, but my mother said go for it."

Spencer smiles. "That's the one. There was no clashing."

"Well, that's all nice and good, but I'd rather be making memories with you, Princess, then listening to them," Phillippe breaks the moment. "Can I steal you away for a few—?"

"I think Spence wants a rematch first," I tell Phillippe without looking away from Spencer's eyes, a strange silverly greenish-grey in this light. "And we'll take it over there so I won't embarrass him again."

I ignore the murmurs as I stand up with my glass. Spencer follows me to a tiny high-top table beside the bar.

"You pulled me away," Spencer says in a low voice. "Are you supposed to do that? I thought I wasn't getting special treatment."

"You're not," I tease. "This is how I treat all the guys."

He lifts his glass. "Trying to get them drunk by chugging multiple beers? I'm happy to be pulled away by you anytime, especially if it gets you away from French guy."

"I like most French guys, but not him." I lean closer and Spencer follows suit. "He won't be here much longer."

"Good to know."

Our faces are close together, close enough that I could kiss him if I rose on my tiptoes to get a little closer.

But I don't. Not yet. Because when I kiss Spencer, it's not going to be with an audience of men. I'm not kissing him on this date.

I can't say the same for when Spencer will kiss me, because I know it will just be a matter of time.

It's inevitable. I know that now. We will kiss, and it will change everything.

But I'd like to sort out my feelings before that happens, because once it does, Spencer will take a big part of my heart.

He doesn't realize how much of my heart he's already holding.

So I lean back before he takes advantage of the moment. "I remember the first time I saw you drunk." I cup my hands around my glass to stop myself from reaching for his hand. "It was that royal dinner with the Danish prince, and you sat next to this older woman who was bored and wanted you to be her drinking buddy."

Spencer makes a face. "Marjorie Turner. And I've never been able to drink a martini after that night."

"You smelled so bad," I reminisce with a grin. "And I still wanted to kiss you." His eyes widen. "Oops. Should I not have said that?"

"Did you want to kiss me other times?" he demands. "Tell me."

I shake my head with a giggle, and let my gaze slip to his mouth.

I'm glad Spencer doesn't take after his father too much. Duncan has the chiseled good looks found on romance novel covers—for which he modeled for many years—but he's almost too perfect. And he's also like a second father to me, so having Spencer look like him would be weird.

Spencer showed me a picture of his mother once and it was obvious he took after her: the same high, sharp, cheekbones and almond-shaped eyes with the thick lashes. And the mouth—wide and full, with lips curving down unless he smiles, and always with a hint of dryness because he refuses to use lip balm.

A tiny sigh escapes as I wonder how soft those lips are.

"You giggled," Spencer points out.

"That was a laugh," I argue. "Never a giggle. I'm too refined for that."

"You may be refined but don't forget, I've heard you belch like a sailor."

I laugh loud enough to catch the next table's attention.

"Tell me more about when you wanted to kiss me," Spencer invites, looking very pleased with himself. He has a somewhat arrogant smile when he's in public, and one that doesn't reach his eyes when he's tired. But I like this one.

I like that he looks so happy.

"You only get one of those memories," I tell him with a shake of my head.

"A day, or ever?"

"Depends how well we're getting along."

"If you tell me about the times you wanted to kiss me, we'll get along fine."

"No, because that reminds me of the times we *didn't* kiss." My smile slowly fades. "And I might kind of blame you for those."

Stop picking fights with him.

Again, not sure if that's my mother's imaginary voice or mine.

I give myself a kick. This is a new Spencer that I'm trying to get to know, but we always fall back into our old ways. Bicker, bicker, argue. Stab, slash, and parry like one of Odin's sword fights. There is so much past between us that words sharpen when they don't need to, and barbs are thrown unintentionally.

It still hurts. I shouldn't want to hurt him.

Spencer straightens, his eyes full of regret and something else I can't read. "I don't think I'm the only one to blame. You're a strong, independent woman. You could have kissed me any time you wanted to."

"You're right," I say lightly, draining a third of my beer because it's getting a little warm in here with all the talk about kissing. "I could."

Present tense. Does he notice?

Oh, I think he does.

"Did you have fun at the beach?" he asks politely, his gaze fixed on my lips.

"I did." My tone is equally polite. "And you?"

Spencer wrenches his gaze up to look me in the eye. "It had to be volleyball." He rubs a hand at the back of his neck.

"I like volleyball. I'm good at it."

"You are."

"And you... not too much?"

"It's hard to be good at something when I feel like I lose my cool when you're around," he admits.

"Sure, if you had some cool to begin with," I tease, desperate for us to get back to the easy banter. One of the other men will interrupt us any minute now, and I want to leave this on a positive note.

I don't want to leave him at all.

"I have cool," he protests, clutching his chest. "You wound me."

"I thought you were wounded when you took that ball to the side of your head. You need to learn to duck, Spence."

"You were too much of a distraction, Lyra."

My breath catches. His words pull a string in my belly, and in a minute, Spencer will be able to unravel me like a wool sweater.

Is that a bad thing?

"You've seen me every day of my life when I'm home." I tread carefully, keeping it light. Keeping it easy. Not wanting to say the wrong thing. "When were you losing your cool then?"

"I thought you wouldn't think I was cool if I kept losing it."

I move my hand on the table just enough so that it's brushed up against his.

It's the first time I've initiated contact since he got here. It's the first time I've touched him, and it's a heady sensation.

Spencer covers my hand with his, and I try to keep breathing normally.

"I've always thought you were cool, Spencer," I say in a soft voice, staring at our hands. They look good together. Spencer has some colour after being outside yesterday and again today. His forearm is now the colour of nicely toasted bread. "Talking about being cool is really lame, by the way," I add.

He laughs. "I think I held my own. With the volleyball. Was that the plan? For you to try to embarrass me?"

I shrug. "Maybe I just wanted to see you without a shirt."

Spencer widens his eyes, his smile touching every part of his face. "Ah, now we're really being honest. What else did you want?"

I'm all for honesty and for flirting and suggestive comments, but he's asking me to admit things I might not be ready to say aloud.

What are you waiting for?

It's not easy. Give me a break.

I look into my glass like it should have the answers, and when nothing comes, I take a long drink.

"Lyra," Spencer begins, moving closer to the table, his expression intent. I've seen that expression before, when he's negotiating a deal, or trying to sway an opinion.

Or trying to win an argument.

"I've been here a week. We need to talk."

"We could have talked years ago, but you decided that you needed to explore your relationship."

There I go. It's like the waitress has dropped an entire pitcher of beer on the table between us and there's no way we're going to be able to sop it all up before everything is sticky and smells of yeast.

Spencer straightens, his smile leaving his eyes without even a quick goodbye. "Which is exactly what *you've* been doing for years as well. And this," he says in a sharp voice, with a frustrated flick of his fingers toward the table of men patiently waiting for me. "We should have talked before you decided to do this."

"I didn't think that was necessary. Besides, when do you think that should have happened? Before you declared yourself madly in love with Abigail, or after?"

"I didn't declare anything," he mutters.

"Well, you didn't exactly say you weren't. This was a spontaneous decision. I didn't take the time to talk to anyone."

"Really? You didn't tell anyone that you decided to become the Suitorette to get back at me and Abigail?"

Again, there it is. Spencer has always been able to see through me, more than my brothers. He understands what I say and don't say, my behaviour. While others see me as impulsive and thoughtless, Spencer knows every action is rooted in a reason.

I was hurt that he picked Abigail. I thought I lost him. And this was the best way I could come up with to lash out at him.

But I'm not about to tell him he's right. "You nearly gave me a heart attack showing up here," I say lightly. "I thought something was wrong. My dad…"

"I could see it on your face, and I'm sorry about that, but there wasn't a way I could warn you."

"A warning would've been nice."

Spencer lifts his glass. "Pot calling kettle black. It was a spontaneous thing."

"You don't do spontaneous."

"Oh, I know, but I just did. Lyra, I don't want to keep talking in circles with you."

"Neither do I, so tell me the truth about why you're here."

"Isn't that what we're supposed to do on a date?" He gestures to the men at the other table, now staring at us with varying expressions. "A date without an audience."

It would be so easy to blurt out everything I'm feeling. To turn my heart inside out and dump it all in his lap, to get it all out there in the open.

But I can't, not until I know for sure how he feels. It's a good start; there is mutual attraction. We can flirt and have moments. There's chemistry. But unless I'm convinced Spencer Laz has true feelings for me, everything is going to stay locked up tight.

"I'm here for you," he says with frustration. "I don't know how many times I can tell you that."

"You're here for me now but—"

"Now is what matters," he insists. "I've known you my whole life, and it's time we decide if there's a future for us. I've always

thought of you as mine, and maybe that's not the right thing to say, but that's how I feel. I'm a part of your family, but it's always been different with you. You're mine."

"Because I'll help you really become part of the family?"

Spencer takes a step back. "Don't say that. You feel it too. You always have."

I have. It's on the tip of my tongue to admit it, to agree with everything Spencer is saying, but one thing—one little thing—holds me back.

"How did you breakup with Abigail?" The question comes out harsher than expected.

"How?"

"Yeah, *how*? Did you tell her you wanted me, that it was over between the two of you? Or was it her? Did she end it? Probably because you couldn't hide this recent confusion you're going through."

"Lyra..."

"Spencer." I grip the edge of the table because I know. I know without him agreeing, and it hurts. He didn't pick me over Abigail.

And he knows I know. "It wasn't like that," he begins.

"I don't care," I say, as calmly as if I was born a princess and educated in hiding my emotions.

Because I have been.

"The truth is, you have never picked me."

"That's not true."

"It is. But you know what? Every one of those men over there, and the rest of them back at the hotel? They pick me. They want me. And maybe they don't have the history and *does he* or *will he* that we have, but they do know who they want. They don't have to figure anything out." I take a deep breath. "They want me. No side clauses or addendums, no confusion because they thought themselves in love with someone else and then got freaked out because their toy was going to be taken away."

"You're not my toy."

"No? Then why have you been playing with me for years like I was?"

And then I walk away from him.

25

Spencer

THAT WAS—SHE SAID...

Lyra thinks I've been playing with her? That nothing means anything, that I—

That was harsh.

It's also true.

I don't need self-reflection or internal monologues to realize right then and there that Lyra is right about everything.

I've always admired her bravery, but now I see her as truly fearless because she's willing to risk it all to get it right.

She wants me to acknowledge how I've treated her. That I've been afraid, have taken her for granted. I've been content with our relationship and didn't want to rock the boat because I was scared.

She's made mistakes too, but I have no doubt Lyra would admit to each and every one of them.

By the time I've recovered, Lyra has already swept nice-guy Liam away to the ring toss game mounted on the wall at the end of the bar. It would have been better if she'd dragged away Phillippe because I would have been all too happy to interrupt.

I walk back to the table on shaky legs that has nothing to do with the rest of the beer I downed.

She's right.

I have been toying with her for years, never telling her how I feel because that would have meant admitting it to myself. And admitting that I was in love with Princess Lyra—what would that mean? I'm treated as a part of the family and outsiders would think being with Lyra would make it official. That becoming part of the royal family of Laandia was my plan the whole time?

Clearly, Lyra shares that line of thinking too.

I've always wondered and worried about what it would do to my relationship with the princes if I was in love with Lyra. The brothers are as important to me as my sisters, because for years, they were all I had. The thought of putting a wedge between us because I'm in love with Lyra—

I'm in love with Lyra.

It hits me right there, in the middle of the Island Hops Brewery in Saint Pierre, while off to the side, Lyra laughs with another man like she doesn't have a care in the world.

I'm in love with Princess Lyra of Laandia, and the thought makes me miserable because even if Lyra feels the same—and from the way she looked at me, I think she might—she's not going to believe me.

"You okay, dude?" Charlie asks as I slide into the seat beside him.

"She walked away from you pretty quick," Luc C. says, not even bothering to hide his smirk. "Looked pretty upset."

Smile. Phillippe is smirking.

I know I haven't been the most popular amongst the men, but I've tried. I've tried to make friends. But this is ultimately a competition, and it's every man for himself. I can wish them well in real life, but there's no way I want any of them to end up with Lyra in real life.

Or in the reality world.

I want to end up with Lyra, and it scares me how much I want it.

"I've been having arguments with Lyra for as long as I've known her," I tell Luc C. with a rueful grin rather than a sharp retort. I don't need a retort, because I know there's no way Lyra would ever pick him in the end.

Luc C. doesn't have a chance with her. Neither does Phillippe.

"What was this one about?" Charlie asks. Maybe he's just trying to get information, but I'd like to think it's a gesture of friendship.

"She got upset because I've been hiding my head in the sand about how I feel about her. I can't blame her. I'm upset at myself."

"How do you feel about her?" Derrick wants to know. "Honestly."

This feels like we're on some sort of talk show, discussing the events of the world in front of cameras and a live studio audience.

It's surreal, almost as much as it is unbelievable that I am sitting here about to confess my true feelings like I'm making a grand gesture in a romantic comedy.

Only, I'm not running across an airport to catch Lyra before she leaves me forever. I'm talking to a group of men I barely know, and Lyra is across the room with Liam.

And I see him kiss her.

A shaft of pain hits my heart and I can only stare. I stare at Lyra in another man's arms, with another man kissing her. Liam is kissing her, and she is kissing him back.

And then she pulls away and looks straight at me.

I push my chair back. "I've got to get out of here," I mutter as I head for the door. I don't even care that the cameraman follows me.

I have no desire to go back to the hotel, back to that hotbed of hot men, to face them. Any one of them can steal Lyra away from me, even if I'm the one in love with her.

If she's in love with me, why is she kissing other men?

The image of Lyra with those lips that I've been obsessing over since I got here pressed against Liam's is going to haunt me for a long time.

Maybe forever.

It happened so fast; there was cute banter and knowing glances, fun reminiscences, and then it got ugly. Is there too much baggage for it not to get ugly?

And then the shockwave so intense that I'm surprised the others couldn't feel it. I'm in love with her. Can't they see it? Isn't it scrawled on my forehead in red ink?

I came here to figure out my feelings for Lyra, but now that I've done that, what next? Because that doesn't mean I'm going to end up with her. She's made that perfectly clear.

I have no idea how Lyra feels. Because if she feels even half of what I do, what is she doing kissing other men?

That is the question that stabs at me as I walk through the tiny town. I don't let myself question why I was kissing Abigail for all that time, because then it's easy to justify Lyra's actions.

What did I think would happen if I showed up here? These men are fighting for Lyra. Kissing is going to be involved.

I would have kissed her if we hadn't been on a date with six other men and it wasn't guaranteed to be televised to the world.

But that's what I signed up for, isn't it?

I trudge down the road. A car slows beside me and I don't bother to turn, thinking it's someone from the show sent to make sure I don't disappear into the ocean. And then I hear Odin's voice.

"We really shouldn't have guys from the show walking around or we might lose you to the women from town," he calls out the open passenger window.

"No one would want me," I tell him, taking a few steps to slump against the car, head drooping.

"That doesn't sound like you. Get in."

My body suddenly aches with exhaustion, and I'm not sure I have the energy to open the door. I stand there so long that Odin finally reaches across to open it for me.

I manage to get in by myself, but I feel like I'm moving someone else's body.

"Spencer, tell me what's going on." Odin grips my arm with a worried expression. "What happened? Is it Lyra?"

"Lyra is fine. She's better than fine. She's currently enjoying a beer with a group of very nice men, laughing at their brilliant comments between bouts of kissing them. Maybe not all of them." I rub my eyes, praying the image will disappear. "I hope not all of them."

"She kissed someone?"

"I think she's been kissing someone since she got here, but this time I got to see it in person."

Odin starts the car. "This was on the date? Where's everyone else?"

"I left."

"Was it the kissing, or any other particular reason?"

"Do you remember when you first figured out that you were in love with Camille?"

"In love—"

I forget for a moment that Odin is also Lyra's brother as well as one of my best friends. And then I don't care. "Think back at the moment when you knew you were in love with her. And then picture her kissing someone else."

"Ah."

"Yeah. Ah."

He drives quietly for a moment, and I know he's trying to think of what to say. "You said love?" he asks finally.

"Yeah."

"Like, being in love with Lyra, love?"

"I'm in love with your sister. I should probably tell her this first, but I've been an idiot and didn't realize it until I did, and then I turn around and she's kissing someone else because she walked away from me because we can't stop fighting. Or she won't stop pointing out what I've done wrong, which, apparently, has been a lot of things."

"Sounds like you've been a real idiot," Odin says drily.

"I'd say I've been a lot of things, but this is a PG show."

"That bad, huh?"

"I've made a mess of things, O, and I don't know how to fix it. And I have no idea if she even wants me to."

"Want to come back to the house to figure things out?"

"No, this is something I have to do on my own. I thought I could walk it out, but then you showed up."

"Ria called and said you might need a pickup from a friend. I'm surprised you don't have a camera following you. They like the tender moments between the contestants."

I turn around in the seat. "I must have lost him. Guess he figured you're not a contestant, and this isn't a tender moment. Thanks for the pickup, by the way."

Odin shrugs. "You needed me and I came. Same thing you've been doing for us your entire life."

"Lyra asked if I'm doing this because I want to be part of your family."

Odin frowns. "You're already a part of the family. Doesn't matter if you're with her or not. I would actually think it might be a deterrent. We're a lot to take on, you know."

"You're the only family I've got."

"Well, Sophie and Stella might take offense at that. She's still around, you know? In case you want some sisterly advice."

"Have you ever asked for some sisterly advice?"

"From Lyra? No way." He laughs.

"That's the woman I love you're talking about."

Odin glances over with a sympathetic smile. "You're not the first man who's fallen for my sister, you know."

"Yeah, but I want to be the last."

26

Lyra

I MANAGE TO DO my Suitorette duty and have individual time with each of the men left on the date. We spend hours in the brewery to film it all. It's a nice enough place, but all I can smell is yeast and hops.

Spencer left. He walked away, and I'm desperate to find out if that means he's leaving the show—and me—or just headed back to the hotel early.

I didn't want him to see me kiss Liam. I didn't *want* to kiss Liam—it just happened. I won the silly game and gave him a hug and then his mouth was on mine, and I was so surprised that I let it happen.

One minute I was teasing Spencer about all the times I've wanted to kiss him over the years, and the next, I'm kissing someone else.

Who does that?

The Suitorette, apparently.

It doesn't happen with any of the other men, even though Phillippe tries at least three times.

He's so going home tomorrow.

After the men are driven back to the hotel, I sit at the table with Rue, morosely finishing my beer.

She's tapping away at her tablet, not noticing I look like I've lost my best friend.

Which I might very well have.

"You should have kissed more of the men," Rue says without looking up. "You need to work on that."

"I need to work on my *kissing*?" I ask in an icy voice.

"No; not the actual technique, I mean—you need to kiss more of the men. It was only Liam tonight and the others—" She finally looks up from the tablet and freezes when she sees how I'm looking at her.

It's not a good look.

"I don't, actually, need to kiss anyone." I enunciate each syllable to help Rue understand. It's not the first time she suggested I up the episodes of PDA. Almost every date recap, she makes a comment on how it's important to find out how compatible I am with the men and kissing them is the best way.

I wonder how many men she had to kiss that she wasn't really interested in.

"Ah... okay." Rue stands up quickly, her chair leg protesting as it drags backward. "Let's go back to Camille's for the recap." I can read her thoughts like a book—this conversation, any conversation where I'm shooting daggers at her, is above her pay grade.

She wants backup from the big guns.

But I'm not letting her off the hook that easily. "No, I think we should talk about my kissing now."

Rue takes a deep breath. It's not the first time that I've seen someone gather their courage before dealing with me. "The audience likes it when you kiss," she says, aiming for an authoritative tone.

She fails.

"I don't give a flying fig what the audience says," I tell her, my tone slow and serious and much more in control than Rue. This is *my* show and I'm not about to pander to their every wish if it has me doing things I'm not comfortable with. "Have you not heard of consent? *My* consent? Just because I am putting myself out there, and trying to make a connection with these men, I'm in no way obligated to participate in any sort of physical activity with them, and they—and you—need to realize that. I will kiss someone when *I* want to. When *I* feel like it and when *I* have a connection with them. This will not be dictated by you or anyone watching in the far corners of the world. If you want more kissing, find someone else."

I stare up at Rue, standing with wide eyes and an open mouth.

"Do you understand?"

"Please don't walk away," she all but begs with her hands clasped together. "Grayson will fire me for sure if I lose two of you on one date."

"If you ever suggest I kiss someone I don't want to, I will see that you're fired myself. Don't doubt that I won't."

Rue shudders. "Oh, I don't."

"We should have gotten that in the diary room," Hasan says as he lowers his camera. I had no idea he was filming.

"I'll say that again and again, for whoever needs to hear it," I promise. "Did you follow Spencer earlier?"

Hasan nods. "Odin picked up him and took him back to the hotel."

The hotel. "And then?"

"He's still there," Rue cuts in. "He's not leaving unless you send him home."

"I'm not going to send him home," I say quietly, more to myself than either of them. I stand up, suddenly exhausted. "Let's go. Thank you," I call to the owner of the brewery, who is still hovering behind the bar like he has been since we arrived early in the afternoon.

It's dusk now, and all I want is something other than beer to drink and then my bed. It might be because I'm so tired, but the brew master makes me think of Dad. Of Kalle. A rush of homesickness washes over me.

I head over to him, hand outstretched. "Thank you so much for your hospitality and for letting us invade your business for the day," I say, pushing the exhaustion back to manage a pleasant smile. "My father has an interest in a micro-brewery in Laandia, and this—" —I wave my hands— "—is how he envisions his place. I'll tell him to visit and get some inspiration."

"The king is always welcome," the owner stammers. "As are you, Your Highness."

I smile warmly and shake his hand. "I'm just Lyra here."

*

Grayson doesn't let me pick Spencer for tomorrow's one-on-one date.

After today, it's obvious I need to clear the air with Spencer. The expression on his face when he saw me kissing Liam was so many things—haunted, frustrated, angry... and with so much regret in his eyes.

I've told him my side, and it's time I listen—really listen—to him.

I tell all of this to Grayson and Ria after Rue drops me off.

I'm still not happy with her.

"You can't," Ria says in a firm voice. She and Grayson were already at the kitchen table, the whiteboard list of names as well as the remnants of Madame Carol's berry pie tempting me. "The sponsors expect love and drama to last for the entire season, not just two weeks before you skip off for your happily ever after."

I'm not going to be happy with Ria much longer either.

"I'm not going anywhere," I tell them, gathering a fork and the pie dish before I sit down. "But you really have to start feeding me more. At least let me eat on dates."

"Is there anyone other than Spencer?" Grayson asks. "Can you get through one more one-on-one date? I'm really sorry, Lyra, but we need him around for a little longer. Viewers turn in for the drama as well as the romance," he adds apologetically. "We need the tension between the two of you to ramp up a little. The chemistry between you and Spencer is already off the charts and I'd really like to expand on that."

"Do you think that's fair to whoever I pick for the date, knowing I would rather be with Spencer?"

"This show is about multiple men getting their hearts broken. There's nothing fair about that. Look at it as giving someone a chance that they wouldn't get."

I finish my mouthful of pie. "One more solo date and then Spencer. I have to see where this is going, Grayson. This is my life." I try out the princess voice again, the one I use when I expect to get my own way—yes, there are many situations where it comes in handy—but I'm too tired from the day's adventures for it to be very effective.

"Which you're sharing with the world," Ria points out.

"Trust me when I tell you I know exactly how you feel," Grayson says. "I've been where you are, and it doesn't feel good."

If I didn't trust Grayson, this might be very different. "You're very good at this."

He smiles his blinding white smile at me. "And so are you."

"Who do you think I should pick?" I hate myself for asking. I told myself that the picks would be *my* decision, and now I'm handing over control.

Or at least asking for suggestions.

"Honestly?" Grayson looks at Ria and she nods. "I say Tanner. He's going to win over the audience in the first episode, with him being so excited about your brother, and then the stuff with Tema. And if he doesn't win your heart..."

"You're thinking about him for the next Suitor," I finish.

Grayson shrugs. "I have to look for possibilities."

"And Tanner would be a good one. He's a sweet puppy, but I don't think he's for me. So, sure, I'll take him for the next date. Do you want me to send him home after?"

"Oh, god, no. The viewers would hate you. We'll keep him around for as long as we can."

I nod and finish my pie. I don't care who stays as long as Spencer is still here.

27

Spencer

B Y THE TIME JON and Basher—who is a surprisingly good cook—serve us chicken fajitas for dinner, the entire hotel knows I walked out of the date.

It's even a topic of conversation as we sit down for the meal.

A meal I have every intention of missing, but Rand won't let me.

"You need your boys around you," he says, forcibly pulling me out of our room.

"No offense, but these aren't my boys."

"But they could be. At least some of them could be. Like me. I'm your boy, and I'm not letting you sit and stew in here alone."

"That sounds weird."

"Plus, whatever Jon makes tastes amazing and I'm hungry and you need to eat to sop up the alcohol, so let's go eat."

Yes, the alcohol. Turns out the hotel has a very nice selection of bourbon, which I discovered after Odin dropped me off. "Ok, but I'm taking my bottle."

Ashton takes it out of my hand as soon I get to the kitchen. "What do you have here?" He studies the label. "Not bad. Where do I find glasses?"

Rand produces three because I've been swigging straight from the bottle.

I'm more interested in the bourbon, but the smell of food finally tempts me to accept a plate. I sit quietly with a small group in the lobby, the food laid out on the reception counter.

The moon rises over the water and the sound of the waves crashing makes good background noise.

It makes me think of Battle Harbour.

I wonder what Abigail is doing. I wonder if she'll ever stop hating me.

She might not hate me, but I'm definitely not her favourite person.

I wonder what Lyra is doing.

I regretted leaving as soon as Odin dropped me off at the hotel, if only to be able to see how she acted with the other men. If they all went along the same lines as Liam, that would be torture.

I shouldn't have been surprised, since I know the format of the show. There is flirting and kissing, men pulling Lyra aside, and other men breaking in to steal her away. These men are trying to win her heart and they're pulling out all the stops.

Realistically, using physical contact is a great way to push attraction into something more. If I kissed Lyra...

If I kissed Lyra when I wanted to, no one else would have stood a chance.

I stay caught up in my thoughts, not joining the discussion about the date until Phillippe turns to me.

"Why did you leave?" His Quebecois accent is stronger after he's been drinking and it seems those in the brewery had a lot of opportunity to sample the beer while they waited their turn.

Everyone had time with Lyra.

I guess that's only fair, but I don't feel like being fair right now.

A quick glance around shows that Phillippe's question grabbed everyone's attention. I shrug.

"I don't know how you think you're going to get her to fall in love with you if you leave like that," he says under his breath.

"You don't think she's already in love with him?" Liam asks and the table falls silent.

The question is like sticking my finger into a socket. It jars and it jolts and there's a rush of hope that makes me feel dizzy.

But it quickly fades. "Lyra doesn't love me," I mutter. I can only hope she might be able to love in sometime in the future, but now? I don't think so.

"How do you know? Has she ever been in love with you before?" Jon asks.

"I don't know," I admit.

"Have *you* ever been in love before?" Every head turns to Ashton. He chats, he jokes, he's an ass most of the time, but I've never heard him even mention the word love.

"I don't know. I thought I was, but it felt different from this."

"Different people, different love," Boone says, and I'm not the only one who looks at *him* with surprise. I'm not sure if he's the bad boy, or the grump because he seems like a combination of both. "I've never been in love before."

"Me neither," Dylan confesses.

"I'm in love with Lyra," Charlie announces.

"I think I am, too," Luc decides.

I chuckle. "No, you're not."

"Just because you're—"

"You've known her for two weeks," I interrupt. "That won't even get you past the first layer of Lyra. There is so much to her that it would take you a lifetime to really get to know her. And how can you be in love with her if you don't know her?"

"But they want us to fall in love with her," Derrick argues.

"How do you fall in love with a person in two weeks?" Jon wants to know. "You fall in lust. You take all of that attraction and you tell yourself that it's love."

"But it's really not," Rand agrees. "Not yet, anyway."

"The process works, though," Leo points out. "Look at Grayson and his wife. Esme found someone in her season too."

"Maybe they got lucky," Ashton sniffs and helps himself to my bourbon. "I'm not lucky."

A few of the men laugh at that. "You're a billionaire," Phillippe says rudely. "I'd say you're the luckiest of us all."

"I wouldn't say that." I pull the bottle back. "Money doesn't equate happiness."

"Says the guy who lives in a castle," Derrick says under his breath.

I ignore that comment and make myself another fajita.

I have nothing in common with these men, other than Lyra, and that makes it strange.

Also, strangely comfortable.

I don't have conversations like this with the princes. We rarely talk about women, never talk about love. Maybe no one has ever asked me because they thought that I've been in love with Lyra, and being her brothers makes it too weird.

I'll have to ask Odin.

The others have always had a love interest in the back of their mind—Gunnar might have been in love with Stella for years without admitting it to me. I'm friends with Edie, so Kalle might not want to talk to me about her. I really don't know Rand and Jon or Ashton, so it's easier to open up to them.

Strange. Usually, I'm reserved with people. I keep to myself. Even with my friends other than the princes...

I don't have a lot of friends.

I work. I socialize with Kalle some, and Bo, now that he's back in town. Odin and I had a regularly scheduled squash game once a week, and I would spar with him whenever I had the chance.

I have many acquaintances since I know most of Battle Harbour by name, but not many close friends. It's my own fault, and while it's never really bothered me, I get the feeling that this might be the time to work on changing that.

I'm here for Lyra, but maybe I'm here for me, too.

"What do you love about her, then?" I ask Charlie later. The food has disappeared and some of group begins to dissipate into other corners of the hotel.

Like the bar.

"Well, she's beautiful—" Charlie begins and those around me laugh.

"That's a given," Jon says. "Non-physical features."

"She's fun. Funny."

"I get the sense that she can be a little intimidating," Liam says quietly.

I laugh. "You have no idea. I remember once when we were at some event in Washington, Lyra overheard a politician make a disparaging comment about Laandia. She walked right over and gave him the tongue lashing of his life. And don't bother saying anything about tongues," I snap at Phillippe. "She had the guy cowering, stammering out an apology in five minutes."

"She's brave." Charlie smiles.

"Bold," Rand says.

"She was fifteen," I continue. "The king was somewhere in Europe and none of the boys were available, so they sent her to represent the family, and me to make sure everything went smoothly. She was fifteen and she was magnificent even then."

"You've got it bad." Ashton laughs. "Magnificent?"

"She is," Liam says loyally.

"This from the guy still in la-la land because he got his first kiss."

"Don't really need the reminder. Did the rest of you kiss her too?" Why did I ask that? Because I really don't want to know. I've been imagining the worst since I got back and that is punishment enough.

"Jealousy isn't a good look on you," Jon points out.

"I know, but do you blame me? I don't understand these shows. How do the guys handle it?"

"I guess we're about to find out."

One by one, the lobby empties. Some of the men find their way back to the pool table, others head for the pool. It's late, but the cocktail parties run later, and the men seem to enjoy a night off.

The clink of bottles and the laughter coming from the bar area suggests a group of them are really enjoying the night off. I could join them, but I prefer to sit here with my thoughts.

The thoughts are all about Lyra.

Jon has left to supervise the kitchen cleanup, but eventually returns with a glass of amber liquid for me.

"I'm sure I'll regret this in the morning, but thanks." I raise the glass to Jon before I take a sip.

"It won't be a problem unless you get the date rose."

"I'm not holding my breath."

"What are you going to tell Lyra," Jon asks, sinking into the chair opposite me. "Because you'll eventually get a date rose."

"I guess I'll tell her I'm in love with her."

It seems the simplest option, but also the most terrifying. But things have always been so complicated between me and Lyra and so simple seems best.

Jon, who is here for the same reason I am—Lyra—handles it well. "Do you think she feels the same way?"

"I honestly don't know. We've always had a connection, but since I've been here, it feels different. More... real."

"Real is good," Jon muses. "Although, real usually isn't the norm during a reality show."

"I don't know, Charlie really believes he's in love with her," I say lightly, and Jon laughs.

"I've never let myself experience it," I continue, surprising myself with the admission. "I've always tucked it away. Didn't let it grow."

"Ripen." Jon nods. "I've done that before. I understand."

"How do you feel about Lyra?" I ask nervously.

Jon shrugs his big shoulders. The guy is ripped and has a perpetual scowl on his face, but he's surprisingly easy to talk to. "Honestly, I don't feel much about her," he admits. "She seems like a good woman. But I don't think it was the best move for me to come on here. I don't think it's for me. Maybe if we were in the real world…" he trails off.

"This is the farthest thing from the real world," I tell him.

"And if this was the real world, she wouldn't look twice at a guy like me."

"Oh, I don't know. I think you'd have a better chance than Charlie."

"Don't tease him, he's in love with her."

We laugh and the feeling of companionship is so unexpected, and so nice.

I came here with the single-minded goal of finding out if there was something between me and Lyra.

I'm finding so much more.

"Is it bad?" Jon asks suddenly. "You hear so much about the royal family, but is being a princess easy for her? Is she happy?"

"I think she loves it," I admit. "She's amazing at it. They all are—the whole family takes to the royal life—"

"Like they were born into it?" Jon interrupts with a chuckle.

"Exactly. They've all had their issues, and losing the queen was difficult to deal with, but eventually, Lyra will take on more of a role like the princes are doing. Whatever she does will be amazing." I smile ruefully at the thought of an older Lyra representing our country with her usual verve and vitality. "Or maybe she'll chuck the crown and go live on a deserted island."

"You sound like you really know her."

"I like to think so. She knows me better than anyone else," I admit. "And that scares the hell out of me because I don't want to lose her."

"Then don't," Jon says. "Just don't."

28

Lyra

WHEN I PICK UP Tanner the next morning, there are two bicycles waiting for us.

I'm not pleased about that because I think anything with two wheels should also include a motor. But I smile and hug and pretend everything is fine, all the while scanning the crowd of men grouped to greet me for Spencer.

He's nowhere to be found. Neither are Phillippe, Derrick, and Luc C., because I sent them home. The group of men is dwindling, which is how it should be. There are twelve left.

I'm doing everything the Suitorette should be doing. Only it doesn't seem to be working.

Being a princess is easier than this.

As we wave goodbye, perched upright on old bikes with baskets, and tires that make you feel every rock, I wait for Tanner to mention Spencer.

Do the men even talk about what happens on the date? Does Tanner know that Spencer walked out, and if he does, is he wondering why Spencer didn't get a yellow goodbye rose as well?

Tanner asks about Kalle instead.

As we ride into town, Tanner peppers me with questions about my brother. I recap Kalle's hockey career, try to remember the reasons he switched to baseball (other than "because he could"). I'm at a loss when it comes to Kalle's curling, though, but I'm very knowledgeable about The King's Hat pub.

It's good that I've kept up with my brothers' lives, even though I never expected to be quizzed on a date about what Kalle is up to.

Hockey players. I guess there's a bond that never goes away.

Once we make it into town, we spend some time walking around the stores, tiny shops showcasing Saint Pierre's history and French past.

And a few really good bakeries.

We visit the candy store, and apparently, Tanner has a huge sweet tooth. He insists that we pick something out to give to Tema.

The downtown area of Saint Pierre is cozy and quaint, with enough colourful homes and fishing boats to remind me of Battle Harbour. There's another pang of homesickness. It's a surprise because mainly I focus on what's in front of me rather than what I've left behind.

Maybe it's time to spend some time at home.

That's definitely my mother's imaginary voice, because I like my life in Chicago.

But that might change, depending on whom I end up with. *If* I end up with anyone.

Could it be Tanner?

Tanner is sweet and nice and fun, with a personality like a favourite teddy bear that you have to hug.

I do hug him a lot throughout the afternoon: when he presents me with a bouquet of wildflowers, bought, not stolen from a yard; when we get silly trying on hats in a little shop; and when we get splashed as we walk through the waves at the beach.

I do the big, throwing myself at him hug for that—Tanner lifts me up and I wrap my arms and legs around him. It's a perfect Suitorette shot.

So is us running through a flock of seagulls, sending them flying with loud *ha-ha-ha* calls.

I know the viewers will be comparing Tanner to Asani, and Tanner is going to come out on top. It's also going to come out that I like to terrorize birds when they're minding their own business, but seagulls can often be an annoyance from the sixth level of Hell and I think they can handle it.

The entire date is like an interview for Tanner as the next Suitor. I keep Grayson's words at the forefront of my mind, and I make sure the cameras get the best of Tanner.

I ask the questions about past relationships—he's had two serious ones, and the last one resulted in a broken heart about a year ago. I get him to admit that it was tough when he injured out of hockey and how he felt lost for a few years until he fell into coaching kids.

He confesses that he really wants to be a father.

I'd marry him in a minute if I wasn't thinking of Spencer all the time. It's like my mind has divided, quite neatly, into Suitorette/Tanner/ignore the cameras but play to them, and Spencer.

I want to talk to him so badly that it actually hurts.

Other than that, it's a good day and we stay in town until the sun dips low in the sky. A pickup truck collects Tanner and the bikes to take them back to the hotel, and Grayson picks me up in the convertible. I'm happy we don't need video of us riding back to the hotel; on the show they neatly segue the casual events of the afternoon into the romantic part of the evening, when the reality is there's a few hours in between when we separate and change before meeting up again.

"Don't mess up your lipstick," Alexa warns as she helps me get ready back at Camille's.

For the evening date, I wear a strapless, lilac maxi dress, the gauzy fabric flowing around my legs, with my hair up. Alexa does subtle makeup, making me look sun kissed, not sunburnt—which my nose and shoulders certainly are—with a dramatic plum lipstick.

If I get to take anything from my time on this show, it might be Alexa and her boxes of tricks because she always makes me look amazing.

"Isn't the point of it to get messed up?" I tease, sounding more light-hearted than I feel.

I'm going to have to kiss Tanner sometime tonight. After I get vulnerable and open up with insights and personal anecdotes about my life. I'm going to have to kiss him, and I already know I'm going to be thinking of Spencer.

When I'm ready, the car takes me into town where the show has booked the tiny French restaurant over-looking the water.

I've watched the show enough times to know this is where the romance will happen. Over a quiet meal, we'll have private time to share our thoughts and feelings.

To be vulnerable.

I'd rather run through the seagulls again and deal with them pooping on me.

But still, this is what I signed up for.

It's the first typical one-on-one date—I sent Asani home before we got to the dinner part, and Basher and I mixed it up with

Denzel, so viewers weren't able to see the romance blossoming over plates of food that we never touched. Tanner and I are going to have to play the part of a couple falling in love. I'm going to have to do this for him, with the hope that I'm not believable enough for him to start falling for me.

I know Tanner is interested; there is attraction there, but what I really feel for him is friendship.

I can only hope it's the same for him.

"You look gorgeous." Tanner gets to his feet as I walk toward him at the table on the back deck of the restaurant. The admiration in his eyes looks real—and so is mine when I get a good look at him in his dress pants and shirt with the sleeves rolled up to show tanned forearms.

I'm happy to see his shaggy hair is still shaggy.

"So do you," I tell him.

The ambience is perfect—candles, the scent of good food, a glass of chilled Sancerre before me. Thin clouds scud across the rising moon and the wind has picked up, sending waves crashing against the jetty.

It would be a perfect night for romance if you weren't looking at the three cameras focused on getting our every word and expression.

This is where it's going to seem like Tanner and I are falling in love.

I hope Spencer never sees it.

We sit, we make some inane toast, and now it's Tanner's turn to ask the questions. I brace myself, preparing to be vulnerable.

"Why do you live in Chicago?" Tanner begins. There is food before us which we are not allowed to eat. They told me to have a snack before we started shooting and I'm glad I did. "I would think New York would be more your speed. Toronto even."

"Have you ever been?" I counter, tracing the edge of my wine-glass.

Tanner shakes his head. "Boston and Philadelphia, but not Chicago. I tend to stay in Canada mostly."

"I love Canada. But Chicago is beautiful. It's kind of a silly story about why I ended up there." I take a deep breath because it's time to start giving this vulnerability thing a shot. Or at least the personal anecdotes. "You've seen Ferris Bueller's Day Off, haven't you?"

"Is that the one with the kids in detention?"

"No, but that's another John Hughes movie. He made the best teen movies of the 1980s."

"I'll take your word for it. I've never been one for movies."

"That might have to change," I say lightly, and Tanner grins. "Anyway, in the movie, Ferris ditches school for a day. He plans this whole elaborate sickness just so he can play hooky with his girlfriend and his best friend. And they go to Chicago. When I saw the movie, I wanted to be one of those characters."

"The girlfriend?"

I grimace. "No, I wanted to be Ferris. He was the leader, the planner, the elaborate prankster." I smile at the memory. "He talked his way into the best restaurant without a reservation, he managed to get on a float in this parade. He just grabbed life. I've always loved his sense of adventure, his confidence, and I thought if I lived in Chicago, every day could be like that." I pause. "It's silly."

"Why? That's who you are. You have this passion for life that's incredible."

"I try," I admit, trying to hide the sudden lump in my throat at the thought of someone actually seeing me for once. Tanner is dangerous, and if things were different— "You're from Halifax?"

"Originally from New Brunswick, but open to relocate." He grins.

"Are your parents still together?"

"Yes, they're very happy." Tanner drops his gaze. A pause, and I think that's all he's going to say. But then— "How old were you when your mother died?" he surprises me by asking, as well as by the gentleness in his tone "The queen, I mean."

"She was the queen but she was still my mom." He's the first of the men who has asked about her.

The accident that took my mother is public record, as is the fact I was in the car with her. But I rarely talk about it.

"I was seventeen," I say.

I was seventeen when my mother picked me up at a friend's place, and then lost control of the car on an icy bridge during a surprise October storm.

I was seventeen when I woke up in the hospital to find Spencer hunched in a chair beside me, clutching my hand with an expression of such sorrow on his face that I knew right away. He still said the words though and held me as I cried. We both cried, because the queen had been a mother to him as well.

"That must have been difficult."

I still miss her. I think about my mother every day. I *talk* to her, but I'm not about to tell Tanner any of that. How it took three years of therapy for me to get past the guilt that was crushing me.

How half of the crazy bad choices I've made were because I was grieving.

How I dumped all of that into letters to Spencer, and he listened and understood.

I nod. "For the entire country. She was an amazing queen." I smile sadly. "And a pretty great mother."

That's it. That's all I can do.

I motion to the water, at the waves crashing louder than before. "There's a storm moving in. You can tell by the wind."

"It's still hard to talk about her," Tanner points out, and I'm surprised he's not letting it go.

"I don't talk about her." My voice is steady, without a hint of apology. I've perfected it over the years because I only talk about my mother with those who knew and loved her.

"Fair enough." He rattles the ice in his glass, takes a sip. "You don't remember that we met before."

My breath is shaky, but I manage the subject change with relief. "I think I'd remember you."

"It was the second game of the Juniors' championship. My first year, but it was Kalle's second. We won, and you somehow made your way to the locker room."

"That's where the celebration was. I remember now. There were a lot of players hugging me." I scrunch my nose. "There was a lot of sweat and man-smell."

"That's a locker room. Two of your brothers were with you."

"Bo and Gunnar."

"And Spencer."

My smile fades at the mention of his name. It's not fair that Tanner is on this date with me. He doesn't seem to think anything at all is wrong.

It's all wrong.

Tanner is great. He's the whole package. He ticks all the box-es—he's got the face, the body, the personality...

Maybe not all the brains, with all the concussions in his past, but he's a sweet guy.

In another life, I would have fallen for him, and probably broken his heart.

In this life, I don't want to break his heart. And I don't want to be on this date with him.

"You never left his side," Tanner says, his smile rueful. "All these guys kept coming up to meet you, and you would smile and talk to them, and then you'd go back to Spencer, like he was your security guy. Not your brothers, but Spencer. He's, like, your person."

"He's..." I don't know how to describe Spencer right now. I don't want to say too much, because if I start talking about him, I know the façade of this date will come crashing down.

I've played the part of a woman falling in love with the hockey player so well tonight, and if Tanner keeps talking about Spencer, it's going to ruin everything.

And Tanner keeps talking. "The other day at the pool, I was watching the two of you."

"I thought you were watching Tema," I manage in a light-hearted voice.

"That kid." Tanner smiles and I hope they get a full-faced shot of that smile. I hope that changes the subject, but no.

"It didn't matter who you were talking to, you were constantly looking for Spencer." Tanner toys with his fork. "He's the same way. He can't take his eyes off you when you're around."

His words jolt me. "He's always been protective of me. We've been friends a long time." I don't want to talk about Spencer, so why am I drinking in every mention of him like it's the best glass of wine I've ever had? I don't want to talk about Spencer because it's not fair to Tanner, and I like Tanner. I really do.

Just not like I like Spencer.

Love. Love Spencer.

"I think you're more than friends." Tanner looks at me with a sad smile, and he knows. "It's good that he's here."

He has to know this is all wrong.

I get to my feet. "I can't do this," I declare.

29

Spencer

I FORCE MYSELF TO hang around the lobby with the others, waiting for Tanner to report back on his date with Lyra.

Even saying that in my head makes me grit my teeth.

But after the bonding of last night, I need to wait with the others. It's been a long afternoon and even longer evening as images of Lyra with Tanner begin to haunt me. I may still be jealous that Tanner has gotten this chance, but at least the regret has calmed to a dull roar in my mind, and I honestly wish Tanner the best. He's a good guy.

If I'm not the one who ends up with Lyra, I could handpick a few of the men for her.

If I want to torture myself, that is.

I don't want to think about that. I'm not ready to give up yet, but I'm not sure what I'm going to do if I don't get the next one-on-one rose.

Finally, close to midnight, Tanner returns, as smiling as he was when he left.

He's immediately accosted by the others, all wanting to know how it went with Lyra.

"I'm hopelessly in love with Princess *Tema*," he says with a laugh.

"What about Lyra?" Charlie asks. "Are you hopelessly in love with her?"

"That would be too easy, if I thought I had a shot." Tanner shrugs his shoulders. "I don't think I have a chance in hell with Lyra."

"What do you mean?" Rand asks.

"I think there's only one guy here that's got a chance." And Tanner looks right at me. "I hate to say it, but it's you, man. It's all you."

30

Lyra

RIA MANAGES TO TALK me into staying longer with Tanner, long enough to get a few shots of us hugging in the moonlight.

He seems to sense that I don't want to kiss him.

Rue presses for a more intimate shot, but Tanner seems content to keep his arms around me. He drops a kiss on the top of my head, but that's it.

I want to thank him, but that might be weird. I do give him a long hug when I say goodnight.

Tanner is a good guy, but not for me.

The next morning, they get me up early for another date.

Another day, another date—and then I remember this is the wedding dress date.

They let Sophie, Camille, and Odin join me for this date. Bo declines for his family, even though Tema clearly wants to be a part of it.

I'm fine with that. I know it's selfish, but if Tema was there, it would be all about Tema, and this is my show.

All the men are included because it's the wedding dress shoot, so I'll get to see Spencer.

I've watched the show enough times to know this is a big deal, but Odin left his season too early, and also didn't really watch the show, so he has no clue about the implications.

"Everyone gets dressed up in wedding clothes and there's some sort of competition and the top few get pictures taken and one wins time with Lyra," Sophie explains as we're driven to the hotel to find my wedding dress.

"And why is that important?" Odin wants to know.

"Because it will give her a visual of what it might be like to marry the person," Sophie says, sounding so patient even as she rolls her eyes.

Marry.

That's the show's endgame, but I haven't decided if it's mine yet. My initial goal was to just find someone to take my mind off Spencer.

Super hard, now that he's shown up.

He'll be there for this group date. I couldn't leave him out, even if I wanted to.

No one is in sight as we pull up to the hotel, and I can't even see faces waving from the windows. They must have them sequestered somewhere.

"What do the men wear?" Odin wants to know as Alexa ushers us to the ballroom at the back of the hotel.

"Tuxedos. Suits. Maybe there'll be a kilt." Sophie grabs Camille's arm with excitement and she laughs.

"What do I have to wear?" Odin asks in a sour voice.

"You don't have to wear anything if you don't want to be here," I snap at my brother. "This is about me, you know. You had your turn."

Odin looks surprised, but nods his head. "Sorry, Lyra. I'd like to stay and I'll wear whatever you want me to."

"Oh, this should be good," Camille murmurs, and I laugh.

Laughing helps with the nerves.

I shouldn't be nervous. It's the third group date; I don't have to do anything but smile and look beautiful. But it's the rack of wedding dresses at the side of the room that has the knot in my stomach tightening.

I've never been the type of girl who imagined her wedding dress, mainly because I'm a princess and I know if I want a dress, all I have to do is call up a few designers and find something that fits and is in fashion.

It's not a very romantic way to look at it.

But I've also never imagined the day where I need to try on dresses, because it hurts too much to realize that my mother won't be there with me.

I tuck that sadness down deep and join Sophie and Camille as we sort through the dresses to find one that suits me.

The princess styles are the first to go.

Sophie finds an interesting choice—a mermaid style, fitted tight to my body before splaying out below my knees, with a lace overlay that actually looks like scales. I'm ready to try it on, but Camille points out how difficult it would be to walk, as I have "very long strides."

Huh. I've never really considered my stride, except the few times I've been on a runway. And I had no idea Camille notices things like that.

She finds a satin sheath in a beautiful ivory shade that looks pinkish in the right light, but the back is completely bare and dips so low in the front that it might be difficult to keep up.

"Mom wouldn't go for this one," I say aloud as I study myself in the mirror.

"Your mom?" Sophie looks at me strangely. Yes, we are back to being best friends again, but I've never mentioned my mother to her. She missed that part of my life, and even though she knows what happened, she doesn't know how it felt.

How it still feels.

I catch my breath because I never meant to say that out loud. "I mean—"

"It must be hard, knowing your mother won't see you like this," Camille says in a soft voice. "I know it was for me."

I turn to my sister-in-law. "And you were by yourself," I realize. "That would have been horrible."

Camille's lips quirk. "Well, I was marrying your brother, so it wasn't all that bad."

"Do you ever...?" I pause. I don't know why I never thought of talking to Camille about this before. She lost her mother, so she must have some understanding of how this is for me. "Does it ever feel like she's... *there?*" I ask in a whisper. "Your mother?"

"Of course. There's a bird on Miquelon that always makes me think of her when I see it."

"Was it her favourite bird?"

"No, she hated it." Camille smiles, but there's a sadness in her eyes. "She would complain about it every time she saw it. It makes me laugh when it's around, and I like to think that's what she would want. For me to laugh instead of crying."

"My mom definitely would want that. When I hear different songs, I think of her. But being here, trying to find a 'husband'—" I use air quotes around the word because I'm not a hundred percent sure that's what I'm looking for. "I've been thinking of her a lot more."

"It's something you'd want your mother around for," Camille agrees, giving my hand a squeeze.

"Yeah."

Sophie is quiet through this exchange, since she still has her mother, however unpleasant a person she might be. "Lyra? Look at this one."

She's holding a white dress with ruffles like a flapper's dress, but it's the one on the rack beside it that grabs my attention. "Yes, but this one." I snatch it from the rack and hold it against myself.

"Definitely try that one on," Camille instructs.

"Your mother would think it's perfect," Sophie adds.

It takes a bit to get into it, but finally, with Alexa's help, I stand in front of the three-way mirror in the dress.

And it might well be "The Dress."

"I think I found it," I whisper. Alexa has run off to find a headpiece that would go with the dress, Sophie went to find a bouquet, and Camille has gone to find Odin, so I'm alone with the moment.

I haven't had too many moments like this since I've been here.

"What do you think?" I ask my mother. I know she's not here, but she should be. Maybe not here, on the set of The Suitorette, but if this were real life, she should be with me.

And it... it hurts my heart that she's not.

I take a few deep breaths because tears are threatening and the last thing I want is to be found crying over a dress.

It's not as easy as it should be, taking a deep breath in this dress. Strapless heavy satin hugs my torso; a sharp, upward-pointing fabric accent marked the straight neckline.

Just below my hips, six strips of silvery white tulle fall in ruffles, almost completely covering the satin.

"Strict at the top, party at the bottom," I say to my reflection. I want to smile; I want to jump up and down with delight that I am wearing such a beautiful, perfect dress, but the sadness is there, too strong for me to ignore.

A shrill bird song catches my attention and I turn to the window. A solitary bird sits on a branch like it's looking in the window.

"I know that's not you, Mom, but I'm going to pretend it is," I whisper. Just for a moment. Just until the sadness—which she wouldn't want me to be feeling—dissipates.

I sniff and give a shake of my head, and it's gone.

But the bird stays.

31

Spencer

THERE ARE TWELVE OF us on this date.

I have no idea how this is possible. How can I talk to Lyra, let alone get near her with this many men, all wanting the same thing?

I want to be annoyed at Lyra for letting this happen. For not giving me a chance to talk to her, explain why I walked out of the last date.

And then I realize she expects me to be annoyed. Possibly even wants it because we communicate the best when we're angry at each other.

And I'm sure she knows why I left the brewery.

I tuck the irritation down deep and follow the group out to the back lawn of the hotel.

There's no beach area here; the waves come straight from the North Atlantic, and while the constant crashing is picturesque as well as relaxing, no one should step foot in the water. It's cold, it's rough and it's rocky, with a wall built up to keep the worst of the waves off the lawn.

We group around Grayson and Rue, with six camera people standing around. At least this part isn't being filmed.

It's taken some time to get used to the constant cameras, but anyone who ends up with Lyra will need to expect that.

"Let me explain what's going on here," Grayson calls over the din of the men who aren't hiding their excitement.

I should be that excited.

I am that excited—I can't wait to see Lyra, but I'm also nervous about what they're going to make us do.

While wearing suits and tuxedos, and, in one case, a kilt.

We all agreed that Jon has the best calves for the kilt.

"I'm happy to report that we won't be going anywhere near the water today," Grayson says loudly. "On my season, I ended up in the water, and can we say *chafing*?"

Laughter all around, and Grayson grins.

He's very good at this host thing.

"You all look amazing once you're cleaned up... but you might not *stay* clean." He motions behind him, where a bit of an obstacle course is set up, with a throne-like chair at the far end.

Rue claps her hands. "Gentlemen, this is going to be fun. Now, first thing will be the catwalk, where you can show yourself off to Lyra. Who is coming out—" She checks her watch. "Any minute now. Get in line, please, and cameras start rolling."

It's chaos for five straight minutes, and then it just—works.

Lyra comes out of the ballroom door on Odin's arm, followed by Sophie and Camille. My sister is in purple, while Camille is wearing hot pink, which should clash with her hair but instead, gives her an amazing glow.

And the way Odin glances behind him suggests he clearly thinks so too.

But once I see all of Lyra, she's all I can look at.

I've seen Lyra in all types of dresses. I've been her escort at countless parties and galas, and I've held her in my arms as we've danced.

I've seen her look beautiful—she is beautiful—but she's never stolen my breath like she does now.

Odin escorts her to the throne at the end of the runway and steps away, leaving Lyra facing us.

There are mutters and whispers, whistles and cheers, and Lyra waves before dropping into a curtsy even better than the one she once gave to the Queen of England.

But instead of settling onto the throne to let us start, which is what I think she's supposed to do, Lyra starts down the wooden runway.

Hips swaying, arms swinging, and silver shoes peeking out from under her skirt, Lyra looks like she was made for a catwalk.

The guys erupt with cheers as she reaches the end, blows a kiss to the group, and turns to retrace her steps.

"And that's how you do it," Grayson cries over the din. With a last wave, Lyra takes her seat. "Rand, you're up."

Rand, cheeks as red as his hair, dressed in a bold striped grey suit, does his best to copy Lyra's walk, even dropping a curtsy when he pauses in front of the throne.

She's laughing as much as the rest of us, and it lightens the palpable nerves.

At least mine, anyway.

One by one, we head down the wooden runway, each trying to put their personality into the walk and how we pause in front of Lyra.

There are a lot of bows and a few curtsies, although no one pulls it off like Rand. Boone, who is the most intimidating one here, drops to one knee and kisses Lyra's hand. Dylan, the firefighter, strikes a pose before he starts stripping off his jacket and tie, and managing to get his shirt off before he reaches Lyra, and then tosses it to her.

Jon stalks like he's possessed by a panther, and Leo pretends to dance.

"No fair—he was just on Dancing with the Stars," Rand grumbles good-naturedly.

Ashton struts, hands in pockets, looking like he does this every day, even though he's wearing the most obnoxious bright blue suit with a loud paisley print. Tanner pretends to skate, and Basher, ever present drumsticks in hand, plays a drum solo as he strolls toward Lyra.

And then it's my turn.

I was so busy watching the others that I never planned what I would do. But as I step forward, it just comes to me. Holding Lyra's gaze, I walk toward her, hands in the pockets of my dark purple velvet suit like I'm taking a stroll across the square in Battle Harbour to the coffee shop.

At the end, I stand for a moment before her before I extend my hand.

32

Lyra

Of course I take his hand, because I know exactly what Spencer is doing.

I rise from the chair—super uncomfortable in the bum area—gripping Spencer's hand.

"You look exquisite," he says simply.

"Thank you," I tell him.

His hand slides to my back. "Do you remember the Christmas party the mayor had?"

"Of course." I grin, adjusting my stance.

And then Spencer swoops me into a waltz.

There's no music, but the steps come back as though we practiced them all day yesterday. I had been sixteen, and Spencer was home from his second year at university. The new mayor—married to Duncan's ex-wife—had been hosting a Christmas dance, even though my father would have one the next week as well.

Out of loyalty to his father, Spencer didn't want to go. My brothers tried to persuade him, but it was me who convinced him. Signe did her best to ignore Spencer, even though she had been his step-mother, and Spencer didn't want to deal with her rudeness for the night. I came up with an idea of a dance, so that it would be impossible for Signe to pretend Spencer wasn't there, since everyone would be talking about him.

We practiced for two days straight.

And now, Spencer leads me in a Viennese waltz, the very same dance we did then.

It feels so good to dance again.

It feels so good to have Spencer holding me, his back straight and strong, his hand holding mine like it's something precious.

"You've still got it," I tell him as we make the turn at the end.

"You bring it out in me," he counters.

The warmth in my chest grows as we waltz, the hem of my dress swirling around me. At the end, pausing before my chair, Spencer breaks hold and spins me around, before dropping me into a dip.

My laughter bubbles up as I lie in his arms, his hand holding mine pressed against his chest.

And then it dies as our eyes meet. "I need to be here," he says in a low voice. "I need you to see me, Lyra. Because I see you. I always have."

He settles me on my feet and bows over my hand.

Dimly, I hear cheering from the others, but I can't focus.

It's hard to catch my breath.

After the fashion show comes the obstacle course. The winner will get time alone with me.

For the first time, I really hope Spencer wins, so I can ask him what he meant.

It's a good strategy to remind me of our shared past, but bringing back memories only shows me what we didn't have.

Do I want to be reminded of all the missed opportunities?

We were friends. I... I'm still not sure what to call what I felt toward him. But we were never together, and I blame Spencer for that.

Maybe that's not fair, but it's how I feel.

Grayson explains what will happen as I stand with Sophie and Camille, sipping champagne. Odin stands by the men to offer moral support.

Still wearing their suits, they will be divided into two groups for a tug-of-war challenge. The winning group will be then put in pairs to compete in a balloon popping contest, and a three-legged race. The two winning pairs will then compete in a bouquet making contest.

It's the strangest, most random set of events, and it's hilarious.

The Blue team, led by Boone and Jon, beat the Red Team. Tanner and Dylan do their best but are no match for the combined strength of the bad boys.

Watching Jon compete in a kilt is a highlight for all.

They pair up: Jon takes Rand as a partner, Boone has Leo, and the four of them win the three-legged race, mainly because Jon and Boone manage to carry the smaller men across the finish line.

I'm happy to see Spencer and Liam take third place.

The three pairs are then tied together around their waists, given a balloon, and told to pop it.

I have never laughed so hard.

Boone wraps Leo in a bear hug, squeezing, but the rubber doesn't give before Leo is crying out that Boone might break his ribs.

Spencer and Liam push their balloon to their feet and eventually, by stamping over each other's feet, manage to pop it.

But not before Jon takes it between his teeth and bites it, making Rand squeal as it pops in his face.

I'm still laughing as the two of them face off over a mound of flowers, but Rand seems to be the only one who has ever held a flower.

He makes me a gorgeous bouquet in the time allocated, winning the time with me.

But before I can lead Rand away, Leo comes up with a question about the dance, and then Dylan has compliments about my dress.

And then Spencer is there. "This is Rand's time," I tell him, glancing around to see Rand joking off to the side with Jon.

"I know. I'm not arguing today," Spencer tells me.

"Well, I can argue whenever I want," I decide.

"That sounds like the annoyed little girl who couldn't have her friend live with her instead of me."

My eyes narrow and I wish I'd escaped with Rand when I had the chance. "Why are you bringing that up? I didn't have a problem with you there."

"No, but you didn't like it."

"Why wouldn't I like it? You were always on my side. You made my brothers spend time with me."

"They wanted to."

"That's what everyone says, but I don't really believe it. I... liked... you being there," I admit. "When you went away..."

How did we start talking about this? There is so much I need to say to Spencer, and we're talking about when he moved to the castle when he was a kid?

"Did you miss me then?" Spencer asks in a low voice. His silvery grey eyes catch my gaze and hold it, like he held my hand in the hot tub.

And like then, I start to feel like a block of butter left out in the sun. The way his gaze doesn't falter. The determined jut to his chin.

The way that suit fits him so perfectly, even rumpled with grass stains from when he tripped over Liam.

The way Spencer laughed as he fell...

I nod.

"Would you miss me now? If I went away?" Spencer doesn't wait for me to reply. "Lyra, why don't you just give me a rose and we'll figure this out once and for all?"

33

Spencer

I NEVER KNEW WHAT to expect by coming on this show, but it was not that.

It hurts seeing Lyra walk away with another man, although I cheer along with everyone else when Rand wins.

He's a good guy, so I can't begrudge him the win.

They all seem like good guys.

I didn't expect the sense of comradery between us. It's kind of like when I spend time with the princes.

We stand around the back of the hotel and watch Rand, hand in hand with Lyra.

"This is the worst part of it." Liam comes up beside me. "Seeing her happy with someone else."

"It sucks," Boone says in his growly voice.

"But it's not bad that it's Rand," Liam counters. "At least he's a good guy. It would have been really tough to see someone like Phillippe or the Lucs with her."

"So it wasn't just me with Phillippe?"

Liam shakes his head. "Slimy."

"Douche," Boone agrees.

"Who are we bad-mouthing?" Ashton offers me another bottle.

"Phillippe?" Tanner guesses as he joins us. "Or are we back to Lucas?"

I have to laugh. "No one liked him either?"

"Nah," Ashton. "Small-town guys."

"Your sister lives in a small town now," I remind him, clinking bottles with him.

"To my dismay."

"We have you to thank for getting rid of him," Liam says. "You called him out about having a girlfriend."

"I didn't know for sure."

"This is why the show gets a bad name," Eliott grumbles. "Guys like him out for their fifteen minutes of fame."

"Instead of the heart of a good woman." Ashton rolls his eyes.

"Why are you here, then?" Boone demands.

"I think the more important question should be to this guy." Ashton points his bottle at me. "What was with that dance?"

"Yeah! Dude," Leo joins in. "It took me weeks to move like that and you walk about and show me up."

"It wasn't the first time," I admit. "We went to a dance once and Lyra thought—"

"You take dance class with her or something?" Boone growls.

"Something. She took a lot of dance classes when she was younger, and it worked."

"You think now is the time for it to work out for you?" Liam asks sadly.

I shrug. "Like everyone here, if I didn't take the chance, I might never have another one. You guys—any one of you could make her fall in love with you, and if I was left at home watching that?" I shook my head. "I would regret it forever."

It's funny how I'm no longer regretting my decision to join the show.

34

Lyra

I CARRY THE FLOWERS Rand gave me as we walk to a gazebo on the side of the hotel.

"These are beautiful," I tell him for the third time.

"Not as beautiful as you." It's strange for him to sound so serious. I haven't spent much time with him, but all of our interactions have been light-hearted and funny. Rand is a very funny guy.

"What do you do when you're not wooing princesses?" I ask as we settle on the bench. Rand pours us each a glass of champagne and sits close beside me.

He smells nice, a mix of soapy innocence and sexy musk, and his red hair is thick with just the right amount of curl that makes me want to run my fingers through it.

"Good to know that my wooing has been noted." He grins. His cheeks are freckled, but the tan blends them together.

"We would have red-haired babies," I say out of nowhere.

"And you're already thinking of procreation?" Rand nods. "That's very encouraging."

"I'm encouraging until I have a reason not to be."

"What did Asani do to give you a reason?" he asks. "Just to make sure I'm not following his lead."

"He was nice," I relent. "But..."

"But he might have had different views, like how he thought princesses are there to look pretty and help make the world more peaceful?" Rand grins at my surprised expression. "He made some comments in the house before you sent him home."

I frown. "This is information I should have known."

"You would have heard about it if you hadn't sent him home," Rand assures me. "There's a bit of a protective vibe in the house."

"About me?" He nods. "That's sweet, but it makes me think of growing up with my brothers, and I don't really want to think of any of you as a brother type."

"Not even Spencer?"

"Spencer is my brothers' friend, not my brother."

"It's cool. He seems like a good guy."

"How's he doing with the others? Starting late and all." The question slides out before I can stop it.

I should *not* be talking about Spencer when I'm with someone else.

But Rand indulges me. "He's been watching more than interacting. Getting the lay of the land."

Because that's what he does. Spencer observes to find out what he needs to know, then sets the stage for others to shine.

I wonder if he's actually capable of taking the spotlight for himself.

But it looked like he's doing fine with his dance earlier.

Enough about Spencer. "How do you like staying with twenty-five men?" I ask as I finish my champagne.

"Twelve now, until you send the next batch home." He refills both of our glasses and clinks his against mine. "If we're being honest, I'll say that I really don't want to be part of the next batch sent packing."

"You like it here, then?"

"I'm in it to win it," Rand vows. "Win the heart of the fair maiden."

I lean back against the cushions and survey him. "Tell me something about myself that you don't think the others know," I invite.

Rand studies me. "You give off the vibe of being this incredibly amazing, vivacious woman, someone who can conquer the world if you put your mind to it."

"Everyone knows that," I say with a cool smile.

"I'm not finished. That's what you show, what you want others to see. But I think, what I see, is that deep down, you're a little lost. I think you want someone to step up and take care of you, but without telling you they're taking care of you. Like your not-brother Spencer. I'm betting he's always tried to take care of you, but lets you know what he's doing. I don't think you like that."

I don't reply because, *wow*. It's like Rand took a peek inside me. I didn't even know I had a problem with that.

"I'm a teacher in the real world," Rand says. "I'm insightful and observant."

"You don't have to be insightful and observant to know you don't have to worry about getting a yellow rose tomorrow."

Spending time with the men like this lets me really see what they're like. Do I imagine what it might be like to be in love with them? Of course.

When I was with Tanner, I pictured what our life might be like. I imagined a social life full of parties and friends around his hockey career.

I also realized I would need something more in my life, to compete with Tanner's love for his sport.

With Rand, I imagine a smaller life. Maybe in Battle Harbour, maybe somewhere else. I'm not opposed to relocating, but I might have an issue making my life smaller to fit into his.

I've always imagined a life with Spencer.

As we walk back, I know Rand isn't going to be the one, but I've had fun with him and don't want to hurt him by telling him that now.

Maybe I could change my mind.

Grayson meets us at the hotel and gives me a minute to say goodnight to Rand before he ushers me to the car for the drive back to Camille's.

"Good day?" he asks.

"It was a lot of fun," I tell him, leaning my head against the seat. "Do I get to keep the dress?"

"We could probably arrange it. It does suit you."

"Thank you for keeping us out of the water. I'd hate to ruin it."

Grayson laughs. "You saw that episode, did you?"

"Over a million views on YouTube. It's a classic."

"That dance with Spencer is going to be up there," Grayson warns. "How are you feeling with him here?"

"Is this off the record, or for the cameras?"

He gestures to the empty car. "There's only us here."

"It's a little disconcerting," I admit. "I feel like I'm two people—the person I am in my life, and the person Spencer thinks I am."

"They're not the same person?"

"I don't know. I always got the sense that Spencer—and my brothers—don't really give me a lot of credit for being capable."

"I think you're very capable."

"I know I'm very capable. Rand said I could take over the world if I wanted to, and he's right."

Grayson laughs. "I think you could be very scary, Your Highness."

"I know I can be." My smile fades. "But I'm not sure Spencer sees me like that."

"I'd say that is something you need to find out. Not assume, but find out for sure."

"I want to give him the next date rose."

Grayson sighs. "There's a few weeks to go," he hedges. "Lots of men left."

"When you were the Suitor, did you ever wonder that you wouldn't be able to find someone?" I ask in a soft voice.

"I knew it was Bexley right away," he tells me. "But the longer we got into the show, I started to worry that she wouldn't be able to stick it out. It's a lot for the contestants—and I know, because I've been one of the contestants as well. It's part of the problem—sometimes you make this amazing connection with a person, and instead of focusing on it, nurturing, you're forced to keep making connections with other men. That's tough for everyone."

"Which is why I'm ready to explore the connection with Spencer now. I'm giving him the rose tomorrow."

I'm glad Grayson doesn't bother to argue with me.

35

THE NEXT MORNING, RAND and I are the last ones in the hall.

And we're the only ones with a red date rose outside the door. Rand picks it up and gives it to me.

36

Lyra

I'VE NEVER BEEN SO nervous before a date as I am now, getting ready for my date with Spencer.

There isn't much to get ready though—Alexa does a light makeup with extra sunscreen because we'll be spending the day outside, then leaves me so I can get dressed. I wear black running shorts and a pink T-shirt, my hair in a swingy pony-tail.

I change the shirt four times, the shorts twice, each time Tema giving me her opinion. I'm not sure she realizes today's date is with Spencer, or if she's just caught up in my nervous excitement.

She's mentioned Abigail a few times since she's been here, off-handed comments or funny things she's said. I know Abigail is like a second mother to Tema, while I am only the favourite aunt. I don't want to upset her.

I don't want Tema to think I took Spencer away from Abigail. Because I didn't.

I have no idea what goes on in the heads of eight-year-olds.

Eventually, Bo appears to collect her. "You with Spencer to-day?" he asks in his gruff Bo voice, as he picks Tema up and throws her over his shoulder.

I nod.

"You look scared."

"I'm not scared," I protest.

"Good, because you shouldn't be. It's Spence."

Of course it's Spence. But it's not the same.

"Tell Spencer I said hi," Tema cries from upside down. "And Tanner. I like Tanner."

"Tanner likes you, too," I tell her. "And I'll tell Spencer." It makes me feel better that Tema seems fine about my date with Spencer, but then again, she's eight and has no idea what really goes on during a date.

"Is that all you're going to tell him?" Bo wants to know.

"I don't know what I'm going to tell him. I don't know anything," I say, hearing the note of possible hysteria in my voice. "It's different here. He's—"

"He's *Spencer*," Tema points out. "And you like him. And he likes you."

I stare at the back of Tema's legs. It sounds so easy when she says it.

"He's the same Spencer he's always been," Bo points out. "Just be yourself, because that's why he's here. For you."

"Have you seen him?" I ask.

Bo shakes his head. "They won't let me near him. Why?"

"I just wanted to know if that was something he told you to say to me."

He sets Tema down, and shoos her away before he steps into my room. Clothes are strewn all over the place, with a rack brought in to house my collection of dresses.

Grayson was true to his word, and the wedding dress I wore yesterday hangs beside the navy dress from the first night.

I wish I could wear one of the ball gowns today, hiding inside the silk and sequins like it was my armour.

"Lyra," Bo orders and I slowly raise my eyes to Bo. "You're the princess of Laandia."

"Not the only one anymore," I correct.

"You're the only daughter of King Magnus and Queen Selene. You've got thousands of people who follow you on social media—"

"Please, know your numbers. It's in the millions. And I don't know what you're trying to tell me."

Bo turns me to face the mirror. "Look at yourself. You're Lyra Erickson, and you've known Spencer your whole life. Trust yourself. And trust Spencer."

I stare at Bo's reflection rather than my own. "Are you okay with this?" I whisper. "If this ends up being a *this*? He's your best friend and the four of you—"

Abigail, but I don't want to mention her name.

And Hettie, who suddenly appears at the open door. "Lyra, Ria says the car will be here in five minutes," she reports, looking flustered when she sees our serious expressions. "Sorry to interrupt your moment."

"You take over this, Hettie." Bo drops a kiss on my head. "You're my favourite sister," he reminds me.

"I'm your only sister," I say as he heads for the door.

"Not anymore. Sisters-in-law count too."

"Everything okay?" Hettie asks as Bo disappears.

"First-date jitters," I admit with a rueful smile. "And I seem to need some sort of blessing from Spencer's best friends."

"Bo's happy about this," Hettie assures me.

"And you? Abigail is your best friend and I'm kind of taking her man."

My newest sister-in-law smiles at me. "You can't take anything from Abigail that she isn't willing to give up."

"So if Abigail hadn't walked away—"

"Spencer would have realized what we all do. That he needs to be with you."

I turn to look at myself in the mirror. *Yes, he does.*

"Let's just hope he does, or you're going to have another short date," Hettie says over her shoulder as she leaves. "I'll tell them you'll be down shortly."

I spend the next few minutes staring at myself in the mirror.

"This is it," I say out loud. "This is my chance with Spencer."

It's about time.

"It wasn't time before." And I never expected this to be the time, either. I signed on to be the Suitorette to get over Spencer, not go on a date with him.

It shouldn't feel this significant because I've gone on date-like things with Spencer before. We've been to the MetGala. Movie premiers. Birthday parties for Prince William and former PM Justin Trudeau.

I've wandered through the secret passages of the castle clinging to his hand and drank wine on the battlements with him.

But all those times were the same because I never felt like he wanted to be with me. It was as if he had been with me because he was assigned as my date or my guide, or my minder. Someone who was there to make sure I didn't get into trouble.

This time, it's different.

37

Spencer

IT'S NOT THE BEST day for a hike.

The afternoon sun hides behind grey clouds that threaten rain. Rue assures us three times that the rain will hold off until this evening, and everything has been set up for us, so the date is still a go. There's a cool breeze that has Lyra hugging her elbows as she strides along the path before me.

"It reminds me of Scotland."

They're the first words I've spoken since we started off.

Maybe it's the cameraman following us, close enough to hear our every labored breath. And yes, some of my breaths are labored. For a flat piece of land, Saint Pierre has a surprising number of dips and inclines. And yes, I'm far from the best shape of my life. Too many late nights at my desk with fish and chips take out, too many mornings starting with lattes from Coffee for the Sole with full-fat milk and extra syrup.

I can still keep up with anyone, but it takes its toll.

The quiet may also be because it's the first time we've been alone.

Alone, in that there's no other men around. There's always the cameraman.

"Do you remember when we went to Balmoral?" Lyra says over her shoulder. "Dad went a few times, but it was only the one time when they let all of us go too."

"All of us" means I was invited as well. It was soon after Dad and Signe got divorced and he hadn't wanted to leave me alone. King Magnus and Queen Selene thought nothing of bringing along another teenager.

"And the Queen thought you were another prince." Lyra laughed.

"Your mom didn't correct her until the end of the weekend."

"She always thought of you as hers, so she didn't care. Plus, you don't correct the Queen of England."

"No, you don't," I agree but all I can think is *she always thought of you as hers.* "I loved your mother," I add. "Not as the queen, but... you know."

Lyra looks back at me. "She loved you too."

"I never told her."

"And I never told her enough. But she knew."

We're silent again, the path widening, so we can walk side by side. A plane flies low overhead and Lyra waves.

"Try not to acknowledge the cameras," Johnny says from behind us.

"It's Bo," Lyra tells me. "They wanted overhead shots, so he offered to fly around with the camera guy."

"Hasan," I say.

"You know their names? Of course you do. It's no wonder Mom loved thinking of you as a son—you've got more royal qualities than the rest of us put together."

"Because I learn people's names?"

"Because you think of learning people's names."

"The queen knew everyone's name," I point out. "I got it from her." I pause, not knowing how far I can go with Lyra on the subject of her mother. It's always difficult for Lyra to put her emotions about her mother into words.

She put most of her thoughts and feelings down on paper in the letters she sent me.

I had been away at university in Toronto when I got the news about the accident. I don't remember anything about the flight back, just that I managed to get to the Island Airport and somehow there was a plane waiting for me.

The magic of my father—organizing a ride home for me at the same time he was supporting his best friend and grieving for the queen.

All of us gathered at the hospital had been... grim. And then I had been in Lyra's room when she woke, and I was the one who told her that the queen had died.

That her mother had died.

"I miss her," I say softly.

"I miss her every day," Lyra says matter-of-factly. "I talk to her sometimes," she admits. "I don't know what that makes me."

"It makes you a daughter missing her mother. What do you talk about?"

"Oh, I don't know. Life, the stupid stuff I do. Boys."

"Do you talk about me?"

There's a long pause, then, "She loved you."

"You said that."

"So, yeah, I talk about you. Especially since you showed up to mess up my season." But she grins as she says it.

I open my mouth to reply, even though I'm not sure what to say. Do I tell her that I talk about her? Because I don't. I rarely mention Lyra to anyone.

But I think about her.

A lot.

Lyra stops. We've reached the summit of the hill, which feels more like a mini mountain to me. I really wish I'd taken up Kalle's offer to work out more often. "Newfoundland." She points to the sliver of land visible in the distance.

"This place is really beautiful."

"It really is. I had no idea why Odin would agree to give up everything and move here," she marvels. "Now I get it."

"Because he loves Camille?"

Lyra shakes her head. "You can love someone and still not drop your life for what they want. At least I don't think you should. There should be compromise, not just giving up. Odin gave up a lot."

"Would you ever give up your spot in the line of succession?"

"No way. I love being a princess."

I laugh. "You're a good one."

"Even though I don't know everyone's names."

"There's always something to strive for." I take her hand, her fingers soft and cool in mine.

She looks down at our fingers entwined. "I have a lot to work on."

"Why do you say that?"

"My life." She gestures impatiently with her free hand. "It's a mess. You all think so."

"I don't know about that. It's your life. Are you happy?"

"I thought I was. And then I got here, and things slowed down. It showed me what I was missing."

"What are you missing?"

Lyra takes a deep breath and I think she's about to confess some secret dream about being an ambassador to the world, or even to take on more responsibilities at the castle.

I'm not prepared for what she says.

"You."

38

Lyra

I SAID IT. I finally said it.

I said *something*. Not all of it, but it's a start.

But will Spencer...

"I've missed you, too." He stands in front of me, blocking the view, and brings a hand to push back a tendril of hair that escaped my ponytail.

His fingers brush my cheek.

"I missed having you in my life," I correct. "I missed having someone to count on. Who believed in me. Who I could tell things to."

"I kept every one of the letters you sent to me when I was away," he says.

Hope bubbles in my chest. "Really?"

"Every single one of them. But then you stopped writing."

"You had your life, and I wasn't a part of it. I thought you didn't want me."

"I always wanted you, Lyra." His thumb curves over my chin, so close to my mouth.

"Why didn't this happen before?" I whisper, pressing my lips together in preparation for his kiss.

How do you prepare for a kiss you've been waiting your entire life for?

"It wasn't the right time." He doesn't kiss me. Instead, Spencer brings our joined hands to his mouth and presses his lips against my knuckles, bowing his head.

I lean into him, feeling the warmth of his body so close to mine. "Do you think this is our moment?" I breathe.

His cups my cheek, his thumb stroking along my jaw. "If it is, I don't want to mess it up."

"You could hurry it up," I suggest. "Maybe you could—"

"There's a picnic," he says, looking over my shoulder.

"What?"

"Over there." He gestures to the side where a cabana-like structure has been set up at the top of the hill. I have no idea how I missed seeing it. "Sit with me?"

I would do anything with him.

Spencer leads me to the setup—half bed, half couch, full of comfortable pillows and a throw blanket that he lays across my legs before pouring champagne from the ever-present bottle.

"They built this for us." I laugh.

"They built this for you and whoever was going to get this one-on-one date," he corrects. "Who were you going to give it to before—?"

"Before you danced with me?"

"I figured that might seal the deal."

I laugh softly. "Arrogant."

"I learned from the best."

"Me?"

"I was thinking your brothers. But no—I always admired their confidence. It's not arrogance."

"It can be arrogance," I point out with a younger sister's certainty and Spencer laughs.

He shifts and tucks me against him, his arm warm against my shoulders. I lean against his chest, unable to stop my smile. It's surreal that we're actually here—finally together, on a date. Even if it's one orchestrated by the show, it's still a date.

Our first date.

We're overlooking the water, and the white caps multiply as I sit and enjoy the view. Birds swoop in and out of sight, dropping to the beach out of sight over the hill.

It feels comfortable here. Real.

For the first time since I signed up to be the Suitorette, I feel like this is where I'm supposed to be.

And with *whom* I'm supposed to be with.

"Do you remember the first time we kissed?" Spencer toys with my ponytail, rubbing the strands of hair between his fingers.

"See, that's arrogance that you think I would remember."

"Don't you?" he asks looking down at me.

"Well, yeah, but..." Spencer smiles knowingly. "It wasn't my first kiss," I add rudely.

"You were *ten*."

"I'm a princess. People liked to kiss me." I hold up my hand. "I met Logan Paul and Ross Lynch at some party and one of them kissed me. Only I can't remember which one of them it was."

"I must have blocked out hearing about that," he says. "And I have no idea who they are."

"I bet you know who Justin Bieber is." I smile smugly. "Do you remember that picture I had of us? He signed it."

"And you framed it and hung it on your wall," he adds sourly. "I really couldn't stand him."

"Because he kissed me?" A giggle escapes.

"I think you like to kiss people."

"Kissing is always fun," I say, and take a breath. "When it's as far as you're willing to take it."

Something flashes in his gaze. Something that looks a lot like relief. "Is that so?"

"Tell me about what you remember about kissing me," I say. There had been a group of us hanging out down in the dungeons of the castle and someone suggested we play Spin the Bottle.

I think it had been me, which is probably the only reason my brothers agreed.

That had been the age I perfected the temper when I didn't get what I wanted.

"It was my first kiss," Spencer says in a low voice. "Because I was not a princess who people like to kiss. I was thirteen, so that's a long time to wait."

"I thought you and Abigail—" I hate bringing up her name because she doesn't belong in this moment. Not anymore.

Spencer shakes his head. "That wasn't until later. I was nervous. Watching that bottle spin..."

"It's not like you had many choices." I laugh, breaking the moment. "It was me or your sisters."

"Kate was there, too. But I didn't want to kiss Kate."

"You wanted to kiss me?" I ask coyly, looking up at him.

"I guess," he says, feigning indifference until I slap at his chest. "Fine. Yes. More than anything." Spencer shifts again and pulls my legs over his lap. "Happy?"

"Very. What else?"

"Everyone spun, and Gunnar got Stella, and then Kate got him—"

"A love triangle even then. And then Odin got Sophie! I thought she would self-combust."

We laugh at the thought of serious Odin bending to kiss little Sophie, who had been bouncing in her spot with excitement.

"And then it was finally my turn."

The bottle had stopped between me and Kate but she had moved away so it was closer to me. Spencer hadn't wasted any time like my brothers did; he crawled through the circle until he knelt before me. He barely looked at me before leaning in to press his lips against mine.

It was over too quickly, but it left me reeling for days. Weeks.

"You tasted like cherries," he says.

"My lip gloss."

"They became my favourite fruit." He laughs self-deprecatingly. "Every time I had one, I thought of that day in the dungeon. Also, whenever I had a sore throat and had Vicks cough drops."

"You thought of me when you were sick?" I swat his shoulder this time.

"I thought of you all of the time."

I catch my breath at the seriousness of his voice.

"I didn't know it, Lyra, but I've been crazy about you for my whole life. Since that moment I first saw you—"

"I was a baby," I whisper. "That's... ew."

"Maybe not that far back," he relents with a smile. "I don't know when it happened, but it was always you."

"You and Abigail..." I have to bring her up. I have to know where things stand with them because I can't go into this second-guessing.

"She told me to figure it out with you. She could see it—I think she always knew that I was waiting for you."

"That's not fair to her."

"It's not, and I'm glad she broke it off. She deserves to find someone who loves her unconditionally, not as a warm-up act until the main event comes on."

"Am I the main event, Spencer?"

"Yes. You are."

The moment pauses like it's taken a breath and holds it, the air suddenly warmer as Spencer cups my cheek and I lean into it.

I tell myself to remember this moment—the scent of rain in the air, the birdsong sweeping over us, the warmth of Spencer's hand.

The promise of what is to come.

And then everything fades away as our lips meet, soft and sweet and real.

This is real.

39

Spencer

BEING THERE, AT THE top of the hill snuggled up with Lyra doesn't feel real.

It's something I've never allowed myself to hope for. To dream about. Not just being with Lyra, but being with the woman I'm in love with.

I'm in love with Princess Lyra. No—I'm in love with Lyra Erickson.

I don't tell her that as we talk about things of no importance. We laugh.

We kiss a lot, and it's a revelation. Men never think of whether women are good at kissing or not—at least I never have. I just assume they will take my lead—and I've never had any complaints.

Arrogant, yes, but true.

Kissing Lyra is like nothing I've ever experienced.

It's not just the touch of her lips against mine, but the confidence with which those lips move against mine.

Long, languid kisses, with her hands thrust in my hair, until I need to pull away for a break. Tiny pecks while we change position, laughing because Lyra pouts that she can't get close enough to me.

The way her mouth finds the spot behind my ear and how she kisses her way down my throat as she sits, straddling my lap.

Hopefully not all the kissing makes it through the editing process, or I might have some explaining to do to King Magnus.

On the surface, it feels like things are resolved between Lyra and me—that there is an us—but deep down, I know there's more to come.

I know we need to talk about us, but it feels better to wait.

It feels better to keep kissing, and work out the details later. I'm good with details—although with all the kissing I'm doing, I feel like I'm pretty good at other things as well.

We stay entwined for a long time, stopping occasionally for a sip of champagne or a piece of fruit, but are quickly drawn to each other again. There are whispers of nonsense, murmurs of appreciation and—thunder?

"Did you hear that?" I mutter against Lyra's lips.

"No," she says, snaking her arms around my waist. "But—" She feels the cold droplet at the same time I do. "I think it's raining." She groans as she buries her face into the spot where my shoulder meets my neck, her lips brushing my skin because she's already pushed aside my shirt to kiss there.

King Magnus doesn't need to see that.

"Do you have an umbrella?" she whines.

"It's definitely raining." I glance over at Johnny, who has the camera down and his phone against his ear. "We should get off the hill."

"We have to walk down?" Lyra cries, clearly unwilling to move.

"I didn't think you were the lazy sort," I tease, my hands on her waist to push her off me.

"I'm not lazy, I'm comfortable." Lyra stretches and I can't look away from her smile of contentment.

I put that smile on her face, and she put an even bigger one on mine.

I'm still smiling as suddenly, the rain begins in earnest, fat drops that quickly turn into a sheet, soaking us within moments.

Lyra shrieks and jumps, laughing, to her feet. This is the only shelter on the top of the hill, and it's not much of one. Ominous clouds have gathered overhead. "You couldn't have told us it was about to rain?" I call to Johnny, who is trying to protect his camera under his jacket.

"Ria said it wasn't supposed to," he cries back, his long hair already stringy and soaked.

"Our producers are clearly not from the Maritimes." Lyra pops the last strawberry in her mouth. The set up has been ruined, but there's too much for us to carry down. She links her hand with mine and swings it between us. "Guess we're in for a wet walk. Good thing I like to be out in the rain."

I wish Johnny could get this side of Lyra on film.

The three of us are soaked to the skin before the golf cart gets to us.

That's the end of the date. We don't get the dinner portion; by the time we reach the village, it's storming in earnest. Two SUVs along with Ria meet us. She instructs me to follow Johnny.

"Okay, but—" The driver has an umbrella over Lyra and is escorting her to the second SUV. "Lyra," I call over the wind. "Call me later."

"She can't call you," Ria tells me, following Lyra, who stops to look back at me with a confused expression. "No contact with the contestants unless you're on a date."

"But we're—"

I don't even know what we are.

The scent of Lyra's perfume, her shampoo—of her—clings to my nose. The taste of her—a mix of champagne and fruit—is on my lips.

I am overwhelmed with Lyra and I don't even know what to call us.

"She's still the Suitorette," Ria reminds me, all the while pushing Lyra into the vehicle and out of the rain.

I stand in the downpour, as Lyra manages a quick wave before they drive off toward Camille's. The driver of my SUV, with Johnny inside, honks impatiently and I hurry to get in the backseat.

He drives us back to the hotel.

Every ounce of my being wants to be with Lyra. I want to be at Camille's with her, telling her and Odin about our date. Hugging Hettie and Tema and telling Bo that I'm in love with his sister.

But the reality is that I'm being taken back to the hotel, where there are eleven men waiting to hear about my date, just like they waited to hear from Basher and Tanner.

The hard truth is that Lyra has a commitment to the show, and the other men are still waiting for their chance to win Lyra's heart.

I know the contract she signed, because I saw Odin's, and Lyra's would be so much more involved.

We may have found each other, but that doesn't mean she's mine.

At least not yet.

Back at the hotel, they have pulled the heavy storm doors across the back of the lobby. I've been through storms in Battle Harbour, but the driver tells us they're worse here in the Gulf of St. Lawrence, with nothing to protect the little island.

He drops off Johnny and me and drives off into the night, eager to be home.

A group of men wait for me, as I enter the lobby, dripping all over the floor.

"Looks like you got rained out," Rand says, hurrying up to me with towels.

"It sounds like it's going to be a bad one," Jon tells me. "They're worried the power will go out."

"It's okay—Spence here will heat things up and tell us what happened with him and Lyra." Basher bumps my arm as I run the towel over my face.

"How was it?" Tanner asks.

Basher had his own one-on-one date with Lyra. So did Tanner, standing behind him. I'm only one in the process. Who will be next? Jon? Rand? Boone?

How am I supposed to get through that now?

"Good. It was good," I manage.

"What happened?" Jon demands.

"Nothing. We... talked. We..."

"Did you tell her you're in love with her?" Charlie demands.

"No, but we—"

"You kissed," Rand supplied. "Yay, you. But—"

"What happens now?" I ask them. There's going to be another group date, another one-on-one date. There are still weeks to go until Lyra makes her choice. It might be me. I want it to be me. But, "She might pick me," I say. "She might pick any of you, and there's nothing I can do about it. There's nothing any of us can do."

No one argues with me.

"You—" I point to Tanner. "—or you—" this time I point to Basher. "Could end up with her. She might fall in love with you. Or you—" I look at Ashton and shake my head. "Not you."

"Hey!"

He laughs and I sink onto one of the couches, head in hand. "I don't know what to do. I gave it... maybe not my all, but a lot. But she's still here, and there's you. Anyone of you could take her from me."

"Except me," Ashton drawls.

"The lack of control is the hardest thing." I look up with surprise to see Rand with a serious expression on his face.

"I'm not used to it," Basher agrees.

"This is why The Suitorette is so popular with women," Liam says. "They would all love the chance to make the big decisions. To think about themselves for once."

"Yeah," Tanner says with a bewildered expression. "How do you know that?"

"I have sisters."

"Coming on the show means Lyra can make a choice based on what her heart is telling her, not her head. She's not considering logistics about what would happen after—she's making a leap of faith, trusting it will all work out."

"Sometimes it doesn't," Basher points out. "I've got a sister too, and she watches this stuff religiously. She gave me the stats."

"Look at the stats in real life," Ashton mutters. "Nothing is guaranteed."

I look around at the worried expressions. Lyra is in full control of the situation, and I trust her.

But along with Lyra, the show has control here because they have Lyra under a contract. Lyra may know who she wants to end up with, but the producers may not let her pick me.

And after more dates, with the numbers dwindling, who can say Lyra may not second-guess choosing me.

Did she even choose me?

I can't do anything but wait to see if it's Lyra and me at the end, and that might just drive me nuts.

40

Lyra

THE STORM RAGES FOR twenty-four hours.

But what is happening outside isn't as bad as the storm inside Camille's house.

Sophie waits for me when I get back to Camille's. "I thought you were leaving after Bo did the fly-by?" I ask her, giving her a wet hug because I need the warmth. Madame Carol hurries over with a huge towel, clucking at me in French to get out of my wet clothes.

It happened so suddenly. One minute, I was wrapped up in Spencer's arms and the next, we were racing down the hill, trying to outrun the rain, holding hands and laughing.

And now I'm at Camille's, and I don't know when I'm going to see him again.

"Bo told me he saw you were holding hands so I convinced him to wait until the morning. And then the storm, so we stay. Not that it's a bad thing." She grins with encouragement.

"So you could get the details?"

"In case you needed to talk things through."

I burrow into the towel. "I think I might need Grayson for that."

"Want me to get him?"

I shake my head. "Let me eat first. The main thing wrong with this show is that they never let me eat. I've only had strawberries and cheese."

And a whole bunch of champagne.

But it's not the wine that is making my head spin.

After a healthy dinner of Madame Carol's fish pie, we sit around the table with a bottle of wine.

"It's Spencer, isn't it?" Bo begins.

"I knew it." Camille claps her hands. "The first time I saw you together, I just knew."

Grayson glances at me over his glass of wine. "This might be a problem."

"Why?" Sophie demands. "She's found love with my brother. That's what the show is for."

"There's still eleven other men waiting to get their chance with her," Grayson points out. "Does Spencer feel the same way?"

"I think so."

"Of course he does," Sophie adds. "He always has."

"Should you check with him before you ruin my show?"

"It's going to make the show," Odin assures him.

"We still have four weeks to go. Plus, a trip to Nova Scotia for the overnights and hometown visits."

I shake my head even as Grayson's face falls. "I don't want to do all that," I tell him. "I can't. It's not fair to the others."

"Neither is dumping them without a chance. They all gave up a lot to come here."

"What if they can stay?" I glance at Sophie, who is bouncing in her seat, just like she did when Odin kissed her years ago. "I have an idea..."

Sophie stops bouncing. "No," she says, all the eagerness and excitement of me finding love disappearing from her face. "Don't even think about it."

How did she know? I never thought I was that easy to read. "But you'd be perfect."

"But I don't want to be," Sophie tells me. "I haven't given up on finding love on my own terms. In my own way. I don't want to be the Suitorette."

"Was that your idea?" Grayson demands. "Have someone take over for you?"

"It still is," I tell him. "I think Sophie would be perfect. Are you sure?"

"Absolutely positive."

"Well, then. I happen to have another idea..."

41

Grayson

THE STORM IS A pretty bad one, but it has nothing on the persuasive power of Princess Lyra.

I keep the contract on the table between us. It clearly states that she owes us six weeks of footage, plus promotional material, and yet...

It's hard to deny when someone is fighting for true love.

She talks about Spencer. A lot.

I admit, it's a love story. We could play it with missed opportunities and Spencer's legitimate fear of losing her. We'll get the viewers—but what to do with the other month left in her contract? We can't stretch five dates into a six-week season, regardless of how good the editing is, and how much filler we include.

We're locked down at Camille and Odin's for twenty-four hours while the rain comes down in sheets and the wind whips the treetops into a frenzy. Camille isn't fussed about the severity, but then again, she grew up here.

We have fierce storms in Toronto, but the city isn't on an island—or an archipelago, as Ria corrects me—with the closest mainland twenty-five kilometres away.

Ria and I are at Camille's, leaving Rue with the cameras and the men at the hotel. Luckily, we have cell service throughout, so I can check in, as well as get her insight about what to do with Lyra.

Rue has one opinion, with Ria taking the opposite, which leaves me as the deciding vote.

I hate being in this position.

But as the storm breaks around nine o'clock on the second night, I finally agree to Lyra's idea.

With a few concessions.

42

Spencer

WE'RE STUCK IN THE hotel for the duration of the storm and it just about drives me crazy.

Dates are cancelled.

I'm not used to having so much free time, and there's only so many games of pool you can play. Rue finally breaks down and opens one of the conference rooms so we binge all four seasons of Stranger Things.

That's a lot of demi-gorgons.

But it's not as bad as my constant spiral of thoughts about Lyra.

I was so caught up with her on the date that I never told her the important stuff. That I love her. That I want a future with her.

That I want to be with her, whatever that looks like.

I know she loves Chicago and if she wants to stay there, I'll have to look at relocating, at least part of the time. If she wants to live somewhere else, we can look at places together. I love what I do for the royal family, but I can still do that remotely.

There's a lot of options for us, and while the storm beats down, I go through them all.

I can't wait to talk to her about them.

But finally, the sun rises without the cloud cover and the rain stops. I track down Rue as soon as I wake up and I don't find any roses outside the door.

"I need to see Lyra today," I demand.

"You and the rest of the hotel," she says, studying her tablet. "She's unavailable for today."

"What do you mean, she's unavailable? Is she okay?"

"I don't know yet, and she's fine. Oh, wait—this is for you."

"What?" I try and see what's on her screen but Rue holds it to her chest.

"A text from Grayson. You'll get the evening part of your date that got rained out tonight, so be ready for seven."

"I have to wait until then?"

Rue smiles. "Enjoy your free time."

I don't enjoy it.

But eventually, seven o'clock arrives and I'm ready in the lobby, wearing my best suit. Instead of a car to take me to meet Lyra, Grayson shows up.

He looks a little ragged, with shadows under his eyes, but still dressed in his hosting jacket.

"Hey, Spencer. You make it through the storm okay?"

"What's going on with Lyra?" I demand.

He laughs. "You'll find out soon enough. She's here, actually. She's waiting for you at the side of the hotel. You ready?"

"Yes." I turn, about to hurry away, but Grayson puts a hand on my arm.

"We're still on camera, so slow down a bit. She's not going anywhere."

Lyra is waiting for me on the catwalk from the wedding dress date. And like that day, she takes my breath away when I see her.

The sun is setting, the sky a rainbow of orange and pinks, and giving Lyra the perfect background. But it's Lyra who overshadows the sunset, wearing a cream-coloured gown that hugs, caresses, even molds to her curves like the best kind of athleticwear.

When I get closer, I notice there are little beads sewn onto the dress that would give the hand a nice massage if you rubbed her back.

Not that there's much fabric on her back.

Her hair hangs past her shoulders, with the sides pinned up. She's wearing her mother's sapphire necklace, dipping into the low V-neckline of the dress, as well as a tiara that sparkles in the fading sun.

That's when I know this is a big deal, because Lyra never likes to wear a tiara.

"You look beautiful," I say as a greeting.

"You don't look so bad yourself." Lyra smiles, but there's worry in her eyes. "Although I did like that velvet suit you wore for the fashion show."

"Velvet suit. Got it." I nod, ready to show Lyra I will do anything for her.

"The second part of your date was rained out," Grayson begins and I start, because I was so focused on Lyra that I forgot he walked out beside me. "And Lyra wanted to finish it."

"Sounds perfect to me."

A single red rose lies on a small, high table beside Lyra. And a small box.

My heart clenches at the sight, then starts to beat double time. "What's going on?" I ask her in a voice that no longer sounds like mine.

Lyra's smile falls from her face. "Spencer. It's time I ended this."

43

Lyra

"WHAT?" SPENCER STUTTERS.

For a brief moment, I let myself enjoy the confusion on his face, because—come on, he kind of deserves it. Spencer has had years and countless opportunities with me and he's refused to take advantage of it.

Then again, so have I.

Not anymore.

"I'm ending this," I repeat. "This—whatever you call it. The *does he care, will he kiss me*, thing we've had between us. The shared history that neither of us can move past, the best friends but more? Maybe more? I don't know what to call it."

Spencer steps forward, ready to take my hand, but I step back before he can touch me. "Lyra, there's so much I never said to you the other day," he begins.

"Oh, I know." I smile slyly. "We were too busy kissing, which was nice, but that was our moment, and we missed it. So I created another one."

I wave my hand to encompass me, the sunset. "I don't want to miss this one, so let me speak, please."

"But you want to end it." He's on the cusp of frantic, and I've never seen that side of Spencer.

I've seen him strong and confident. I've seen him so focused on his work that he's forgotten to eat. There were times of sweetness and laughter, and comfort, but I've never seen him scared to lose me.

If that's what it is.

I think it is. I hope it is.

"I want to end *that*," I say to put him out of his misery. "What I just said. I want to end the uncertainty. I want to start new. With you."

I bite my lip, forgetting Alexa's instructions not to mess up my lipstick. She spent so much time getting me ready this afternoon, and it was nice to see it pay off by the admiration in Spencer's eyes.

I've spoken in public countless times, on videos posted on social media for my followers. I shouldn't feel this nervous.

But it's good that my dress is long because my knees are practically knocking together.

I've given speeches, introduced my father and other dignitaries. I've even presented an Oscar. But that was child's play compared to this. I've never felt the weight as heavy as what I need to say to Spencer.

I force myself to take a deep breath. And then another. And then: "I love you."

My voice breaks at the end and I steady it as the words float between us. "I've always loved you, and I've waited—maybe a little impatiently—for you to feel it. To say it, but you never did. So I'm saying it."

"Lyra, I—" The smile on his face gives me all the encouragement I need to keep going, and I hold up my hand for him to wait.

"I love you," I tell him again. It gets easier the more you say it. "And I did come on the show as a way to get back at you, as well as to get over you. You and Abigail—that really hurt me." My voice shakes a bit. "In my head, I know it shouldn't, but my heart said differently. But after talking to you, and Abigail—"

"You talked to Abigail?" he demands.

My smile is just a little smug. "I did. I may be a princess of Laandia, but I'm also a woman terrified of telling you what's in my heart and you breaking it as you walk back to her. So I covered my bases. Talking to Abigail helped with that because she explained how it was a friendship between you and a little more. Do you feel the same?"

Spencer, still shocked by me bringing up Abigail, nods.

"You can speak now," I tell him with a laugh.

"I love her as a friend," he says in a rush. "It's always been you. I love you, Lyra."

I put a hand to my mouth. It's what I wanted to hear for so long, but now the words are there… it's so much more than I could have hoped for.

"You love me," I echo.

"I love you." Spencer is firm, losing the confusion and gaining confidence. "I love you and I finally realized this after you walked away from me in the brewery, so this has been a bit of a bad week for me."

I laugh. "A bad week for *you*?"

"A very bad week for me, so if you don't mind, I'd really like to kiss you right now." He takes a step forward, but as much as I'd like nothing more than to be in his arms again, I take a step back.

"In a minute. I'm not done here."

"What more is there?"

I pick up the rose. "I need to give you this, as a sort of way to finish the process of the show."

Spencer frowns. "I don't understand. The show is over? How does that work? I thought..."

"It's over for us, and I'll explain later. Will you accept this rose?"

He steps forward and snatches it out of my hand. "That's a stupid question," he says with a grin.

"I know, but they made me say it. And then this." I pick up the box. "This is one of my mother's rings. I've always loved it, and Dad said it was always mine to use as..." I watch Spencer's face closely, waiting for him to grimace or show some reaction that this isn't what he wants.

His smile only widens, and he doesn't take his eyes off me.

"I would really like you to give me this ring someday, but I can wait—"

Spencer lunges for the ring box, but I hold it out of his reach for another moment. "I said I was ending this. I'm ending our past, and I'm ready to start a future with you, Spencer. A future where we love each other—and we both know how we feel. I'm not sure where that leads us—"

He grabs my wrist and takes the box from my shaking fingers. And then—

Spencer drops to one knee in front of me. "Lyra Erickson, I love you. And there will be no waiting. I can't wait to start a future with you, and I want that future to start right now." He flips open the box and the square-cut sapphire, surrounded by diamonds, sparkles in the last of the sunlight.

"Will you marry me?"

I pull him to his feet so I can kiss him.

"Yes," I whisper, the tears beginning to fall. "Yes."

And then his lips are on mine, and his arms around me, and I hope Johnny gets this shot because it's the very last time I ever kiss anyone for the camera.

Epilogue

Abigail

EIGHT HOURS EARLIER...

It's not so bad being without Spencer.

I miss him, sure, but I miss Hettie and Tema a lot more. I'm glad they got to stay in Saint Pierre, but Tema still feels like my own, so having her away for so long is an aching pain I'm going to have to get used to.

But Spencer being gone isn't as bad as I thought. Eight years without him in my life makes it easier to have him drop out of my life again. It's only been a few months since we were officially together anyway, and it was never some fairy-tale romance to begin with.

That's what I keep telling myself, and for the most part, I believe it.

It'll be easier when Hettie gets back from Saint Pierre, so she can tell me too.

Since I've been back, I've spent most of my time with Hettie, Bo, and Spencer, and a lot of my school friendships have faded. In the weeks that Spencer has been gone, I've jumped back in and made a point to forge new ones. The job at the coffee shop helps, because it's always busy and I'm pretty social, but I make plans with Stella. I join Fenella Carrington for a drink at her club. I visit Mabel at The King's Hat and fill her in on the years she missed with Tema.

I'm creating a presence in Battle Harbour, and it's not as Spencer Laz's girlfriend.

I'm proud of that.

But still, when Hettie is back tomorrow—

The bell over the door chimes and I stand frozen, hand on the coffee spout, until the cup is filled to the brim, and I switch it off before it spills over my hand.

Princess Lyra has just walked into Coffee for the Sole.

With Grayson Grant, host of The Suitorette.

Spencer left me to join the show, and all three of them, along with a bunch of other men, are supposed to be in Saint Pierre so that Lyra can find true love.

They're not supposed to be here in Battle Harbour, unless maybe the time line has changed and they wanted to show a visit to the castle to meet Lyra's family or—

"Best coffee in the whole Maritimes," Lyra is saying to Grayson as they make their way to the counter. "Hi, Abigail."

"Ah—hi."

Princess Lyra has barely strung a sentence together to speak to me, and she's never greeted me by name in a friendly voice.

Of course, she's friendly—she finally has Spencer.

And, of course, she's going to greet me—I work at the coffee shop and will have to serve her.

"This is Abigail," Lyra says to Grayson. "She and Spencer were... together?" She raises an eyebrow. "A couple.? Boyfriend and girlfriend seem kind of high school, and I don't think that's what you were back then."

"We were together, and now we're not. Which you are well aware of." My voice is cold steel. I don't care if Lyra is a princess or a queen—she took my boyfriend.

Even though I kind of gave him to her.

"I'm not here to gloat or whatever you think I'm doing," Lyra says quickly. "I'm here because I need a favour."

"You need a favour from *me*? An extra pump in your drink?"

"No, although that would be great. Hey, Wyatt." She smiles at Silas's nephew, who has sidled up to get the gossip. "Would you mind taking care of our drinks? Two vanilla caramel lattes with unicorn foam, please and thank you? We need a minute with Abigail."

"You're Grayson Grant." Wyatt has a silly smile on his face.

"I am." Grayson offers his hand to Wyatt, who takes it like he's been offered a sack of gold. "Nice to meet you."

"I watched you pitch a no-hitter against New York." Wyatt's voice is dazed and Grayson's face breaks into a mile-wide grin.

"No way!"

"He's a big baseball fan," I explain. "He doesn't watch The Suitor."

"I'm going to start now," Wyatt assures him.

"Always nice to have another fan." Grayson offers his hand to me. "Grayson Grant."

It's a good celebrity name, even as much as it's been spoken in the last two minutes. I take his hand. "Abigail Locke."

"Do you have a minute? I have a proposal for you."

This has to be about Spencer and a tug of annoyance pulls my face into a frown. "I don't need closure with Spencer. It's over, and I'm fine with that."

"I'm really glad to hear that," Grayson says. "Because we'd like you to step in as the Suitorette."

The coffee shop is noisy with regular customers at the tables and the hiss of the steamer as Wyatt prepares Lyra's order, but it's not that loud. I shouldn't have problems to hear what Grayson just said.

"What?" I turn to Lyra, who shrugs. "I don't understand."

"It's Spencer for me; it always has been." Lyra has a strange, soft, shy smile on her face. There is nothing soft or shy about Princess Lyra, so I don't understand why she's smiling like that—

Spencer. Spencer put that smile on her face. I wait for it to hurt. And it doesn't.

It doesn't hurt. It doesn't anything. I'm still confused at why Lyra is *here* instead of enjoying some romantic rendezvous with my ex-boyfriend... "Yes, but—"

"The men they have for this season are incredible," she continues. "And I really like them, but it's not fair for me to continue this, because I'm in love with Spencer."

"You always have been." Again, a surprise that I can say that without sounding like a bitter shrew. Just stating a fact.

Lyra nods, still with that soft smile. "I have been, and I need to tell him as soon as we get back. But that leaves things awkward for Grayson and the show, because I'll be stepping down as the Suitorette." She glances at Grayson. "I told Grayson that he should recruit you to finish the season."

"Me?"

Lyra's blue eyes are steady as she studies my face. "Yes, you. And before you say no because it's me who is asking—" I shrug, because she's right. I am about to say no without even listening to what she has to say.

"I've always been jealous of you," she surprises me by saying.

"Me."

"Yes. You. You've always been close to Spencer, the only woman he's allowed through the barriers."

"I'm not sure if that's the case," I say slowly.

"I think it is. I know it's true. I've always resented you."

"Lyra, this isn't really helping," Grayson mutters.

"She has to know she wouldn't be taking over from me, like I'm offering her my leftovers."

"Lyra," Grayson hisses.

"That's what you were thinking, isn't it?" she demands.

"Now that you mention it," I admit. "The optics..."

"The men aren't mine. Never have been. They're great guys, and I made a secret trip to the hotel this morning before we left to talk to some of them. They like the idea of you."

"They don't even know who I am."

"Oh, they do now. Ashton helped with that." Lyra claps a hand over her mouth. "Sorry," she says to Grayson. "I let that slip."

Grayson frowns at Lyra before turning to me. "There are eleven men left. I've contacted five others, so you would start with sixteen, none of which have a strong connection with Lyra. She actually hasn't been the best Suitorette—"

"Hey," Lyra protests.

"You haven't. She doesn't have a connection, other than friendship, with any of the men, so the season needs help. Desperately needs help."

I smile. I can't help it.

"It would be four weeks, instead of six, so things would move fast. Do you think you could handle that?"

"I don't remember agreeing to anything," I say in a cool voice, even though my heart races at the thought of being the Suitorette.

And it shouldn't, because why would I do that to myself?

Because I've always loved the show.

Because I would like to find love.

And... this might be the sticker: it would be *so much fun* to succeed at something that Princess Lyra failed at.

I don't actually believe Grayson when he says Lyra's not the best Suitorette—the fan in me thinks that was Chrissa, because I never believed she wanted to be there—but it's nice to hear.

I understand when Lyra says she's always been jealous of me, because it goes both ways. I've always been jealous of the place she has in Spencer's heart.

"But you're thinking about it, aren't you?"

I meet Lyra's gaze, see her smug smile. It should drive me crazy that she got Spencer, but...

It doesn't. It seems right they're ending up together.

"What do you say?" Lyra demands. "The guys are great. At least the ones that are left. Jon gives *foot rubs*," she hunches her shoulders with a grin.

"Lyra, you can't—she has to make her own judgements." If Grayson had a way to silence Lyra, I think he would.

"She'll judge they're good guys as soon as she meets them. But the way Jon's thumbs—"

Grayson takes her shoulders and marches her away a few feet.

I think he's telling her to stay.

Do I want to do this? Non-stop cameras, no privacy, just for the chance to fall in love?

"Look, Abigail," Grayson says with a rueful grin. "Lyra suggested you for this, and what I've heard about you, I think you'd be great. But you'd really be helping me out. I could find another Suitorette, but if it was you, it would really close the circle. I think it would be good TV. And I understand how this might not be the most comfortable for you, but I give you my word that we'll keep any mention of Spencer, and your relationship with him to a minimum. I guarantee, the men don't want to talk about him any more than they have to. He's a good guy, but this hasn't been the most conventional season. I think you joining would be able to steer us in the right direction."

"But taking over for Princess Lyra?" I frown at the thought. As much as my first instinct is to agree—because *why not*—any woman would be intimidated at the thought of following a princess, especially one like Lyra.

"I think you'll be amazing," Grayson assures me in a low voice. "I had a long talk with Bo and Hettie—he flew us over, by the way—"

Hettie is in town. The thought is a warm blanket over my shoulders.

"And they told me a lot about you. I agree that the thought of filling Lyra's footsteps might be tough, but I think you are more than capable of it."

Grayson Grant is very persuasive.

"What do you say? Want to find true love?" Grayson asks, his smile warm and wide and white, and much more attractive than he is on television.

"Do it," Lyra urges, not even pretending not to listen. "You'll have so much *fun!*"

I could use a little fun.

Want more happily-ever-afters? Subscribe to my newsletter for bonus scenes—like King Magnus & Tema's!

Then get ready, because Abigail's stepping into the spotlight in *Royal Replacement.*

Acknowledgments

Thank you for sticking with me for my Love in Laandia series!

Royal Rebel is the fifth in the series, and I will *not* say it's the final quite yet! There are ideas percolating, many, many ideas, and you know the saying—never say never. I set out to write a series about the children of the royal family of my made-up land, and Lyra's story is the last (but not least!). But throughout this journey, there are other characters who have made a big impression on me (and hopefully you!) and stories might have to be told.

And now onto the words of gratitude for all those who played a part in getting my books into the hands of readers:

To Regina—Thank you for always managing to make time for me, even when you're swamped with other books! I love your insights of my characters, your funny asides, and especially the emojis! You have no idea how much your little notes in the margin mean to me, and how often I change and adjust because of them!!

Thank you to Dylan for all cover characters!

Here comes to longer part: THANK YOU to all my subscribers and followers! Sandra—love getting your emails and hearing about your kids. Bernadette—love getting your emails too, because they always help make my books better. I can't list you all, but I wish I could. A quick shout out to Yolanda, Chris (@marbooks88), Kelsey (@bookedbykels), Wendy (@kelsomath) and MacKenzie (booking.it.with.mk)! Social media is something I haven't yet grown comfortable with, but you all—and many more—make it easier on me with your shares and your comments.

Even if I don't mention you, know that I'm sending a big, HUGE thank you for your support!

And now for a few fun facts about Royal Rebel:

*Grayson Grant first appeared in Don't Tell You Love Me, got his own book in Don't Want To Be Friends, and then **another** book in Falling for the Suitor, the titular Suitor in my Suitor Science series! I must like this guy!*

I came up with the Suitor reality show franchise because I was becoming a bit obsessed with The Bachelor/Bachelorette. I've moved on from that era... sort of!

Lyra's name—I was on the hunt for Viking-inspired names when I wrote this series, and Lyra isn't exactly Norse, it does have a cool meaning. This is what the internet says about it. "Lyra is a name with ancient and celestial roots that's finding new popularity thanks to its starring role in Philip Pullman's His Dark Materials series, seen in the movie The Golden Compass. Simple yet unique, Lyra hits the sweet spot between too popular and too unusual."

I pronounce it Lie-ra. And it's the name of one of Ed Sheeran's daughters!

Thanks for reading!
Holly xo

READING LIST

Love in Laandia

Royal Rumble
Royal Retelling
Royal Rising
Royal Reluctance
Royal Rebel

Suitor Science

Hating the Chemistry Teacher
Falling for The Suitor
Fraternizing with the Ex
Marrying the Billionaire Best Friend
Loving the Wrong Guy
Finding the One

Don't

Don't Tell Me You Love Me
Don't Want to Be Friends
Don't Stop Me Now
Don't They Know It's Christmas

Love & Alliteration

Perfectly Played
Beautifully Baked
Pleasantly Popped

Charlotte Dodd

The Secret Life of Charlotte Dodd
The Missing Files of Charlotte Dodd
The Best Worst First Date Ever
The Hidden Past of Pippa McGovern
The Last Stand of Charlotte Dodd

Sisters in a Small Town

Coming Home
Hanging On
Stepping Up

Unexpecting
Unexpectingly Happily Ever After

STANDALONES

Cinnamon Rolls and Pumpkin Spice – Coffee Break with the Billionaire

Oceanic Dreams – I Saw Him Standing There

Absinthe Doesn't Make the Heart Grow Fonder